Readers' comments

'I was awake until after midnight reading just one more chapter.'
Lydia

'Another really exciting story'
Hazel

'I really enjoyed getting back into the world of Woodford!'
Annette

Kathy Morgan lives on the Dorset/ Wiltshire border, where she runs an antiques business with her partner. They have a variety of animals, and Kathy enjoys exploring the local countryside with her horses and dogs.

Deadly Philately

by
Kathy Morgan

Kathy Morgan's

Woodford Mystery Series:

The Limner's Art

The Bronze Lady

Death By Etui

The Mystery of the Silver Salver

Deadly Philately

Also by Kathy Morgan:

Silver Betrayal

Snowflake, the Cat Who Was Afraid of Heights

Dear Kate –

I hope you enjoy reading this book!

Best wishes,

Kathy

This book is a work of fiction. Names, characters, places and incidents are the product of the author's imagination or are used fictitiously. Any resemblance to actual events, locales, or persons living or dead, is coincidental.

Printed by KDP.

1st edition September 2021

A CIP catalogue record for this title is available from the British Library.

For you, with love from me xxx

Thank you to everyone who has encouraged me to keep writing!

As many of you know I have recovered from sepsis and covid in the past couple of years since I started to write this book, and the effects of both of those illness can be quite debilitating on the creative process. It is thanks to every one of you who have checked in with me at some time that this book exists.
It is hard to single anyone out, because every message has made a difference, but I will say a special thank you to Vanessa, Caroline, Jean, Sally, Nova, Denise and Elaine.

Although it is my name on the cover, many others have had an input into Deadly Philately. Some of these names will be familiar to those who have been reading my books since the beginning, and some are new to the team. Special thank you to Eve-Marie, Nova, Bob, Jeannette, Lydia, Charlie, Annette, Hazel, Fiona and Martin.

Thank you to Charlotte Jenner Equine Photography for the picture of me wearing a Brackenshire HOOFING gilet, and riding JD!

Thank you Charlton Chilcott-Legg for the wonderful image of the stamps on the front cover, and a map of Woodford!

Of course, all mistakes are mine!

Philately

Philately is the collection and study of postage stamps, postmarks, stamped envelopes, and other material related to postal delivery. The word was invented in 1864 from two Greek word: *philos* meaning ‘love’, and *ateleia* meaning ‘tax-free’.

My first experience of philately was watching my dad with his stamp collection. He had become interested when he was a young lad, and his next-door neighbour gave him his first album. Over time he focused on mint-condition stamps from Saint Vincent and the Grenadines, because he loved their colour and variety, and his collection includes examples from the 1860s. He bought me a series of British First Day covers, starting with the Year of the Child in 1979, but I don’t think I was very interested after that and we soon stopped.

Rowland Hill is the person credited in the nineteenth century with designing a pre-payment system using individual adhesive stamps, replacing the costly system of expecting the recipient to pay which frequently resulted in refusal and the return of the card or parcel to the sender. In England in 1840 two different designs were produced, both with the profile of Queen Victoria: the one penny in black; and two penny in blue. Over the next few decades countries around the world adopted similar systems, and philately was born.

As you can imagine, the volume of stamps produced since 1840 is massive, and so philatelists specialise in their collections. Some people, like my father, collect stamps from a specific country, others collect stamps in a certain condition. Usually stamps with a hint of a postmark are the ones collectors want, but some, like my dad, prefer them in mint condition, unused. Others collect flower designs or buildings from anywhere in the world, the categories for philately are numerous.

Usually the higher the denomination the more collectable the stamp because there are often less of those in circulation, but we have all heard of the Penny Black, and examples of this one penny stamp can be bought for hundreds of thousands of pounds. The Penny Black stamp is valuable not just because it was one of the first two stamps to be produced, or because of its age, but because it was only manufactured for a few months before the colourway had to be changed and a Penny Red stamp replaced it.

Philatelists also collect other postal-related materials, including stamped envelopes. Before individual adhesive stamps were produced, envelopes and parcels were rubber stamped, and these are highly collectable. Postmarks are useful today, particularly when determining how old a postcard may be, and how long it took to travel from the sender to the recipient, for example during the first world war. The UK's Royal Mail offers a service to businesses and charities who would like all post from specific areas to be stamped with a message or logo, and different colours can be used.

Collectors prefer to buy albums from auction, rather than individual stamps, because there is always a chance that no one has bothered to check every stamp on every page, and everyone else has overlooked the valuable one.

Abbreviations:
Brackenshire HOOFING – the Brackenshire branch of the national organisation HOrse Owners having Fun In Groups (My invention! KM).
ICE – In Case of Emergency.
RD – Race Director.
TREC – Techniques de Randonnée Équestre de Compétition. Originated in France, and used to be run in the UK by the British Horse Society. A sport which tests the skills of horse and rider in planning and executing a long-distance ride in unfamiliar country.
TYPS – Thank You PointS for volunteers at Brackenshire HOOFING events.
WES – Woodford Equestrian Supplies.
WSWC – Woodford Streakers Wearing Clothes, Woodford's running club.

Character list in alphabetical order:
Alison Isaac – equestrian coach, employee of Woodford Equine Rehabilitation Centre, sister of Jennifer, daughter of Peter, stepsister of Daniel Bartlett
Amanda – chef at The Ship Inn
Amelia McCann – member of Brackenshire HOOFING
Bilbo – labourer for Grayson Bragg, and part-time antiques dealer, member of WSWC
Caroline Thomas – owner of an outside catering company, and employee of The Woodford Tearooms, cousin of Daniel Bartlett, member of WSWC
Charlie Lichmann – member of Brackenshire HOOFING
Cliff Williamson – owner of Williamson Antiques, ex-husband of Rebecca Martin, member of WSWC

Daniel Bartlett – Black's Auction House employee, cousin of Caroline Thomas, stepbrother of Jennifer and Alison Isaac
Debbi Tolstoy – member of Brackenshire HOOFING
Diana Smalley – member of Brackenshire HOOFING
Doug – Black's Auction House employee
Grayson Bragg – property developer and builder, husband of Patricia Bragg
Hazel Wilkinson – antiques dealer
Hannah McClure – fitness instructor, wife of Ian McClure, member of WSWC
Heather Stanwick – daughter of Kim and Robin, and member of Brackenshire HOOFING
Ian McClure – policeman, married to Hannah McClure, member of WSWC
Ieuan Davies – member of Antiques and Art Fraud Squad
Jennifer Isaac – equine vet, girlfriend of Paul Black, sister of Alison, daughter of Peter, stepsister of Daniel Bartlett
Jill – bank worker
Jimmy Nicholson – member of Brackenshire HOOFING, husband of Phil Smart
Katherine – member of Brackenshire HOOFING
Kim Stanwick – Chair of Brackenshire HOOFING
Krista Tennison – Paramedic, member of WSWC
Linda Beecham – antiques dealer, member of Brackenshire HOOFING
Lisa Thomas – co-owner of The Woodford Tearooms, mother of Caroline, aunt of Daniel Bartlett
Lydia Black – employee at Kemp and Holmes Antiques auctioneers, daughter of Paul Black
Nova – member of Brackenshire HOOFING

Madeleine Powell – manager of the Woodford Riding Club, half-sister of Rebecca Martin, member of Brackenshire HOOFING

Marion Higston – part of the Higston family who are major landowners in the area, and own a local farm, the Woodford Riding Club, a local golf course and fishing lake among other agricultural, retail and leisure businesses.

Natasha Holmes – co-owner of Kemp and Holmes Antiques Auctioneers and Valuers

Patricia Bragg – member of Brackenshire HOOFING, wife of Grayson Bragg

Paul Black – owner of Black's Auction House, boyfriend of Jennifer Isaac, member of WSWC

Peter Isaac – equine vet, father of Jennifer and Alison Isaac

Phil Smart – member of Brackenshire HOOFING, married to Jimmy Nicholson

Rebecca Martin – employee of Black's Auction House, ex-wife of Cliff Williamson, half-sister of Madeleine

Richard – employee of Black's Auction House

Robin Stanwick – married to Kim, father to Heather, and member of Brackenshire HOOFING

Sarah Handley – owner of The Ship Inn

Tom Higston – manager of The Ship Inn, member of WSWC

Tristram Bridger – owner of the greengrocers

Nova – member of Brackenshire HOOFING

William – bank worker

Zoe Sherrett – fitness and Zumba instructor, member of Brackenshire HOOFING, member of WSWC

Also featured:
Blackie – Amelia McCann's horse
Dougal – Patricia Bragg's horse
Ernie – Alison Isaac's horse
Flo – Alison Isaac's horse
Highland – Charlie Lichmann's Fresian horse
Jasper – Jennifer Isaac's horse
Lucy – Jennifer Isaac's greyhound
Maggie – Kim Stanwick's horse
Max – Madeleine Powell's patterdale terrier
Rosie – Amelia McCann's horse
Woody – livery pony at Woodford Riding Club

WOODFORD, artist Charlton Chilcott-Legg 2021

Chapter 1

Wednesday 16th October 2019, 6:00pm

'Watch out. Bilbo's up to his old tricks again. Look at that!' said Hazel Wilkinson indicating across the busy antique auction sale room, as a young man placed a heavy box of silver plate candelabras, trays and serving dishes on top of a large slim book and then pushed another book in front of it.
Linda Beecham had already noticed what the big and brawny part-time antiques dealer was doing. 'Blatant. Does he think we can't see him hiding that stamp album?' she laughed, making a note of where the album was so she could check it out when the others weren't around.
'To be fair, I didn't see anything in that album to make it worth hiding from the rest of the buyers. I wouldn't put my hand up for it in the auction,' said Cliff Williamson, dismissing Bilbo's actions, but he planned to have a second look at it, as soon as it was decently possible.
'I didn't even look in it. Stamp albums don't interest me anymore.' Linda shook her head causing her long grey plait to gently sway down her back, as she thought about the prices she used to sell them for. She had not

paid attention to the album when she viewed that area of the Black's Auction House sale room, but Bilbo's actions had piqued her interest.
'Those were the days, weren't they? When we used to pay through the nose for an album like that one.' Cliff agreed as he remembered a handful of past successes. He and Linda were in their early forties and had both joined the antiques trade when they were teenagers, after the glory years of the eighties and early nineties. But they had clear memories of making a good living from the philately market.
'Oh, these will be the good old days I'm always hearing so much about?' said Hazel Wilkinson. She was a retired school teacher in her sixties who favoured long flowing skirts and floaty tops, and was dabbling in her hobby of collecting and selling antiques, in particular china items and ephemera.
Linda and Hazel individually rented space to sell their vintage and antique stock in Williamson Antiques on Woodford High Street, owned by Cliff Williamson, who also sold items in there. Together, the three dealers spent a few minutes sharing stories of big successes with a variety of goods, and then drifted apart to continue viewing the auction before its official start in thirty minutes time. Over the course of the next half an hour, deliberately out of the sight of the other two, each retrieved the stamp album labelled and catalogued as Lot 98, from its hiding place under the box of silver plate and behind a box of old brass bits and bobs. Surreptitiously, they flipped through the pages looking for treasure.
By the time the auction started, the three were back in their usual corner of the room and had been joined by another four dealers, including the huge musclebound

young man with short, cropped ginger hair, nicknamed Bilbo, who had originally hidden the album.
No one mentioned it.
'It's a busy auction today,' observed Linda as she scanned the room which was packed with familiar faces and a few she didn't recognise.
'Mmmh,' nodded Cliff. 'I haven't seen any of the usual Chinese buyers though. Is there a big Asian sale I've missed?'
Linda shrugged 'Not that I know of. If there is one, then I'm missing it too. You're right; I can't see any Chinese in the room. That's odd. Asia Week isn't for another month, so perhaps they've gone back to see their families in China before they get too busy on the auction circuit.'
They both forgot about the curious absences as the auction started promptly with Lot 1, an unexciting collection of corkscrews, and in less than an hour Paul Black, the auctioneer, introduced Lot 98. He had a number of pre-bids on his books and started the bidding at six hundred and twenty pounds. The dealers looked to see who was bidding for clues as to why this lot was so sought after, and felt panicky at the thought they had missed something important. Linda had a chance to bid, but was soon outbid by someone else in the room. She didn't manage to see who, and then the bidding stalled because Linda wasn't willing to pay four figures for something she didn't understand. The anonymous internet bidders took over and started bidding against each other in quick succession. The rules are strict in an auction room: the auctioneer must only accept bids from two people at a time until one stops bidding, and then a new bidder will be accepted. But these rules do not apply to bidding over the

internet and any number of bids can be accepted in the order they are received. First click first served.
Paul checked that the internet connection had not broken, which happened during almost every auction. The rural town of Woodford in the county of Brackenshire was located in the South West of England, and while technology was essential to an antiques auction business like Black's Auction House, it could also be troublesome. When the internet failed, the outside caterer, Caroline Thomas, did a roaring trade. She set up her catering van in the courtyard well in advance of the start of the auction and supplied the buyers and sellers with the usual bacon rolls and cups of tea which fuelled the majority of antiques-related events. She also provided a good range of homemade soups, flat breads wrapped around a variety of organic salads, vegetables and meat, superb fresh coffee, and always had the mobile pizza oven fired up. Once the auction started, the locals would wander in and buy whatever was left. There were gentle teasing rumours that she would nobble the internet connection at every auction, ensuring a twenty-minute break in the bidding and an opportunity for her to sell a few more refreshments.
The screen displayed the price jumping up in increments of one hundred pounds until it hesitated at a bid of two thousand three hundred pounds. Everyone in the auction room was silent, transfixed, watching the big display screen to the right of Paul's head. Another internet bid appeared, and then there was a pause while the cursor in the box 'Internet' blinked, and Paul prepared to accept any bids from the people in the room. But then another bid was made over the internet, and the box marked 'Room' on the screen remained empty. The people in the auction house let out a breath.

The dealers looked at each other, wondering what was so special about this item. No one seemed to know or were willing to tell. Bilbo stood huge and solid with his arms folded across his massive chest, his gaze far above everyone else's heads, and no chance of eye contact.
Again there was a pause in the bidding online, and quickly Paul said 'With the Internet at three thousand one hundred pounds, I'm looking for three thousand two hundred pounds.' He scanned the faces in the room. The dealers' eyes darted to see if any of them would bid, but no one signalled. Linda kept her face impassive and her arms by her side.
'Three thousand two hundred pounds, yes or no?' Paul asked. This time the wait was longer, but the bars at the bottom right of the display screen stayed full, indicating that the connection was good. A low murmur started in the room. Only the auctioneer Paul and his assistant, his nineteen-year-old daughter Lydia, could see who was bidding online and which country they were in.
'Fair warning, fair warning, I'm going to sell Lot... Ah, there we are with the Internet at three thousand two hundred pounds, I'm looking for three thousand three hundred pounds.' Everyone's attention was on the screen again. This time no last-minute internet bid appeared, but someone in the room was bidding and for a few minutes the bids were between one online bidder and one person in the room. The noise level rose as the questions 'Who is it?' and 'Who is who?' were repeated over and over again. Paul was having trouble making sure he caught someone's bidding signal in amongst all the movement.

‘Settle down, settle down,’ he called. ‘I don't want to miss a bid because you are all behaving like nosy parkers.’
Eventually Paul brought the hammer down to a bid in the room for Lot 98 at three thousand five hundred pounds and moved onto Lot 99. Everybody wanted to know who had bid such a large sum of money for a stamp album most would have thrown into landfill. Unsatisfied and with nothing exciting in the next few lots, or at least not that they were aware of, the huddle of antiques dealers moved out into the courtyard to mull over what had just happened while drinking tea and eating sausage sandwiches.
‘Come on then Bilbo, what was in that stamp album?’ Linda, dressed in her usual uniform of jeans and T-shirt, pulled on her warm parka in the chill autumnal air while she asked the question everyone else wanted to ask, but were too embarrassed to reveal their ignorance.
Bilbo shook his head and shrugged. ‘I don’t know,’ he mumbled, before suddenly receiving an urgent telephone call on his mobile, which no one else had heard ring. With a farewell wave, he walked through the wrought iron gates of Black’s Auction House onto Woodford High Street.

Chapter 2

Friday 18th of October 2019, 11:15 am

Paul Black was worried. It was two days after the successful antiques auction, and as usual there were a few outstanding payments. Encouraged by the unexpected high price for the stamp album, and fearful they would miss out on something else tasty, the buyers were free with their bids, and a number of other lots made much higher prices than expected, although none as surprising as Lot 98. The terms and conditions of Black's Auction House stipulated that prospective buyers had to register before bidding, and if successful must pay for the goods before the end of the auction, and no items would be collected without payment. This resulted in a lot of administration for credit and debit card payments, frequent checking of the online banking system for BACS payments, ensuring the correct items went home with the person who paid for them, as well as the collection and secure storage of a large quantity of cash. Many items were posted to their successful bidders, and Paul and his team would be busy for the rest of the week ensuring items were well packed and posted to the right address. One antique due to be posted to China was a nineteenth century cold painted Vienna bronze of a bear, dressed in jacket and trousers standing next to an inkwell in the form of

a bee skep, which had come down at a very high hammer price, but as yet the payment had not appeared in his bank account.
Paul went to run his fingers through his collar-length brown hair, only to remember with a shock as the palm of his hand scraped over the short ends that he had gone for a drastic cropped haircut earlier in the week. He clicked on the refresh icon, willing the eighteen thousand, seven-hundred and fifty-pound payment for the bear to appear. Instead, a small payment of two hundred and forty pounds, followed by another of ninety pounds came into view. Usually both or even one of these would make him happy, but the big one was stubbornly refusing to show up.
Slamming both hands down on the desk, he stood and went over to the safe. Paul had three safes. One was an old heavyweight traditional-looking chest safe which stood on four ball feet on the floor in the open reception area. This was also the office of Rebecca Martin, his assistant, and it was used as a convenient dumping surface for boxes and files. He and his staff used this one as a temporary secure storage for goods brought in for auction by customers. Later they were moved to a safe fixed in a more secret location, and to house the cash once it was counted and ready to be banked. Customers did not know it was mainly for show and appreciated seeing their potentially life-changing belongings locked away in a solid metal box with an ornate lock and huge key. Once the customer had left, the items would be transferred to another room which had an electronic floor safe for which only he and Rebecca, his assistant, knew the combination. The floor safe was not so easily loaded onto a trolley and wheeled out of the building as the chest safe. Nor did anyone have a choice of six sides to cut into and

steal the contents. The auction business was housed in a former chapel, and an original safe still existed. Built into the stone wall three feet deep, only Paul and his father knew about this safe. Old Mr Black bought the building and converted it into the auction house in the nineteen eighties. It had been easy to hide the existence of the safe by positioning a row of substantial floor-to-ceiling cabinets along the wall, one of which had been modified so that the back would slide open, and for a long time only he knew it existed. It was a rite of passage when Old Mr Black revealed the secret safe to his son, and marked the day when he took a step away from the business and handed the reins over to Paul. In recent years, payments with cash had considerably reduced, but there were still a few antique dealers and elderly private buyers who settled their invoices with folding money. Although the denominations in the newer material tended to spring rather than fold. It only took twenty or so customers, each handing over between fifty and three hundred pounds, for the quantity of cash in Paul's floor safe to build up. As with so many rural towns, Woodford had lost three of its five banks, and the remaining two were no longer open all day, or even every working day. The bank with whom Black's Auction House had their business account had recently taken the decision to close their branch on Market Day, a Thursday, which also coincided with some of Black's daytime auctions, and meant there was no opportunity to bank any of the cash until the next day. Paul did not like predictable routines like transferring large sums of money along Woodford High Street to the bank after an auction. Between them, he and his staff set up a series of decoy runs between the two buildings, just in case anyone was hanging around, intending to rob them.

Today Paul was one of three people who were doing the banking. The buyer of the stamp album had paid in cash, and once the hammer price plus twenty percent buyer's premium were added together, the bulk of notes was substantial. Some of the sellers chose to be paid in cash, but not the person who had consigned the stamp album for sale, and the cash pay outs after the previous day's auction were minimal, only totalling two hundred and forty-seven pounds. One last refresh of the screen yielded no new payments, so he shut down the computer. Returning to the safe, he pulled out a cloth bag with the notes he and Rebecca had already counted, double checked, and put into the correct plastic bag. Emptying the bag, he divided the packets of notes into two inside pockets in his jacket, and two outside pockets which he zipped tightly shut. Feeling conspicuous, he headed outside. As he walked through the huge wrought iron gates at the entrance to the auction house, he studied the people nearby, looking to see if any of them were paying particular attention to him. Most of the people he recognised as locals or regular visitors. There was Tristram Bridger, the owner of Woodford's green grocery, standing outside his shop, chatting with the customers. Linda Beecham was in the window of The Ship Inn drinking coffee with another familiar dealer, Bilbo. PC Ian McClure was off duty and strolling up the High Street with his wife Hannah, who was a fitness instructor and ran a studio in Woodford with her best friend Zoe Sherrett, each parent holding one arm of their toddler, Oliver, so he could energetically swing between them.
Although Paul liked to think he was being paranoid about being watched, his instincts today were correct. Of the seven people tasked to monitor Paul's movements only one attracted his attention for

appearing to be acting suspiciously. A scruffy young woman was standing outside the charity shop, ostensibly on her phone. Paul did not recognise her as local to Woodford and the way she was holding her phone while watching him was unsettling. He glanced around to see if there were any likely muggers in the vicinity she could be calling, but could see no one who fitted his idea of what a mugger looked like. The woman finished talking on her mobile, and immediately Paul discounted her when she bent down to pick up the fallen note and hand it to the man who had dropped it as he came out of the charity shop. No one preparing to rob him of his takings would bother with an act of honesty like that.

Chapter 3

Friday 18th of October 2019, 11:30 am

Paul walked down the High Street, scanning the faces and body language of people coming towards him, and making frequent glances to check who was behind him. He was conscious of the bulk and weight of the cash distributed evenly between the pockets of his jacket. Usually he would stride confidently along the pavement or in the road, dodging cars and buses if the town was full of tourists. But today he had an unusual sense of unease. He couldn't explain it but was sure something bad was going to happen.

His heart sank as he drew closer to the bank when he saw there were a few people standing on the steps outside waiting to enter. The last thing he wanted to do was stand in a queue out in the open. He walked towards them, intending to continue on past and enjoy an early lunch in The Woodford Tearooms, after which hopefully the queue would have cleared and he could walk straight into the bank. He saw a familiar battered red truck belonging to one of his regular customers, Grayson Bragg, and stopped for a chat until the door to the bank opened and four people came out in rapid succession, allowing those who had been standing on the steps to go inside. Paul followed them in, and had to shuffle forwards so that he didn't keep causing the automatic door to open. All three cashiers' windows were open, and he could see the friendly and familiar face of long term bank employee Jill behind one of them. Next to her was a young girl who didn't look old enough to have her own bank account, but who Paul knew had been at the branch for at least five years and who was also friendly and helpful. The third window was staffed by a thin grey man whom Paul did not recognise, but his name plate stated he was 'William'. There seemed to be a problem with the customer at his window who had the hot flustered look of someone being thwarted in their attempts to get a routine task completed. Paul saw the haughty look on her face, the smart white capri pants revealing slim tanned legs ending in white high heeled sandals. Her expensive-looking haircut and shiny brown hair which could not possibly be natural, together with bosoms defying gravity, and the jewellery she flaunted on her ears, fingers and neck told him exactly the kind of bank customer she was. He had hoped he was wrong and that today she would be reasonable, but she was a regular customer at the auction house and he'd enough dealings with her to guess how this was going to play out. He wished he'd gone for the early lunch break instead.

'But I have always done it like this' she was saying.

'I'm sorry, but the rules have changed and cash can only be paid into an account with a valid bank card or paying in book.'

'Oh yes, I forgot. It's a new rule, isn't it? That's okay. I've got one of those' said the woman, clearly relieved as she fished around in her shoulder bag before producing a battered grey wallet. Sorting through the cards she pulled one out and pushed it through the slot at the base of the window.

William picked it up and looked at it closely. ‘Are you Mr N.G.Bragg?’ he asked.
‘Yes, that's my husband.’
‘But you are not Mr N.G.Bragg?’ William stated carefully. Paul had a bad feeling about this. Meanwhile, Jill and the young girl were simultaneously saying farewell to their clients and calling for the next one.
The woman laughed. ‘Well, obviously I am not Mr, I am Mrs Bragg. That's my husband's card.’ There was a collective slumping of shoulders in the queue. They all had a bad feeling about the way this transaction was going.
‘Do you have your card with you?’
‘Oh no, I don't have a card. This is my husband’s account.’
‘I am sorry but only the owner of the card can use it.’
‘Don't worry about that; he's given me permission. In fact, I keep it for him. He doesn't know how to use PIN numbers and holes in the walls and all that. I look after his bank card and the PIN number. Don't worry, this account belongs to my husband and he's fine with me looking after it for him.’
The queue exchanged glances. Mrs. Bragg still did not seem to appreciate her predicament. William was holding the bank card. Paul knew what was coming next. He had witnessed things like this before.
William continued in same pleasant tone he had adopted throughout their exchange. ‘Mrs Bragg, I am sorry to tell you that only the owner of this account can use this card. It is an offence to use someone else's card, and the owner should certainly not be divulging their PIN number to anybody else. Not to me, not to their partner, not to their mother.’

‘We know all that,’ Mrs Bragg laughed more nervously than before, and it was clear the penny was dropping. ‘If you'll just give me his card back I'll tell him to change the PIN number, and then I won't know it, okay?’

William kept the card on his desk. ‘I am sorry, but I have to deactivate this card and your husband will be sent the new one. It should take five working days.’

The penny dropped. ‘Oh, for God's sake, this is ridiculous. We can't last five of your working days without any money. It's Friday now, which means the new card won't come through until next Thursday at the earliest.’

William shook his head. ‘I am sorry. Here is the cash you wanted to pay in,’ and he pushed the clear bag of bank notes back under the window.

Grumbling, Mrs Bragg opened it and took out a few of the notes. ‘This will do for fuel and food I suppose.’ She pushed the bag back to William. ‘Right, pay what's left into his account.’

Jill and the young girl were trying to call their next customers, but they were both watching the scene. Eventually, reluctantly, they walked forward.

William gently pushed the bag back. ‘I am sorry, but you cannot pay cash into an account without a valid bank card or paying-in book.’

The woman exploded. Paul was surprised it had taken her this long. ‘But I am paying money into my husband’s account! It's not as though I'm bloody well stealing money out of it.’

‘Money laundering rules mean you cannot pay money into an account which does not belong to you. Where is your husband?’

‘He is waiting for me in the car outside. You know what parking in Woodford is like. Every week he pulls

up outside, I pop in here, pay the money into his account using his bank card, and then we're driving out of town in no time. I keep telling you we do this every week. It has never been a problem before.'
'He should not have told you the PIN number for this card. It is a breach of security.'
'Well, he did. This is ridiculous; I'm going to get him.' She glanced at the queue and said, without a hint of contrition, 'Sorry about this. These jobsworths are so ridiculous. We'll only be a minute once my husband comes in and sorts this mess out.'
Any sympathy the people waiting to be seen may have had for her evaporated. Woodford was a town where generally people were respected, and criticising someone for carrying out the job they were paid to do was not appreciated. Paul stepped aside to allow her through the automatic door. The queue of people turned and looked through the glass at the woman who could be seen angrily gesticulating through the window of the battered red truck parked on the double yellow lines. The driver's door opened, and Paul's customer, Grayson Bragg, a grey-haired man in his fifties wearing jeans ingrained with paint and concrete dust emerged. The woman flung herself around the front of the truck, and slumped into the seat he had vacated. He marched up the steps, slowing to allow the automatic door to function, raised his eyebrows at Paul, and strode over to William's window, prompting the heads in the queue to turn back as they followed him.
'Come on, mate. What's all this about?'
'Hello, are you the owner of this bank card?'
'Yes.' The queue could see that Mr. Bragg was making an obvious effort to be polite. William had clearly been through this sort of exchange before and had an apparently naturally pleasant manner. 'My wife comes

in here every week and pays the cash into my business account with that card and with my permission. Can we hurry this up mate? I'm parked on the double yellows outside and I don't want a ticket.'
'I see. I am sorry, but it is against security policy to tell anyone your PIN number, so I am very sorry but your card has been deactivated. I have ordered a new one for you, which should arrive at your registered address within five working days. I strongly recommend you do not tell anybody, not even your wife, what the PIN number for that card is. Now, is your wife a legal signatory on your business account?'
'Eh? She's only paying money in, not signing contracts or paying bills or nothing.'
William waited.
'No, no she isn't. It's my business, right? It's in my name, not hers.'
'Well then I'm afraid that from now on you're going to have to take possession and responsibility for your bank card and bank account. If you would like your wife to pay money into your account then she would need to be legally added to it. Although I see this is registered as a personal, not a business account.'
Mr Bragg glanced out of the door in the direction of his truck. 'Okay, okay, got it. But can you at least give me my card back? I can't manage without money until next week.'
William shook his head. 'I am sorry but this card is no longer functioning.'
Gritting his teeth, Mr. Bragg said 'Right, thanks a lot, mate. Trish says she has already taken some spending money out of this lot, so I'll pay in the rest. I suppose that is allowed? I am allowed to pay money into my own account?'

Nobody in the queue stirred. The customers at Jill and the young girl's windows were quietly studying their own bank cards. Jill and the young girl were both trying to look professional and were waiting for their customers to move away so they could call the next ones. Paul wondered who to feel sorry for: William, or Mr. Bragg?

Tentatively, William said 'The legal money laundering rules state that money may not be paid into a bank account without a valid bank card or paying in book. At the moment you do not have a valid bank card. Is there any chance you have the paying in book for this account with you?'

Paul silently counted the seconds. One … Two … Three ...

But the anticipated explosion did not materialise. Mr. Bragg. silently collected his bag of money and walked past the queue without looking at Paul, waited for the automatic door to fully open, and strode out to his car, closely followed by the two customers who had been prolonging their interactions with Jill and the young bank worker. Paul hoped the traffic wardens were working in another town that day. Two people came in behind him, and he shuffled forwards, all thoughts of muggings and robberies gone as he prepared for his turn at the cashier's window.

Chapter 4

Saturday 19th of October 2019, 6.25 am

Rebecca Martin awoke with a start. Her heart was pounding as she fumbled in the dark for the noisy mobile phone on her bedside table. An unfamiliar number showing up on the screen at that time of the morning was unlikely to be a cold call; more likely to be the bearer of bad news. She sat up and answered it.

'Hello?'

'I'm sorry to disturb you, but I must urgently speak to Mrs Rebecca Martin.'

'Speaking.' The caller's accent was Welsh and immediately Rebecca felt calmer because none of her children were in Wales.

'Hello Mrs Martin, my name is Ieuan Davies, and I work in the Art and Antiques Fraud Squad. We need to get into Black's Auction House immediately, and as a key holder we would appreciate your assistance to gain access without causing any damage.'

Rebecca almost smacked her forehead with her free hand. What an idiot, of course, just because someone had an accent, it didn't mean they couldn't be in Woodford. She turned the bedside light on so she could concentrate on what he was saying.

'My team are ready to break into the building at six-thirty sharp. This will cause considerable damage and

will leave the premises unsecured. If you can bring the keys and let us in before that time, there should be no damage to the property.'
Rebecca thought quickly. She had no personal experience with police raids, but in her mind's eye she could see the doors to the auction house being smashed in. As she lived fifteen minutes away and was still in bed, this was going to be a challenge.
'I'm going to struggle to get there in five minutes without breaking any speed limits, and I am sure you don't want me to do that. Is this a joke? Paul lives next to the building. Why haven't you asked him to let you in?'
'Yes, we are aware of Mr Black's home address and have tried to contact him, but he is not answering his door or his phone, and you are next on the list as key holder.'
'Please, please don't break in. I will be there as fast as I can.' A thought occurred to her, and her voice deepened as she spoke slowly and deliberately. 'But if this turns out to be a hoax, I will hunt you down and kill you.'
'I assure you this is no hoax.'
Pushing fears of what happens to people who threaten police officers to one side, Rebecca leapt out of bed, tore off her vest, pulled on a pair of jeans over her pyjama shorts, and added a bra and t-shirt, before shoving her feet into the pair of red pumps from under the chaise longue which doubled as a dumping ground for discarded clothes not ready for the laundry basket. She tried ringing Paul as she dived down the stairs, grabbed the car keys from the hook in the kitchen and ran out of the front door. The shock of the cold Autumnal air hit her, and she turned and ran back through the door before it had a chance to shut behind

her. She took a long black woollen coat from the hook and ran back out to her car. The third time she reached Paul's voicemail she gave up trying, and concentrated on driving as quickly and safely as possible into town.
Black's Auction House was positioned at the top of the High Street, directly opposite The Ship Inn. Although the roads and pavements were deserted on her journey into the town, the scene outside Black's Auction House was crowded. There were headlights shining in every direction from numerous dark coloured cars, three dark grey vans, and one white van, all with their blue lights flashing, and people dressed either in police uniform, jeans and warm jackets, or a smart suit. Rebecca's heart rate, which was already racing from the speedy drive, went up a bit higher. All doubts that the phone call had been genuine vanished.
Taking a moment to twist her curly black hair into a band on the top of her head, Rebecca took some slow deep breaths in an attempt to regain some composure. Stepping out of her car, she was immediately surrounded by five people; two in police uniform, and the other three dressed for an evening in their local pub.
'Mrs Martin?' one of them asked in a soft Welsh accent. Rebecca nodded. For nineteen or so years she had been 'Mrs Williamson', but when her marriage ended a couple of years ago she reverted to her maiden name but kept the pronoun 'Mrs' for convenience. It meant that both she and her mother were 'Mrs Martin', but as her mother had moved to Spain and before that she had been the local equine vet there was rarely any confusion or need to explain. The man was roughly the same height as her five foot eight inches, with steady blue eyes and short fair hair, and a musclebound body dressed in dark T-shirt under a black bomber jacket

and jeans. He continued. ‘My name is Ieuan. I am the person you spoke to on the phone. Sorry to wake you, but we must have immediate access to the building. Do you have your keys with you?’

For a moment, Rebecca panicked. Keys! She hadn't thought to bring them with her. They lived in her handbag and in her haste to leave the house while trying to contact Paul, she left her bag behind. Closing her eyes, she could feel a chill of fear at her stupidity. She was already feeling at a disadvantage, aware of the garlic bread she enjoyed last night. Then her eyes snapped open as she remembered something which could at least reduce her embarrassment.

‘No, I haven't, but I will go and fetch Paul’s. Just give me a minute,’ and with her head held high, she strode through the middle of the circle of men and women and out the other side.

Mildly Ieuan said ‘If you don't mind we’ll come with you,’ and the six of them moved in formation past the auction house and into the alley which led down to Paul’s front door. Rebecca's nerves were all over the place, and she fought the urge to giggle as the uniforms and jeans struggled for priority behind her in the narrow space.

Deciding it wasn't worth asking them to look away for security, she unhooked the spare key from behind the gutter which ran down the side of the house, and let herself in. After giving the door a cursory knock, Rebecca was surprised to hear the tell-tale beeping of the house alarm, and deftly she disabled it before it could wake any neighbours who were lucky enough to still be sleeping through the commotion outside. Paul and Jennifer, his fiancée, didn't usually set the alarm while they were in the house, so she guessed they were

away, although Paul hadn't said anything about it the previous evening.
'Paul? Jennifer? Are you here?' she called out just in case. Without commenting to her entourage, she collected a bunch of keys from the hall stand, reset the alarm, re-locked the front door, replaced the key in its now not-so-secret hiding place, and marched back down the alley. The mildly menacing, silent presence of the men and women following behind was beginning to annoy her.
She continued along the pavement past many more uniforms, jeans and a few suits and skirts to the beautiful pair of wrought iron gates. A local blacksmith had forged them to Paul's specifications, and they displayed the name Black's Auction House surrounded by artwork depicting chairs, vases, picture frames, and even a collection of jewellery. Rebecca unlocked and pushed the gates, leaving the uniforms to fix them open to the walls on either side. She walked purposefully up the paved path, aware that the formation behind her had gathered more members and now resembled a sweeping bridal train. The urge to giggle became stronger.
She hesitated for a moment, wondering whether to keep walking straight ahead for the huge doors of the auction room or turn right to the glass doors behind which she and Paul had their offices. It occurred to her that she had no idea what this drama was all about. She stopped in her tracks, causing some of her train to overshoot.
Turning to address Ieuan, who had maintained his distance a little to the right of her the whole time, she asked. 'What exactly are you here for?'
With a slight motion of his head, he indicated to one of the other jeans to produce the documentation. Rebecca

took the paper and scanned it, but other than the words '... To seize all goods, electronic and paper documentation, and any other information relating to...' she couldn't understand any of it.
Ieuan explained 'We have received a report of money laundering in relation to one of the items sold during the auction which took place here on the evening of Wednesday sixteenth of October. This is part of an ongoing international operation, and we must act quickly to seize the evidence. If you could let us into the building and direct us to where the administration for Black's Auction House takes place, we will be able to leave you in peace sooner rather than later.'
Rebecca was aware that for a number of years the authorities had been cracking down on people who chose to launder money from drugs, arms and prostitution through the legitimate business of antiques dealing, but this was her first experience of what that may entail. Assuming Ieuan and his team would want her to show them the paperwork for the vendors and buyers involved in Wednesday's auction, she led them over to the glass doors to the offices, unlocked them and neatly stepped inside to switch off the alarm. Once the alarm was disabled, before she could go any further Ieuan put his arm in front of her in a move which was surprisingly effective considering there was no contact between them, made her take the few steps back through the door and out of the way as the jeans and suits surged forwards, leaving only Rebecca and Ieuan outside with the uniforms.
It was then that Rebecca noticed the three dark grey vans had been driven into the courtyard, two were positioned outside the sale room, and the third was parked with its back and side doors open next to where she was standing. For the next few minutes, she

watched helplessly as almost the entire contents of the offices were carried out of the building and packed into the vans and the boots of some of the cars. Less than forty-five minutes after the early morning phone call, she was being escorted from the premises. Paul's keys had been confiscated, the vans and most of the cars had been driven away, leaving only one marked police car, one unmarked 4x4, and the white van outside the gates. Ieuan told her 'We will forensically go through everything to do with Black's Auction House as far back as we can, comparing the records we have seized today with those already collated for the case we are investigating. We will need to interview both yourself and Mr Paul Black, and all of the other employees of Black's Auction House. This could take several months, but we will be working as quickly as we can. Until then, no unauthorised persons may have access to this site and I'm afraid that includes both you and Mr Black. Do you understand?'
Rebecca nodded, even though she didn't have a clue what was going on.
Ieuan rummaged in the pocket of his jeans and produced a card, which he handed to her. 'If you or Mr Black have any questions, any more information, or if anything happens that you are concerned about, don't hesitate to contact me on any of these numbers, okay?'
Again, Rebecca nodded. Concerns if anything happens? What did he mean? His and his colleagues' presence were the only events which had concerned her so far this week.
'Good.' He nodded. 'I would like to thank you on behalf of the Art and Antiques Fraud Squad for your cooperation. We always get what we want in the end, but it isn't always as easy for the civilians involved as you have made it this morning. Now, is there anywhere

in this town where my team can get a bacon butty and a cuppa?'
Rebecca became aware there were still a few jeans loitering behind her. Ieuan gestured towards them 'Some of us still have a full day ahead of us going through what's left.' He tipped his head towards the former Chapel. 'We're going to need a good and regular supply of fuel,' he winked.

Chapter 5

Saturday 19th of October 2019, 8:30 am

'Look at him; he's like a man possessed!' Jennifer gasped, as she peered up through her wet fringe, sweat stinging her eyes.
Jennifer had decided to join her boyfriend, Paul Black, and the running club on their regular Saturday morning run. While Jennifer was struggling to breathe, Paul was running up the hill ahead of her with other Woodford Streakers Wearing Clothes, at a good pace and showing no signs of slowing down. Elbows and knees pumping like pistons in a steady rhythm, he looked strong and healthy. Unlike Jennifer. Her legs had independently made the decision to stop moving, and she felt faint.
'I wish I had his energy this morning.' Cliff Williamson took advantage of Jennifer's impromptu stop to pour water into his mouth and over his face. 'Or Caroline's fitness levels. Blimey, she's already running back down to us. How can someone who works with food all day be so fit?'
'You're doing fine Cliff, considering how much you had to drink in The Ship Inn last night.' Jennifer was grateful to him for hanging back with her, but knew it was only because he was hungover. On a normal run, he and Paul would be racing each other in the

testosterone filled competitive way some men do. His red face was contrasting badly with his auburn hair and freckles.
‘Paul and I drank the same amount, but it seems to have affected us differently. I am floundering halfway up this hill and he is already almost at the top.’
‘I suppose that is what happens when one of you celebrates the sale of a redundant dinosaur piece of desk furniture for over fifteen thousand pounds plus commission at your auction, and the other one is his wing man.’
‘Jennifer Isaac, I will ignore the fact you have dismissed me as Paul’s wing man, and instead ask has living with an antiques auctioneer not taught you anything? Redundant dinosaur piece of desk furniture! I can't believe you said that. The bronze inkwell is a piece of fine art by Franz Bergmann who was THE bronze foundry owner of the time. The buyer still hasn't paid for the bear, so Paul's going to have to wait another few days before offering it to the underbidder. It's looking as though the one who bid it up so high was a hoax bidder.’
Caroline had joined them and adopted Jennifer’s teasing tone. ‘Come on you two, keep moving. Standing around chatting about a pretty ornament won't get that running stamina up.’ Despite her fast run up the steep hill and part way back down again, Caroline was looking relaxed and happy. Her shoulder length, straight dark brown hair was caught up in a neat ponytail, a red sun visor shielding her eyes from the increasing strength of the early morning sun. Jennifer felt worse than ever, sure that her own long dark brown hair was plastered to her sweaty face and back in rat tails.

Caroline began to jog back up the hill, beckoning for them to follow her. Cliff fought off the stiffness creeping into his legs and caught up with her in a few long strides.
'You are also an antiques philistine Caroline,' he teased. 'All of these years you have lived in the town of Woodford, one of the great antiques centres of the county of Brackenshire, you ply your trade at every sale Paul has, your family's cafe thrives on local and visiting antiques dealers, and you still do not appreciate a fine and rare antique when it turns up in our local auction. I don't know what they teach you youngsters in school these days.'
Caroline laughed. A quick check over her shoulder confirmed that Jennifer was too far back to hear. 'I do know that Paul is planning something special for him and Jennifer and the money he earns from this sale will be going a long way to paying for it. Let's hope the buyer for the bronze bear pays up as soon as possible, because that extra commission will make a big difference to Paul's plans.'
Cliff rolled his eyes and nodded. 'He's told you too?'
'Yes, he has booked me and mum to do the catering and said he asked you to be his best man. I'm not sure that springing a surprise wedding on Jennifer is a good idea. We did try to talk him out of it, but he was adamant.'
Cliff groaned. 'Believe me, he and I have almost come to blows over this mad plan, but he is convinced she will love it. There's still time to persuade him to change his mind.'
'I don't think there is. We only have two months. Most brides like to plan their weddings for at least a year, if not longer.'

'He thinks he is doing her a favour because she keeps saying she is too busy to plan anything whenever he asks her about it.' His short curly auburn hair gleamed in the sunlight, his freckled tanned face creased into a frown as serious brown eyes looked at her. Cliff and Paul had been friends for many years, and recently Paul had supported Cliff through one of the lowest points of his life. Cliff thought that his friend was making the wrong decision by not involving Jennifer in the planning of their wedding, and wanted to help him to make the right one. 'He is head over heels in love with Jennifer and I know he thinks he is being romantic by doing everything. Jennifer works very hard, and Paul doesn't want to put extra pressure on her by landing the job of planning a wedding on her shoulders. I understand he thinks this is the right thing to do, but I don't.'
'Mmmh, I agree with you. I also think he is making a very big mistake. He has even chosen her wedding dress!'
'To be fair, he has got her mum and sister on board with this, so perhaps we don't know her as well as they do.'
'Perhaps.'
They both grimaced, neither believing it was a good idea, and with an unspoken challenge they raced over a particularly vicious incline to the plateau at the top of the field, where the rest of the group had been resting for several minutes.
'Better late than never,' teased Bilbo.
Paul was leaning heavily on the metal five bar gate, sweat collecting in beads on the short hair around the nape of his neck and running down his forehead. 'I think I am sweating beer' was his only comment at their arrival. Caroline and Cliff walked over to join

him, Caroline only breathing heavily while Cliff kept having to stop to catch his breath before moving forwards a few steps and stopping again.
Eventually he managed to regulate his breathing, and glancing around to make sure none of the rest of the group were within earshot he said 'We were just discussing your mad wedding plans. Caroline agrees with me that you should involve Jennifer in them.'
'Shhh!' Paul hissed, as he found the last vestiges of energy and rushed to check on Jennifer's progress up the hill. Reassured that she was still battling her way up the slope, he turned back and joined the other two at the gate.
'She can't hear us,' Caroline assured him.
'Look, you two, I have made my feelings clear on this subject. Now shut up about it. I want to marry Jennifer more than anything in the world, and if that means I need to do all of the planning and preparation so she can have a stress-free wedding, then that is what I will do. I made too many mistakes in my previous relationships by not putting the effort in and I do not intend to screw this relationship up in the same way. The commission on the sale of that bear is going to make this the wedding of Jennifer's dreams, and we don't need anyone throwing rotten tomatoes from the side lines.'
Cliff and Caroline shared a look and kept quiet. While they waited for Jennifer to reach them, they gazed in silence at the spectacular sight of Stormy Vale. The fields, woodlands, villages and hamlets of the county of Brackenshire were laid out before them in green and brown. In the distance they could even see the blue waters of the English Channel.
This was Jennifer's first outing with the local running group and she wasn't sure there would be another. The

four friends had shared Cliff's car before dawn broke to drive to neighbouring Brackendon, where they joined three other car loads of runners, and together they were running home, a distance of approximately nine kilometres. She had seen Cliff and Caroline having a chat as they ran up the hill ahead of her, while she could barely draw in enough breath before her body automatically expelled it again. Now they had reached the top she knew they were waiting with Paul and recovering, as she continued to flounder. She felt terrible that the rest of the club were also waiting for her at the top, probably cursing her slowness and checking their watches to see if they were going to be late for whatever they had planned for the rest of their Saturday. She wished they would go on ahead and leave her to make her own way home, but the club had a strict 'one for all, all for one' policy, and they kept reassuring her they wouldn't. Her legs insisted she stopped again. She understood why you never see a runner with a smile on their face. This was bloody awful. Never again. Never, never again was she ever doing this again. Never.

By the time she forced her unwilling body to the top of the hill, the other three had joined the rest of the group gathered around and sitting on some hay bales, but as Jennifer staggered over to them she knew she didn't have the energy to jump up. She lay flat on her back on the grass instead.

'Oh' Paul groaned as he slid off the bale and lay on the ground next to her with his eyes shut. 'I am in need of something to drink.' He opened one eye and squinted up at the other two, adding 'and I don't mean anything alcoholic.'

‘There's a water trough over there.’ Caroline gestured towards the fence line where a herd of cows were staring curiously at them.
‘I hope the standard of refreshments for the Woodford Half Marathon will be higher than that. Black’s Auction House are the main sponsor, and I don't want my company’s name going on fly-filled cow-spit contaminated water.’
Caroline sighed heavily. ‘Paul, ever since you offered to sponsor the race day every decision the committee makes has the postscript of “I don't want my company’s name blah blah blah” and we are all heartily sick of it.’
‘All right, all right. Keep your hair on. I was only joking.’
‘Well, it's not funny anymore.’ Caroline spoke for everyone else present, and several people who were not.
Chastened, Paul kept quiet.
‘Thank goodness it is next weekend,’ said Caroline. ‘Then we can all breathe a sigh of relief when it has been a fantastic success.’
‘Oh god, next weekend,’ groaned Cliff. ‘I can’t believe it has been over a year in the planning, and yet is has come around so quickly.’
‘I’m looking forward to running it,’ said Bilbo. ‘How many entrants do we have?’
‘Eighty-two, as of when I checked my emails last night. We have had a few drop out recently with some weird flu bug which seems to be going around, and of course the inevitable injuries and last minute realisation that they haven’t trained enough. With all of the drop-outs it means that we have no waiting list any more, which is great, but we do still have eight spaces to fill. There are eight members of Brackenshire’s

finest constabulary running in fancy dress in aid of Macmillan Cancer Research.'
'Oh yes,' said Ian McClure, a police officer based in Woodford, 'my dinosaur costume is washed, pressed, and hanging on the back of our bedroom door. Although I think we are down to seven now, because one of the team is off work after being awake all night with an annoying cough and a bit of a temperature.'
'This bug does seem to be flooring people at the moment. There are bound to be more cancelling their entry between now and next Saturday,' observed Paul. 'I'll put a post up on the WSWC facebook page and see if we can fill those places.'
'Thank you,' said Cliff.
Paul sighed. 'It's ironic that we decided to organise this race because we wanted to run it, but we're both so busy organising it neither of us can compete.'
Jennifer rolled her eyes. It wasn't the first time she had heard this complaint.
'Come on, let's get this over with.' Jennifer was keen to put an end to the torture, and the others had assured her they were less than one kilometre from home. She beckoned the others to join her as she opened the gate. 'I'm afraid if I stop much longer, someone will have to come and fetch me in their car.'
Paul pushed himself upright and was quickly by her side. Giving her a kiss on the cheek, he said. 'You know, I'm proud of you, don't you? You have done really well to get up that field. It's all downhill from here, I promise.'
One by one the rest of the group walked through the gate as Jennifer stayed at her post, and each one gave her a few words of encouragement, and all reassuring her she could look forward to a final downhill section, or reverse hill as Bilbo joked. Jennifer was familiar

with the lane because she visited clients of the Woodford Equine Veterinary Practice who lived on it, and knew they were all lying. Before she could point out that there were two hilly sections between them and home, Paul's shorts began singing the 'A-team' ringtone.
'For goodness' sake, if it's that bloody unlisted number again then I'm calling the police' Paul grumbled as he unzipped his phone from the pocket. 'Whoever it is has been ringing all morning. Oh, it's Rebecca. It's a bit early for her to be calling on a Saturday. I hope she is all right.'
Paul wasn't too worried about Rebecca, and didn't answer her call immediately. Instead, he led the rest of the group back to The Green, jogging at a comfortable pace for Jennifer to keep up with him. It was only once they had all congregated at the bench by the Brackendon Road and said goodbye to the rest of the club members that he called Rebecca back. His face drained of colour as he looked across the road to the left of where they were standing, but there was no sign of the police presence on the road or pavement outside his auction house. From what he could see, the gates appeared to be locked as usual, but with a panicked yell he took off across the road. The others, startled by his yell and his sudden sprint away from them, instinctively followed. Rebecca appeared from the alley, and beckoned for them to follow her to Paul's house, where she had let herself back in and had helped herself to coffee and milk while she waited for him to finally answer her calls. She spent the time formulating a plan, but until she was sure it could work she decided to keep quiet. It didn't take her long to brief Paul on the events that morning. Cliff, Jennifer and Caroline had to get ready for work, and Jennifer

had promised to drive Cliff to collect his car from Brackendon, so feeling helpless in their friends' time of crisis they left Paul and Rebecca to try and find out what they could do to resolve the situation. Paul, still in his running clothes, hurried around to his auction house to speak to someone in charge.

Chapter 6

Saturday 19th of October 2019, 9:00 am

Lisa Thomas watched through the serving hatch as one after another a dozen policemen and women trooped through the door of The Woodford Tearooms. None were in uniform, but since moving to Woodford a few years ago, Lisa had learned to spot a member of the police force a mile away. Checking her watch, she debated whether to give her daughter Caroline a ring to see how long before she would be coming into work. Normally on a Saturday morning, one person could easily cope with the early breakfast crowd, but that was because the regulars came in singly, occasionally in twos, and so the morning had started as usual. A couple of antiques dealers, Hazel and Linda, had been the first through the door when Lisa opened up at half-past seven, and had sat at their usual table and ordered their usual Saturday morning breakfast of coffee and croissants, and so it had continued with regulars placing their familiar orders, until ten minutes ago when an influx of seven new customers had walked in and were now sitting around a couple of tables they had pulled together, and now the latest group of new customers were trying to join them. So long as the kettle was permanently boiling and the bacon and sausages were minutes away from being perfect, there was normally no problem. A mass entry of a dozen hungry people who all expected to be served at the same time was more like a busy lunchtime in Woodford, when there would be at least two if not three staff working together.

‘Caroline? It’s Mum.’ Lisa always announced herself, even though she knew that ‘Mum’ came up on Caroline’s phone whenever she rang. ‘Darling, I know you are not due in for another hour, but is there any chance you are home from your run, showered and ready to come to work now please?’

‘Give me five minutes and I'll be there. I am literally stepping out of the door now. Don't worry; I was expecting you to call. See you in a minute.’

Wondering what was going on to bring all of these people into the town, and how her daughter knew about it, Lisa topped up the kettle and popped eight slices of bread into the industrial toaster in anticipation for the likely orders. Of course, the local breakfast crowd had been talking about the commotion outside Black’s Auction House earlier that morning, but as no fire engines or ambulances were involved, Lisa assumed it was nothing too serious. Surely it couldn't be as bad as the murder of a few years ago, which had taken place early one morning in the doorway of Williamson Antiques, next door to the tearooms. That had been far too close for comfort.

She checked her appearance in the mirror on the back of the larder door: curly blonde hair safely under the control of a blue headscarf with white polka dots, secured in a bow off to one side at the top of her head; blue eyes framed with black mascara which had not smudged – yet; pale pink lip colour on her lips and not her teeth. She stepped back so her five foot six inch frame was reflected in the mirror, and saw a slim figure dressed in dark blue tailored shorts, brown pumps, white t-shirt, and an apron to match the headscarf. She gave herself a quick nod of approval Mary Poppins-style, before picking up her notepad and stepping out into the room, ready to handle whatever challenges lay ahead.

The sun was pouring in through the two bay windows which looked out over the High Street. All of the tables had small vases of freshly picked flowers, the last of the season's sweet peas or roses from Lisa's garden, and one wall was filled with paintings, jewellery, books and ornaments made by local talents. The noise level was extremely loud. She approached the nearest table containing two men and two women.

'Good morning ladies and gents. Do you all know what you would like to eat and drink?'

By the time Lisa had taken everyone's order, Caroline was at work in the kitchen, pulling mugs, teapots and milk jugs out of the dishwasher where they had been stacked and washed the night before, and preparing for the drinks orders. Together, mother and daughter worked efficiently, delivering bowls of the local natural yoghurt containing oats and bananas, baskets of freshly baked croissants, muffins and bread rolls, plates of local ham and fried eggs, a couple of plates of naturally smoked haddock and poached eggs, and several traditional cooked breakfasts.

A knock at the back door revealed Paul Black and Rebecca Martin.

'Any chance we could have breakfast out here please Lisa?' asked Paul, indicating the courtyard normally only used for staff parking. The courtyard was accessed by an unmade road which ran alongside The Green, and was surrounded by a greenstone wall. Lisa noticed that, unlike her daughter, Paul had not been

home for a shower after their run, and a quick glance at Rebecca revealed that she had not had time to do her hair and makeup before leaving the house. Rebecca tended to wear minimalist make-up, but Lisa could see that her skin was bare, and marvelled that she looked great. They were both obviously involved in whatever was the latest event to hit Woodford. Lisa hoped it wasn't another traumatic one, as Rebecca had already lost her father in a violent tragedy which took place in the town.
Deciding that now was not the time to ask tricky questions, she said ‘Of course you can. Give us a minute and we’ll sort out somewhere for you to sit and eat out here. Do you both know what you would like to eat and drink?’
Lisa and Caroline worked well as a team, and once all of their customers who ordered before Paul and Rebecca had been served, they carried a small table, a couple of chairs, and finally food and drink out to them. They were deep in conversation, sitting on an ancient wooden bench outside the kitchen window, from where they could see over the wall and out onto The Green and the early morning dog walkers. Lisa hovered in the doorway, ready to attend to the customers seated in The Tearooms, and her daughter took the opportunity to have a bite to eat while there was a lull in the service. Caroline sat down with Paul and Rebecca on one of the chairs and began to tuck into a bowl of yoghurt and fruit. She was always starving after a run and was sure the customers could hear her tummy rumbling as she served their food.
Between mouthfuls she asked ‘Do you know any more?’
Paul, still in his running gear and suddenly aware that he must smell terrible, pushed away the plate of egg

and bacon butty, unable to face his usual breakfast choice and took another sip of his coffee.
'I will have that if you are not eating it,' Cliff Williamson, freshly showered with his auburn hair still damp, appeared around the corner of the wall separating his antiques centre from the tearooms. 'Do you have any more information about what's going on?'
'You're welcome to it, mate' muttered Paul. He felt the pressure from everyone waiting for him to speak. He had been trying to ignore his phone ringing and ringing with people who didn't need to know what little he knew, ever since he sat down, but even that was holding its silence for the time being. Keeping his eyes on an elderly gentleman who was determinedly ignoring the dachshund at the end of the red lead, who was stopping to poo on the grass, in a low voice, he said 'The police have locked down the auction house and my bank accounts have been frozen. Rebecca knows more than me because she was there this morning, but even she doesn't know exactly what is going on. You think it has something to do with that bloody bronze bear I sold on Tuesday, don't you?'
Rebecca nodded 'From the little the police are telling me, I think the vendor for the bronze bear is being investigated for money laundering, and because he has put several items of stock through Black's Auction House in the past six months, we are being investigated too.'
'The buyer hasn't even bloody well paid for it yet,' said Paul, bitterly.
'So what does that mean? You are now being investigated for what? For money laundering?' Lisa asked.

Paul growled, still concentrating on the elderly man who was now walking away from the dog mess on the grass as fast as his fat arthritic legs would allow him. 'According to some Welsh policeman who has been phoning me all morning, and who I have only just met and spoken to in person, it means that for the foreseeable future, I am unable to work and earn money. The bastard was standing outside the gates and wouldn't even let me walk into my own auction house. It means that this could be the end of Black's Auction House, because no bugger is going to trust me or want to be associated with me. It means that because some selfish lowlife has decided to use the antiques trade and specifically my business to wash money they have taken from drug addicts and sex slaves, my whole life is ruined. I might as well cancel all the plans I have made for the wedding. That's what it means.'

No one spoke. This was new territory for all of them, and they needed time to absorb what Paul was saying. Even Rebecca had not fully understood what the repercussions of the police investigation would mean to Paul's business and to his personal life.

Paul felt as though he was sinking in a deep swamp. He had always been the type of person who was planning his next move, analysing what had been before, and getting stuck in to make things happen. These were qualities his school teachers and parents did not always appreciate when he was younger, but his dad recognised that if Paul wanted to channel those energies into the auction business he would be successful. His dad was proved right, and when Paul joined the family firm from school he focused on being the best team member, employee and customer service person he could be. His efforts were rewarded, and when his father decided to promote Paul as vacancies arose, no one accused him of nepotism. Gradually Mr Black senior allowed Paul to develop his own ways of doing things, and introduce new concepts. It was Paul who created the house clearance section of the business, and as a result the quantity and quality of the items passing under the auctioneer's hammer had risen. It was Paul who moved the auction business further in the direction of antiques and collectables, away from general bric-a-brac. Although not a fan of online auctions when they were first mooted, Paul was in the process of tweaking the system of ensuring that Black's Auction House had the best reputation with potential buyers who wished to view items over the internet, and buy without paying extortionate packing and postage costs. The action of the police that morning had brought all of that to a halt. He had no timescale to work within, no problems to follow up, no challenges to resolve, no success to celebrate. He didn't know what he could do to resolve the situation, or where to start the recovery. He didn't know if the business could recover. Foremost on his mind was the wonderful surprise wedding he was planning. Before he met Jennifer he would waste his time on affairs, enjoying the secrecy, the duplicitous behaviour, the power to start and end a relationship. But his love for Jennifer overpowered everything else, his need for her replaced the thrill of the drama. If he had no business behind him, no means to earn a living, no self-confidence in his decision-making, what did he have to offer her? Paul remained quiet as he tried to control the unusual feeling of panic which threatened to engulf him.

Eventually, after finishing the egg and bacon butty, Cliff broke the silence. 'That's rough. Surely the police must have some evidence before such drastic measures

can be put into place? And as we all know, you would not get involved in anything like this so therefore there can be no evidence. There must be more to it. Surely they can't ruin someone's business, your livelihood, yours and Jennifer's future, without something more concrete than a buyer putting goods through your sale room. You must have some rights and protections in this matter?'
'According to this chap, Ieuan Davies, apparently not.' Paul's tone did not invite further comments, and the atmosphere grew thicker. No one knew what to say. There were no words of comfort they could offer. Cliff was desperate to order a cup of tea now that the egg and bread from Paul's breakfast roll was sticking to the roof of his mouth and the salty bacon had exacerbated the dryness, but didn't feel it was appropriate. His usual post run hunger and thirst was compounded by excessive drinking of alcohol in The Ship Inn the previous evening. Ironically, celebrating the very thing which appeared to have the potential to ruin his friend's business.
A knock on the serving hatch which separated the kitchen from the cafe gave Caroline and Lisa an excuse to leave. But Rebecca and Cliff had to stay where they were, glancing uncomfortably at each other and at Paul, who had turned his attention to a small beetle as it explored one of the table's legs.
After several minutes of silence, Paul spoke in a lighter tone. He could feel the panic subsiding as he began to see a possible way out of the swamp, although his body was still firmly held in there. His brain had been formulating a short-term plan to get them through the immediate future, and he was ready to put it into action. 'Don't worry, Rebecca. My insurance will cover your wages for the next six months. I bloody

well hope we're back in business before then, but I know of two other auction houses which were investigated and even though they were eventually found innocent, they were forced to close down. An antiques business just cannot survive with that kind of disruption to its cash flow, let alone the atmosphere of suspicion once the police get involved. So much for innocent until proven guilty. I'm going home for a shower and get changed, and then I'll be on the phone to Larissa, my lawyer. Saturday or not she'll know what to do.'

Chapter 7

Saturday 19th of October 2019, 9:45am

‘Oh Madeleine, I am so sorry I am late!’ Jennifer eased herself out of her car, bent to pat the little black Patterdale Terrier, Max, and gasped as her calf muscles reminded her that she had been running up hills that morning. She unclipped her dog Lucy’s harness, and Lucy leapt out of the car to play with Max.
Madeleine Powell, although only in her mid-twenties, was the manager of Woodford Riding Club, and loyal servant to Max. Her brown eyes watched Jennifer with concern. ‘What on earth has happened to you? You look as though you've been run over!’
‘That is exactly how I feel,’ complained Jennifer. ‘I thought I would join the Streakers and go for a little run with them this morning before work. Oh my God, I think they tried to kill me! I thought we'd be doing a five kilometre run, but they made me do nine kilometres!’
‘Good grief, why did you think that was a good idea? They are serious runners, Jennifer. Have you ever run before?’
‘Nope. And I'm never going to again. I thought I was fit from all of the walking and horse riding I do, and I often run around with the dog or when I'm training the

horse online or at liberty. You know how many miles we cover out in that cross-country field.'
'I agree that you and I have walked several miles in preparation for the training event tomorrow, but I don't think walking is any preparation for running.'
'Of course not. If I had known how far they were planning to run I would never have joined them.'
'So, you won't be pounding the pavements on a Saturday morning wearing one of their "Woodford Streakers Wearing Clothes" club running vests with the other Woodford runners?'
Jennifer pulled a face. 'To be honest, I wasn't planning on wearing one of those anyway. But after this morning I definitely won't be. I'm not sure I'll even be able to get out of bed tomorrow. Hello Jasper!' she called to the handsome grey horse who was watching her from the other side of the fence.
'He must have recognised the sound of your car engine. I told you, after you turn him out on the track he waits until you have driven out of the yard before joining the rest of his herd, and when he sees your car drive in, he brings himself back up here.'
Jennifer walked on stiff legs over to the fence, wondering if that was a blister she could feel under her right foot, and rubbed the grey neck. 'Good morning, Jasper' she murmured. She and the horse breathed together for a while, before Jennifer dragged herself away. 'That's better, although my legs still feel like injured jelly. Lead me to this poorly pony. Who is it?'
Madeleine rolled her eyes. 'No prizes for guessing. Somehow Woody let himself into one of the resting fields again, and when I retrieved him this morning he had a large gash along his left side. I think he must have caught himself when he rolled under the fence, as I can't see where else he could have done it. He seems

pretty happy with himself and undid my plait while I was administering first aid.'
Jennifer laughed as she looked at Madeleine's long dark curly hair, which had been hastily wound up into a loose bun and secured with a bright yellow hair band. Madeleine and Rebecca Martin had only discovered that they were half-sisters when Madeleine moved to the town to work at the Woodford Riding Club, and their familial likeness was sometimes disconcerting. Together, Jennifer and Madeleine walked across the yard to one of the stables where a pretty bay New Forest pony was watching them. He nickered as they approached him, obviously pleased to see them. Madeleine brought him out of the dimly lit stable, so that Jennifer could see the damage in daylight.
'I cleaned it up and slathered it with gel, but I wasn't sure if it needed to be stitched. What do you think?'
Jennifer examined him thoroughly from head to tail, and everywhere in between. She and Woody were old friends due to the number of times he got himself into trouble, and he was happy for her to check him over. It had crossed her mind more than once that he was self-harming to get more attention, but her scientific brain knew that horses and ponies do not behave like that. He was unique among her equine patients, as even the most accident-prone ones only managed one, at the most two incidents a year. Woody seemed to have a new one at least once a month.
'I think he has got away with minimal damage this time. It is superficial, and not too long, but you were right to call me out to check. I think that if it had been any wider we would have had to try and stitch it, although the chances of it holding and keeping clean for long enough to work would be minimal. I thought you had added another strand of electric tape along the

bottom of his fence to prevent him from rolling underneath?'
'We did. Gray put that in two weeks ago. Unfortunately, someone,' she said pointing at Woody, 'has worked out that he can disable the electric current by grabbing hold of the handle to the electric tape at the gateway and manoeuvring it free. Then he walks over to a section of fencing, and all he has to do is his usual trick of flattening the tape with his head and neck, and wriggling under the wooden rail. I have it all on CCTV. The daft thing is that once he has opened the tape he is perfectly capable of opening the latch on the wooden gate behind. No other horse on the yard would even think about any of that, let alone put it into action, but Woody does. In fact, I am astonished he was still in the stable when you arrived.'
'He is very bright. I think that he needs more work to keep that brain of his occupied.'
'Mmmh, the trouble is, because he keeps doing things like this I can't work him until it heals, and it is also difficult to turn him out with the others because inevitably he lets them out too.'
'True. Although that wound is not too bad at the moment, if he performs his usual athletics it will open up even more, and there is no way you can put a saddle or even a bareback pad on him without interfering with it. He needs a slow and steady job, one which involves walking in a straight line for several hours at a time.'
'Maybe you should long line him around the town if you want to do something to keep fit?' teased Madeleine.
'Ha ha, that sounds too much like hard work! At least he hasn't broken into the posh yard,' Jennifer indicated the superb facilities across the other side of the car park.

'Yet' groaned Madeleine. 'I dread the day he does that.'
Grayson Bragg, a local builder and property developer, was responsible for the purpose-built red brick barn with a clock tower in a separate yard, well away from the riding club, and where the old dairy used to be. He had been married to a member of the Higston family who owned the Woodford Riding Club and the land around it, and together they had three children, all of whom had grown up loving horses. Although he and their mother had long since divorced, it became clear that his two daughters and their mother were serious about competing in the discipline of dressage and wished to manage their horses in a different way to the riding school ponies and liveries. All of this was long before Madeleine joined the business, but even then the horses and ponies in the Woodford Riding Club were more likely to be found happy hacking around the local area and participating in Easter Egg hunts and Christmas Fancy Dress competitions, than scrubbed and plaited so they could strut their stuff in a dressage arena. Grayson had paid for and project managed the small dressage diva paradise according to the wishes of his ex-wife and his daughters.
This part of the equestrian interest was not under Madeleine's jurisdiction, and the facilities were not available to the riding club. The dressage horses had use of a powerful hot shower, a solarium, a well-equipped tack room, a superb rug room with racks and heaters and a dedicated washing machine, and six well-appointed boxes where the expensive animals with bloodlines which could be traced back through the decades were housed in fourteen foot by fourteen foot stables on deep bedding, almost every inch of their bodies wrapped up in bandages and rugs. As well as

their own horses, they regularly accepted other people's horses for training or starting their ridden life following the Higston women's preferred management system. The horses were turned out for a few hours every day, in individually fenced paddocks so they could not harm each other, and were regularly seen by an army of therapists of varying descriptions. Unlike the horses and ponies next door who were all barefoot, these horses were treated to a set of four shiny new shoes with pads every four or five weeks, and the farrier had a regular time slot on a Friday morning, as well as his own mug and preference for an egg and bacon roll at the end of his shoeing session catered for. The atmosphere was calm and purposeful, unlike the often chaotic and noisy scenes next door.

Indeed, the contrast with the horses a few metres away in the riding club under Madeleine's care was striking, although they too had the use of Grayson Bragg's skills. He or one of his employees were always on-hand to build or mend as required, and there was always a lot of maintenance to do, unlike the modern dressage yard next door where occasionally an electrician or plumber was required. One of Grayson Bragg's employees, Bilbo, was dating Grayson's elder daughter, and he was always willing to fix and mend any minor jobs while she was mucking out or training the horses in the evenings.

The riding club's wooden stables were a ramshackle collection of varying sizes arranged in a haphazard fashion throughout the stable yard, as more had been built when the need arose over the years. These days they were rarely used to house horses, but instead proved useful storage for the variety of TREC and agility bits and pieces which were required sporadically throughout the year, and numerous tables

and chairs. Some stables were kept ready for injured horses like Woody, and for horses who were visiting for a day clinic so their owners could relax and watch the other students.
'Perhaps I am looking at Woody's issues the wrong way round, and he is over-stimulated here and would prefer the quiet atmosphere over there?' pondered Madeleine.
Jennifer shrugged. 'I hadn't thought of that, but I suppose it could be possible. Something to think about. By the way, I have roped Paul in to being on standby in case we need someone to drive the horse lorry to pick up any casualties tomorrow.'
'Oh that's great, thank you. It will save me from getting tied up in an emergency. But surely Paul won't have time to spend the day waiting around in case he is needed to drive the lorry for us, will he?'
'Unfortunately he probably will have all the time in the world for a while. The police have shut down the auction house while they carry out investigations.'
'What! Why? There hasn't been another death has there?' Madeleine had been directly affected by the murder of a close relative in the town a few years ago, and was still inclined to think the worst whenever the police were involved in Woodford. 'Is Rebecca alright?'
Aware of her friend's fears for her half-sister, Jennifer put her hand on Madeleine's arm. 'Don't worry, and no, it's nothing like that. Rebecca is absolutely fine; I saw her before I came here. Although she has been caught up in the police investigation too. In fact, she was the first one to respond to the phone call from the police. Mind you, Paul looked ready to commit murder when he found out the auction house is going to be

shut for a minimum of three weeks, possibly six months.'
'Minimum! How long is the maximum?'
Jennifer pulled a face. 'Worst case scenario? It could be shut for good.'
'What? What on earth has he done?'
'Nothing, that's the problem. You know the bronze bear which sold for over fifteen thousand pounds on Tuesday? We think the police believe the vendor is involved in money laundering, and that Paul's business is involved. Of course he is not, it's a nightmare. I mean, how easy is it to prove you are innocent of something like that?'
Madeleine shrugged. 'I have no idea. I'm not sure I really understand what money laundering is. At least, I know it means turning money gained illegally into apparently kosher goods, but the ways and means are a mystery to me. It must be very lucrative, considering the sums of money involved. Although it was a big sale for Black's Auction House, that amount of money doesn't sound very big as part of a money laundering scheme. Apparently, there are whole streets in exclusive parts of London where the houses are worth millions of pounds and have been bought with the sole purpose of washing dirty money, and no one lives in them! I must be in the wrong line of work.'
'Me too. I think it is the opposite of horse ownership, where you turn good money into no money. Actually, that sale isn't very big for Paul's business. He regularly sells items for more. For example, only last week another lot went for several tens of thousands of pounds. Anyway, I'd better go and earn some money, even if it is only pennies compared to those figures. See you in the pub tonight?'
Madeleine nodded. 'See you there.'

Chapter 8

Saturday 19th October 2019, 11:30am

Madeleine waved goodbye as Jennifer drove out of the yard on her way to the next equine patient, with Lucy strapped into the back seat, and then returned to the cottage to collect the keys for a small off-road truck. Max was already waiting on the passenger seat, having loaded himself into the cab with eager anticipation. This was a twice-a-day job, and he loved the routine. He had a happy time inspecting new smells and jumping in and out of the cab while Madeleine spent the next forty-five minutes poo picking the hardcore track which ran around the outside of the three acre field. She had plenty of time to think about the latest troubles to come to the town of Woodford as she scraped up horse manure and threw it into the flat bed of the truck. Since moving to Brackenshire from Hampshire a few years ago as part of a witness protection programme, Madeleine had settled in very quickly to life as the manager of the local riding stables, Woodford Riding Club, although her personal life had been thrown into disarray at the time. One positive thing to come out of a tragic event three years earlier was that she discovered a family she previously didn't know existed, and learned that Rebecca Martin, and her sister Annette, were Madeleine's half-sisters.

Madeleine had thought she had no living family and that she was moving to a new place where no one would know her and she knew nobody, but ended up finding three lovely new relations, because Rebecca and Annette's mum, and therefore Madeleine's stepmother, Jackie, also welcomed Madeleine into her heart.

As she drove along the track, stopping every few feet to clear up the horse droppings, her mind turned to the challenge of how to solve Woody's propensity for getting into trouble. She had tried to make his environment as pony-proof as possible and wondered what else she could do to help him to be safe. The land at the Woodford Riding Club had originally been a dairy farm, but in the way of so many others the family had pulled out of farming over twenty years ago. When it was the thriving farm, Upper Woodford Farm had covered over one thousand acres and had been a mix of dairy, beef and arable farmland. The Higston family still owned the land, and were active farmers in next door Brackendon, but Upper Woodford Farm now comprised of woodland, a golf course, campsite, fishing lakes, and the equestrian centre she managed, as well as providing a significant section of the upcoming Woodford Half Marathon route.

There had always been horses on the farm, and the riding club started by accident in the nineteen fifties when Harold Higston allowed his daughter Marion to keep a pony in with the two working draught horses. He and his wife, Susan, regularly hunted the draught horses in the winter and Marion came along on the end of a lead rope until she could prove that she was able to stop little Bubbles from charging through the herd of big hunt horses and past the Master of the Hunt. Once the hunting season finished, the draught horses were put back into harness and used to pull the ploughs and carts around the farm, coping easily with the hilly land and quirky field shapes. Marion still wanted to ride her pony, especially as the weather was warmer and dryer during the summer months, but Mum and Dad couldn't keep up on foot and their bicycles weren't much use across the fields. The obvious solution was for Harold and Susan to acquire a riding horse, and then another, and then another. Over time, Marion's friends came to ride her pony or brought their ponies, and their parents rode Harold and Susan's horses or their own. The children grew up and took over the parents' horses, the parents needed new horses, the ponies needed new riders, and within five years the Higstons had fourteen non-farming horses on their land, a number of wooden hunting fences built into the field boundaries, and a flat dressage paddock which was rolled and maintained with great attention to detail. The Woodford Riding and Pony Club was formed.

Sixty years later and Marion no longer had her own horses, but her grandson was studying with a classical trainer over on the European continent, and her daughter and two granddaughters competed in all of the local and national dressage competitions. She walked her two labradors around the fields every day, checking on the horses as they grazed on the track or in the fields, and whenever there were visitors she could be regularly seen taking a keen interest in their activities.

Out in the fields, Madeleine had transformed the former grazing into an enormous equestrian facility offering variety and flexibility to the occupants and visitors. Grayson had enjoyed the challenge of her plans, and had almost single-handedly built, dug and created according to Madeleine's designs, and was now in demand across Brackenshire as the go-to builder for small and large projects along similar lines. Although not a horseman, with one ex-wife, one present wife, and at least two daughters and a son deeply ensconced in the equestrian world, his knowledge and experience of constructing tracks, jumps and buildings were second-to none.

Madeleine had designed the fencing to form an interconnecting track around the edge of three fields which made up the twenty-five acres of land formally allocated to the riding stables, and with a small section running into and around parts of the stable yard. The track provided year-round turn-out and exercise, was grass in places and hardcore in others, so that the UK weather, working bare hooves, and the metabolic needs of the horses could be catered for. The fourteen horses and ponies were divided into herds of three or four depending on who they got on with and what their individual needs were. Some needed to be off the grass completely during the summer and were fed measured amounts of haylage which was made on the farm; others benefited from being off the grass during the daytime with limited access to haylage and out on the grass at night; while the third herd, which included Woody the escape artist, seemed to be able to thrive on adlib grass and haylage with no restrictions. At certain times of the year all of the horses could be turned out together in the field, and no horse was ever left on their own.

Woody's insistence on seeing every fence and door as a challenge was time consuming and frustrating. Madeleine decided she needed to look at the problem from another angle, and it was time for her to find something to keep his intelligent brain occupied because his owner wasn't in a position to do so, or try

to provide a calmer environment, similar to the one in the dressage yard next door. She was sure he wouldn't be allowed through their gates, and she didn't think he would be happy either, but something in his care and management did need to change. She wondered if his owner would be prepared to let him go out on loan to someone who had the time to give him and perhaps a quieter environment than the busy riding club.
Madeleine looked across the fields, which opened out onto many bridleways. The investment the Higston family and Grayson had agreed to put into her plans were paying off, with rarely a day passing without riders hiring the facilities. There was a three-acre field set up with permanent obstacles including bridges, steps, slopes, tyres, hula hoops, bending poles, challenging corridors and corners, and strips of material hung vertically to form curtains for riding through. The ten-acre field beyond it housed a variety of cross-country jumps and ditches, two marked grass dressage arenas and an area of brightly coloured show jumps. The seven-acre field was closest to the yard, and contained pens and field shelters for visiting horses, as well as a series of four round pens creating a cloverleaf pattern, and a fifty metre square arena with an all-weather surface where more show jumps and dressage markers could be set up. At the entrance to the property was a small indoor school measuring twenty by forty metres. All of this combined with access from the fields to many miles of bridleways, quiet country lanes and shared tracks, meant that Woody was not short of access to entertaining facilities, he was short of someone to engage with him on those facilities. The other horses were content with the company of each other if they were given any time off work, but clearly this was not sufficient for Woody.

Once the track was cleared of poo, and Madeleine had emptied the truck of its load onto the muck heap, she and Max trundled back to the yard to be met by a very angry livery owner. Madeleine listened patiently to the short, red faced woman who stood blocking her way, with her surgically enhanced boobs thrust forwards like weapons, her impossibly brown hair plastered to her head after an hour's horse ride, and her hands firmly placed on her shapely hips. As the woman ranted about some minor misdemeanour another livery owner was meant to have committed, Madeleine wondered if there could ever be a day when she would finally tell this unpleasant woman to pack up her belongings and leave the yard for good. Unfortunately, she knew this was never going to be possible, because this particular livery owner was Patricia Bragg, married to Marion Higston's ex-son-in-law Grayson Bragg, and was allowed to keep her horse at the Woodford Riding Club for free as she was by extension part of the family, although that invitation did not extend to the dressage yard next door. Because Patricia had been at Woodford Riding Club for longer than Madeleine, she treated Madeleine like the new girl. Not in a kind way, but as someone who needs to be regularly told how things should be done. Patricia had been surprisingly open to many of the changes Madeleine had introduced, but everything else had to be found fault with and grumbled about. Madeleine felt sorry for her, because in a way she was trapped in the shadow of Grayson's first family and was beholden to them if she wished to have access to the fantastic facilities at the yard. Despite her chippy manner with people, she was diligent and caring with her horse, who was a gentle dark brown Highland pony called Dougal. No expense was spared on either her or

Dougal's wardrobe, the pair regularly participated in the lessons and clinics Madeleine taught, she also spectated or rode in clinics with visiting trainers, and she was always eager to learn about all aspects of horsemanship.
On the whole the livery owners and those students who hired the Woodford Riding Club's own horses were conscientious. Certainly none of them were as rich as this woman, or if they were they weren't shouting about it in the same way, but there were one or two Madeleine thought who could take a leaf out of her book and spend a bit more time looking after their horses.
Patricia liked to tell everyone she came across that she had married her first true love, that she met her future husband when she was fourteen years old and he was twenty-two, and they married on her sixteenth birthday. Of course, it was no secret in Brackenshire and beyond that he was a serial adulterer. He had been married for the first time at eighteen-years old when his new wife was already pregnant with their son, and had been chucked out of the family home when it came to light that he was dating Patricia, while his wife was pregnant with their youngest daughter. Patricia had been five months pregnant when they married, and within a year another underage girl gave birth to his son. To Madeleine's knowledge there were at least another four of his children with different mothers knocking around the area. Whether Patricia was aware that everyone knew about her husband's true behaviour was unknown, but everyone agreed she must be living in cloud cuckoo land if she didn't. He appeared to be the polar opposite of his wife, and was a down-to-earth tradesman who worked hard, was friendly and polite to everyone he met, and unless you knew his wife or had

seen their home, you would never guess that he had more than a couple of pounds to rub together. Two weeks earlier had been their fortieth wedding anniversary, and to celebrate they had hired the function room at the yacht club where Grayson kept a boat he owned in partnership with three friends. The four men used it to go fishing at least once a month, making use of its luxury cruiser build to motor over to the Channel Islands or France. The wives rarely set foot on board, preferring to quaff cocktails and push salads around their plates in the yacht club's lounge which overlooked the marina. Once a year they held a drinks party on board, safely moored to the pontoon.

The anniversary party was a very posh do according to Patricia, and none of her fellow livery owners had been invited, even though she saw them almost every day and had been at school with a couple of them. Despite not being invited, everybody at the yard had been treated to a step-by-step account of the organisation of this party for a good eighteen months in advance. They all knew how much the catering was going to cost and what was on the menu; the insurance value of the stonking ruby jewellery set of earrings, necklace, bracelet and ring her husband had bought for her; how much her new ruby red dress, matching shoes and handbag cost; how expensive the champagne and wine were; and what the band were charging. After the party, Patricia and Grayson had flown off to some fabulous Caribbean Island 'for our fourth honeymoon'. As is typical of such types, Patricia claimed to hate social media, telling anyone within earshot that it was for people who have too much time on their hands, and yet she maintained a Facebook account so she could spy on everyone else, get involved in arguments with people she had never met and could never influence, and occasionally show off about her own wonderful life. Her current timeline was filled with photographs of her looking fabulous at the party, a lovey dovey one with her husband, and then obviously staged 'relaxed' family photographs with their three grown up children, seven grandchildren and various other family members. Stunning views of azure sea and white sand interspersed with multicoloured drinks followed, and now she was back on the yard, behaving more badly than ever. Instead of paying Madeleine to look after her horse while she was away, she had bullied a relatively new livery owner into doing it, promising to look after hers in return. Of course, all of the other livery owners knew the reciprocal arrangement would never happen, and had long since managed to come up with a series of convincing excuses why they couldn't help her.

Madeleine listened as Patricia complained, and agreed that the other livery owner probably should not have left her horse's hi-vis boots wrapped around the fence to dry because they could have been ruined by one of the horses pulling them off. Madeleine then pointed out that there were no horses on that section of the track at the moment, and so the boots were probably safe. Before Patricia could get started on another topic, Madeleine gently and politely gave her no option but to come into the office to pay her horse feed bill, which was already four weeks overdue, and for which she failed to apologise. When Patricia's card was declined, followed by a second card and then a third, for which the woman blamed the riding club's card machine or the bank or the weather, Madeleine was more embarrassed than she was. Patricia attempted to get hold of Grayson to see if he was anywhere nearby and could come and pay Madeleine, but his mobile phone

kept going straight to answerphone. With an airy promise that she would go home and try phoning through the card details ‘by which time your machine should have sorted itself out’, the woman drove out of the yard in her expensive, clean and shiny 4x4, which had never towed anything or been driven off road.
Frowning, Madeleine tested the card machine with one of her own cards, and sure enough the ten pound charge was immediately taken from her account.

Chapter 9

Saturday 19th October 2019, 3:00pm

Jennifer's rounds kept her busy for the next few hours, with booked appointments interspersed by a couple more emergencies and it was well after her timetabled lunch break at midday before she finally had a spare twenty minutes to eat the sandwiches she had dashed in and bought from Higston's Farm Shop on her way to another equine patient. While she was driving in between appointments she had already eaten the packed lunch Paul had made for her the previous evening, consisting of a cheese baguette, apple, hula hoops and penguin biscuit, but she was still hungry. As she sank her teeth into the first sandwich her mobile rang. Glancing at the screen, she could see it was her sister, Alison.

Through a mouthful of sourdough with rare beef and horseradish, she mumbled. 'Hang on, I'm eating,' before chewing and swallowing. 'Hi Alison. Sorry about that. For some reason I am absolutely starving today. I haven't stopped stuffing my face. How are you?'

'I'm fine, thank you. You're not pregnant, are you?'

Jennifer groaned. 'No, I'm not. Don't you start! Why is it that everybody thinks women of our age should be having babies? You're only a year younger than me;

how do you feel when people start going on at you about it?'
'Sorry, sorry it annoys me too. It's just that my friend is pregnant and she does nothing but eat at the moment. Her diet is mainly junk food, which is strange because she would never normally touch a chicken nugget or cheeseburger. Have you got a few minutes for a chat if I promise not to judge you with out-of-date stereotypes?'
Laughing, forgiving her sister, Jennifer checked her watch and nodded, before remembering that Alison couldn't see her over the phone. 'Yes, I have time for a quick chat. What's up?'
'I'm at the Woodford Riding Club preparing for a couple of private lessons this afternoon, and I've had an idea about Woody. Madeleine said you've already seen him this morning? She's worried he's going to be hanging onto his sick note and will miss the start of the school half-term, which will disappoint a lot of the children and compound his boredom.'
'Yes, I saw him the little monkey. He's lucky he got away with just a shallow wound this time, but he can't do anything else to himself, or he may not be so lucky. Madeleine knows what she is doing; I'm sure he'll be fit and healthy before the holidays begin.'
'She also said you have been out with the running club this morning?'
Jennifer groaned again. 'First and last time. I am never doing that again.'
'Oh, that's a shame. I was going to join you! I thought I'd start doing the Couch to 5K programme, and then come out for a run with you once I had completed it. It takes about nine weeks, running three times a week, and I was thinking I could do it with Woody. Obviously Woody will be doing other things on the

days I'm not running with him, and he could easily be working on the running days too, but I wondered if perhaps he needs a bit more one-on-one time before the holidays start and this could help both of us. He never seems to get into trouble when the yard is full of children at weekends and school holidays.'
'Couch to 5K? I don't think I know it, but if it keeps Woody out of trouble for a whole nine weeks then it will be the first thing to work since I have known him. I say go for it.'
'Thanks, I will. Which programme did you use to start running?'
'I didn't use one. I just put on my trainers and my one good sports bra and joined the others this morning.'
'This morning was your first run? You mad woman! Although I suppose that was brave of you. I hope they looked after you.'
'No, they bloody didn't. We drove over to Brackendon and ran back.'
'How far was that?'
'Nine kilometres. I had no idea that nine kilometres is twice the walking distance when you run it.'
Alison was laughing at her sister's grumpy tone. 'Feel free to join us if you would like a gentler introduction to running. I would love to have a human to run with, as well as with Woody. I'm sure Lucy would like to come too.'
'I doubt it. Greyhounds are not keen on long distances. I'm glad I didn't bring her this morning. She'd be far happier zipping around The Green for five minutes while I warm up, and then curling up in her bed instead of pounding out a five-mile run.'
'I think you are probably right, but we won't be doing anything like five miles for the first few weeks. Go on, join me. It will be good to do something together.'

Jennifer sighed, reluctant to commit to anything which involved running again, but recognised the plea in her sister's voice. 'I'll think about it.'
Alison had uprooted her life in Shropshire and moved to Woodford a while ago, but had been so busy working she had not had much time to establish a social group. She was a riding instructor, and had picked up work through Madeleine at the Woodford Riding Club. She was also the person responsible for the care and rehabilitation of the horses at her father and sister's veterinary hospital, as well as having her own two horses to keep fit and compete.
Alison said 'Great, let's start next week. By the way, what's all this about Paul being done for fraud? I'm surprised you haven't already rung me to tell me about it.'
'Oh, that didn't take long, did it? I might have known the town's gossips would be busy and get the story wrong. Paul isn't "being done" for fraud; there is a query over the provenance of something he sold in the auction on Tuesday, that's all. I'm sure it will be sorted out in a day or two.'
'Is that all? The way I've heard it Black's Auction House has been closed by the police. Poor Paul. Rumours like that can cause major damage to a decent business.'
'Who did you hear that from?'
'Someone at the yard. Not Madeleine; one of the other liveries, you know that awful woman who's always complaining about everyone else? She was furious about it. By the way, we haven't had any cancellations yet for the orienteering practice tomorrow, so we'll be busy. Madeleine checked the route again yesterday, and so long as we don't have any more rain tonight, it should all be fine. There is just that section coming off

the Trailway into the Bluebell Woods where the ground is still very muddy. But I'll check it first thing in the morning when I put the Ticket there, so if it's bad we'll warn everyone to make sure they stay in walk through that section.'

'Yes, we had a brief chat about it while I was working up there this morning. If that is the only place where the going is dodgy then everyone should have a super ride. I'll bring one master copy of the map with me tonight so you two can check if I have made any mistakes before I draw the other two. If Madeleine thinks we need to mark that section it will be easy to do before I laminate them.'

'I think I should be doing this practice because my map copying is rubbish. You are much better than me. Anyway, my client has just turned up, so I'd better go. I am glad to hear Paul's situation is not as bad as the rumour mongers would have us all believe, and I'll see you in the pub later.'

'I don't think anything bad is going to happen; Paul wouldn't allow it. It's one of the many things I love about him. He loves a challenge, and I have no doubt he will resolve this one. It's just a stray bit of paperwork or something like that. Once he's worked out what is going on it will all be resolved in a couple of days. See you this evening.'

Chapter 10

Saturday 19th October 2019, 6:00pm

'Pint please Tom, and whatever Cliff's drinking tonight.' Paul pulled out a bar stool and slumped onto it. After his phone conversation with his lawyer, his first instinct was to curl up under a blanket on the sofa at home, and rock his body backwards and forwards while humming to himself. His lawyer had promised to find out what she could about the police investigation, and start proceedings to ensure he had access to his computers, but nothing could start until Monday, and even then she warned him it was unlikely there was anything she could do to speed up the process. He had conducted their conversation on his feet, and at the end of it he stood looking at his mobile phone for several minutes before the urge to sink into the sofa overwhelmed him. No sooner had he sat down he was back up again and pacing the room. He managed to regain some control, found a notebook and pen, and for several hours he sat at the dining table and brainstormed the problem, writing down names of people he suspected of laundering money through his auction, lists of items he could remember which had sold for improbable amounts, and working out ways of minimising the disruption the closure of the auction house site was doing to his business. By the end he felt

as though he was pulling himself out of the clutches of the swamp onto a plank of wood which had fortuitously appeared, but solid ground was a long way into the distance. Before his thoughts could overwhelm him again he left the house, and crossed the road to the pub where he knew that a few hours in the company of other people would help to prevent him from sinking back down.
'I'll get these Paul. Who knows how long it will be before you can get access to your bank account. Two pints please Tom. Is Sarah around?' Cliff put a ten pound note on the bar of The Ship Inn.
'Two pints of Brackenshire Best coming up,' said Tom, as he reached up and unhooked two tankards for Paul and Cliff. All of the beer drinking regulars had their own tankards, thanks to a local craftsperson. 'Sarah's upstairs in bed. She's had a bit of a temperature and an annoying cough for a few days now, so because she is knackered and doesn't want to give any of our customers the lurgy she's taking a few days off. I heard you've had a bit of trouble with the law, Paul.' In his twenties, and part of the ancient Brackenshire farming Higston family, Tom had turned his back on the family business and found his niche in the pub trade. He started working for Sarah Handley, landlady of The Ship Inn, a few years ago as the pot man in the kitchen, had worked his way through the various jobs and was now firmly established as the manager, enabling Sarah to pursue other interests. He was a good-looking young man, with short curly black hair, blue eyes, and the rugby player's physique which kept him a regular member in the local team. He was quiet by nature, but had the ability to bring his energy up when necessary, and had been able to step in on the

rare occasions when disputes in the pub threatened to get out of hand.
'Just a bit of trouble,' said Paul, as he ran his hands over the unfamiliar stubble on his head. 'The police are investigating something, but I expect to be back up and running next week. Thank you, Cliff, but I'll get the next one. Make the most of it while I have a bit of cash still available. Jennifer will be joining me once she's finished work. Can you reserve a table for us please Tom? Are you joining us Cliff?'
'Thanks, yes I will.'
'I'll put you on a table in the snug,' said Tom. 'It might afford you some degree of privacy from the local gossips. You're good for a tab if you need it, Paul. Let me know what you want your limit to be set at, and I'll create one on the till for you.'
As a rule The Ship Inn did not operate on a tab or account system, so Tom's offer was a generous one. Running a village public house was hard enough without having hundreds or thousands of pounds tied up in money owed by locals who may or may not eventually pay. But Tom had already discussed it with Sarah as soon as he heard the news about the shutting down of Black's Auction House, and they had both agreed that Paul's credit was good with them.
Paul was touched by the offer. 'That's really kind of you. Thank you, Tom, but I'll be fine, honestly.'
'Hi, do you mind if I join you?' Jennifer's sister, Alison, appeared at the bar next to Paul. She and Jennifer looked alike, with the same friendly brown eyes and straight brown hair, although Alison wore hers longer than Jennifer.
'Of course not Alison, what are you drinking?'

‘I'm getting this round in,’ said Cliff, as he indicated the change Tom had put on the bar in front of him. ‘Glass of red rioja?’
‘Thanks, that sounds perfect. If you're sure?’ said Alison.
‘We were just about to take our drinks into the snug,’ said Cliff as he slid a ten pound note onto the bar. ‘We'd better have some crisps and nuts to keep us going too please, Tom.’
Paul had been trying to catch Cliff’s eye throughout this exchange, but Cliff was studiously avoiding him. It hadn't escaped Paul's notice that Cliff knew what Alison's favourite tipple was, and Cliff knew he had noticed. With relief he saw another customer enter the pub. ‘Madeleine, come and join us. What are you drinking?’
‘Oooh are you buying, Cliff?’ asked Jennifer as she followed Madeleine through the door.
Cliff exchanged the tenner for a twenty pound note, and graciously added Jennifer's drink to his bill. It was the kind of pub where everyone bought a drink for everyone else, so although it could prove expensive on one evening, you could easily go a week or two without having to put your hand into your pocket.
Tom hadn't had time to set up a table for them, and as no one else was in the snug the group rearranged a couple of tables and several chairs so they could all sit together, albeit with the girls on one side sitting on the comfortably worn velvet bench which ran around the wall so they could discuss their plans for the orienteering practice, and the two boys sat on the chairs on the other side so they could sit in silence and wonder at the conversation going on opposite them.
Madeleine produced a folder and began running through the list she had written on the first page. ‘I

have already put out all the signs for parking, toilets and refreshments, and I've checked that we have enough loo roll and soap in the toilet. You are going to put up the route signs directing everyone to Woodford Riding Club early tomorrow morning?' she looked at Jennifer, who nodded. 'Although thinking about it, everyone knows where they're coming to, so you only need to put up the one opposite the entrance as usual.'
Jennifer nodded. 'Yes, I suppose so. We've run a few of these events for Brackenshire HOOFING now, and I think I just got into the habit of putting them all out.'
'Yes, I'm the same. Don't worry, I'll put that sign up when I get up tomorrow, so that's something you can cross off your list of jobs to do.'
' "Brackenshire HOOFING" ' laughed Cliff. 'It makes you sound like a geriatric dance troupe!'
'Or barefoot fanatics,' laughed Alison, before turning to Madeleine 'which I suppose you are?'
'That's right,' grinned Madeleine. 'Well, I am. It isn't a requisite for HOOFING membership though; we do allow horses with shoes. I should think in the Brackenshire branch there are probably half wearing shoes and half barefoot.'
'What does it mean then?' asked Cliff
'HOOFING stands for Horse Owners Fun IN Groups' explained Jennifer. 'It's a national organisation, with local clubs all over the country. It's only been going for about four years I think?'
'Yes, that's right. Our Brackenshire group was started a couple of years ago.' Madeleine turned to Alison. 'Are you still alright to put the tickets out before ten o'clock tomorrow morning?'
Alison nodded 'Yes, they will be out in plenty of time before the first competitors start looking for them.'

‘Tickets?’ queried Cliff. ‘All your horse riders are going to have to collect tickets on their way round? Won't they get soggy if it rains?’
‘Not tickets as in bus tickets,’ explained Alison. ‘We call them tickets but they are coloured A4 pieces of laminated paper with a letter or a number on them.’
‘The competitors will be carrying a score card and pen,’ said Madeleine. ‘Every time they see one of our tickets they write the letter or number onto the scorecard. And yes, if it rains, the scorecards can get very wet indeed!’
‘What's the point of that?’ Cliff didn't look impressed. He liked to go out on a run and keep moving and he had assumed that horse riders would be doing the same.
‘It means we can tell if someone has followed the correct route or not,’ said Alison. Seeing that both Cliff and Paul looked confused, she continued ‘This isn't like an organised trail run. There won't be little bits of red and white tape and huge signs indicating which way to go. The riders will have ten minutes to copy the route from the master map onto an A4 section of Ordnance Survey map, before they start the ride. It's all paper maps and compasses; old school navigating.’
Cliff began to look interested. ‘I used to enjoy map reading and compass skills when I was in the scouts.’
‘I might have known you'd be in the scouts,’ jeered Paul. ‘I went to one meeting and decided it was a waste of time. All that wearing a uniform, marching and saluting wasn't for me.’
‘I've still got my woggle somewhere,’ mused Cliff
While the boys continued with their reminisces of Scouting, the girls returned to their planning meeting.
‘You're coming to lay out the tickets with me, aren't you, Jennifer? We're going to start running tomorrow.’

Alison beamed at Madeleine. 'Do you want to join us? We're going to start the Couch to 5K programme together.'
'Ali, I've been having second thoughts about running,' confessed Jennifer, as her fingers scrabbled around at the bottom of a packet of crisps. She was sure she had only just opened them. These crisp manufacturers were getting really mean with the quantities they put in these bags. 'My legs and back are killing me today, and my feet don't feel too great.'
'I'd love to join you!' said Madeleine, ignoring her friend's moans. 'But do you think it might be a good idea to wait and start on Monday? It will give us something to do after sitting and standing around all day tomorrow while other people have fun with their horses. Jennifer should have recovered from her madness this morning by then. Do you still want to do it with Woody?'
Alison looked relieved that someone else was as enthusiastic as she was. 'Yes please, if that's okay with you and his owner? That's a good idea, let's start on Monday. The programme is three days a week so we could do Monday and Wednesday mornings and Friday evenings, ending up in here as our reward for sticking with it.'
'So, this is where you are all hiding!' Caroline Thomas bounced into the room carrying what looked like either a gin and tonic or a sparkling mineral water. Cliff guessed it was gin and tonic. 'Mind if I join you?'
'Come on in,' said Madeleine as she shuffled along the bench to make room for Caroline. 'I'm afraid we are discussing our final preparations for tomorrow's training practice at the yard, but I promise we will stop in a minute.'

'Actually they were discussing putting off the start of their nine week running commitment,' corrected Cliff, before taking a large drink from his pint.
'No, we're not putting it off,' argued Jennifer 'It is just that we will be setting ourselves up for success by starting on Monday, when I've had a chance to recover from your attempt to kill me this morning.'
'Good idea,' agreed Caroline. 'It's three times a week, isn't it? You could do Monday, Wednesday, Friday and then relax in here, smug in the knowledge you have run three times in the week.'
'That's what I said,' smiled Alison.
'I think you will enjoy it far more if you start at the beginning,' Caroline said to Jennifer. 'In no time at all you will be able to enjoy coming for a run with us.'
Jennifer didn't look convinced.
'Come on, we only have a few more things to check,' Madeleine wanted to reach the end of her list.
Caroline scooted over to join Cliff and Paul, and the three of them began to discuss the half marathon they were organising for the following weekend. The two groups were both deep in discussion, when suddenly Jennifer thought of something which affected the race organisers.
'Um, you do realise that all of the race numbers are stored in the auction house?'
Everyone looked at her, appalled. 'Bugger,' said Paul, which Jennifer thought was very restrained of him. 'And the crisps, biscuits, squash bottles, tables and marquees. In fact, almost everything except the food which Caroline and her mum will be supplying.'
Thinking quickly, Caroline said 'Don't worry about any of that. I can get catering packs of everything at short notice, if the police still haven't allowed access

for you to retrieve the food and drink. Just concentrate on how you can substitute the race numbers.'
Madeleine said 'Brackenshire HOOFING have two marquees you can use, and I'm sure we have volunteers who will put them up and take them down.'
'Both the Woodford Riding Club and Brackenshire HOOFING have competitor bibs which could be used by runners in some way? They are not the light material you can pin to your running shorts though.'
'There must be a way of getting them printed up before next weekend,' said Jennifer. 'And supplying safety pins shouldn't be a problem.'
'Good idea. I suppose it's a good thing we decided to start low-key, and didn't buy in race trackers or anything complicated like that,' said Cliff. 'Are the stop watches in there too?'
'Yes,' said Paul, quietly. 'I'd better let Hannah know. This is her first time as Race Director of a race, and I'm letting her down.'
'No you're not; we can sort this. What about signs, arrows, bunting, all of that kind of thing?' asked Caroline.
'That's all stored at the Woodford Riding Club, thank goodness,' said Paul. 'Gray has made a huge gantry for the Finish line, and is going to set up a corridor of bunting for the finishers to run through at the end.'
'But the Marshalls' coats are all in there too, with the food and race numbers,' said Cliff.
'I'm sure we can rustle up enough hi-viz from our horsey contacts to cover that,' said Jennifer. 'And if we have to, then we can form a working group and make the race numbers. But before we go any further, and before you give Hannah the bad news, why don't you contact the police and ask if the race boxes can be retrieved?'

'Yes, I will ask,' said Paul, who looked so dejected that Cliff put his arm around him and gave him a hug.
'Surely they can look through them and see there is no way they can be connected to any money laundering,' said Caroline.
'Are you all ready to order?' Tom appeared with his notepad and pen and broke up the tense atmosphere. Everyone scrambled for a menu and peered through the doorway at the specials board on the wall next to the bar. They all chose both starters and main courses and another round of drinks which Caroline volunteered to buy.
Once the important task of choosing food and drink was completed, and satisfied there was no more they could do to help the Streakers, Madeleine continued to tick items off her list, occasionally checking emails and text messages for confirmation of volunteers for the various tasks. As well as TREC, the club who were coming to the Woodford Riding Club the next day, the Brackenshire branch of HOOFING, also participated in a variety of other disciplines, and in the two years since its inception had rapidly expanded to a membership of sixty-two, with three regular venues of which Woodford Riding Club was one. Satisfied that they were as prepared as they could be once the first course was delivered to the table, everyone tucked into their food.
By the time the second course had arrived, Paul was still quietly fretting. He had completely forgotten about all of the other events which the police's decision to refuse him access to his property was going to affect. Paul was always willing to get involved in community activities, and his auction house had space for the running club's belongings. As well as a large amount of the kit they needed for the half marathon, there were

bits and pieces he had ordered for his and Jennifer's up-coming surprise wedding locked away in the auction house. Wedding invitations, order of service, wedding favours. Fortunately Rebecca had all of the contact details for the people like the wedding dress designer and the humanist minister, so that Jennifer wouldn't get suspicious when text messages were sent to Paul's phone about such things, but most people involved were friends of Paul's, including Caroline and Lisa, and it wouldn't be unusual for them to phone him or send cryptic messages. The Ship Inn had a licence for wedding ceremonies to take place on their premises, which looked out onto the town of Woodford's common land, known as The Green, where the duck pond and trees provided a superb back drop and scene for photographs, when weather allowed. The Ship Inn had a large conservatory which opened out onto The Green, and was perfectly placed for the wedding ceremony. They were used to catering for large weddings, and inevitably the locals would join in with the celebrations as they went on into the evening, but Paul wanted his and Jennifer's wedding reception to be a small and intimate affair and had booked The Woodford Tearooms for their twenty or so guests. His plan was to have the ceremony in The Ship Inn's conservatory, photographs on The Green, The Finish gantry for the half-marathon was going to be transformed and festooned with white ribbons and bells, and positioned so the happy couple could pose beneath it, and then everyone would meander down to The Woodford Tearooms. No invitations had been sent out yet, but all guests had been quietly personally invited and sworn to secrecy. If the police refused him access to the wedding-related bits and pieces then it

wouldn't be a disaster. But if the race equipment was lost then that was another matter.
His phone had not stopped buzzing with messages from dealers and fellow auctioneers, all wanting to know what was happening. The only person whose call he answered was Natasha Holmes, a fellow auctioneer and the owner of Kemp and Holmes Antiques Auctioneers and Valuers, who were based in Brackenshire's county town of Swanwick. After several years as sworn enemies, Natasha and Paul had recently found mutual respect for each other. She had always dismissed him as a serious auctioneer because his chaotic personal life which tended to impinge on the professional, but in recent years he had demonstrated sound business judgement with no dramas to blur the edges. Paul, along with many other people involved in the antiques trade, had the impression that Natasha was only in the position she was in because of a suspiciously unlikely relationship with a much older, and richer, man. Whereas Natasha's impression of Paul had been correct, the rumours around her relationship with her business partner Bertram Kemp were unfounded, but as this was difficult to prove, Natasha had chosen to keep working hard and not waste time denying them. Paul was impressed with the success of Natasha's auction house, and had enjoyed many chats over a drink about the pressures and challenges they both faced. He pictured her cool expression, those green eyes slightly narrowed under the sharp black fringe as she concentrated on what he was saying. Paul's daughter, Lydia, worked for Natasha, and he was aware that in the close-knit antiques community any scandal relating to him had the potential to affect Lydia and therefore the reputation of Natasha's auction house.

‘Natasha. No prizes for guessing why you are calling.’
‘I thought I'd like to hear what you had to say rather than listen to the gossip.’
Paul sighed. It was refreshing to hear Natasha's direct approach, as opposed to the gossipy false messages of support from those who relished the scent of scandal.
‘Oh God, I can imagine what's being said about me. There isn't much I can tell you, because I don't know what has happened. The police say they have been keeping tabs on a criminal gang who are money laundering by selling certain antique items through auction houses like yours and mine. They have shut down my business and frozen my bank accounts, both business and personal, because I am guilty by association, the implication being that I have enabled these people in their activity and have gained from it.’
‘That's exactly what everyone has been telling me, Paul, so perhaps in some small way I can put your mind at rest about the gossip. No one has said they think you are guilty. It's more a case of this could happen to any of us.’
‘Really? I'd have thought the knives would be out and my reputation as a trustworthy auctioneer was trashed and in the gutter.’
‘Now you are fishing for compliments,’ Natasha gave a low throaty laugh.
Paul guessed that she was sitting in her pristine black leather and chrome furnished sitting room, holding a tumbler of whisky. With her sleek black bob and strong red lipstick, he always thought she should have been born in the nineteen thirties. He could imagine her in a flapper dress dancing the Charleston.
‘I’ll make sure Lydia is shielded from exposure to any negative comments, while this situation goes on,’ she said.

‘Thank you, Natasha, I appreciate it.’
‘Keep in touch, bye.’
‘I will thank you. Bye.’
‘Natasha Holmes?’ asked Cliff, who had been listening to Paul's side of the conversation. ‘The wagging tongues have reached her end of the county, have they?’
‘Yes,’ Paul nodded.
‘I'm sorry mate. This is going to be tough. I'm not sure how much damage limitation you are going to be able to employ. What did she have to say?’
‘She was surprisingly supportive,’ mused Paul. ‘Since Lydia started working for her, I have seen a better side to Natasha Holmes. She's quite a caring person underneath it all.’
Cliff gave his friend a sideways look. He didn't like the sound of this. He knew that Natasha and Paul had developed a good working relationship, but Paul had a history of failed romantic relationships due to his inability to stay faithful. Or should that be desire to chase after any woman who crossed his path? Two divorces, numerous one-night stands and endless women discarded after two or three weeks. Now he was engaged to Jennifer Isaac, making theirs the longest relationship since his second wife, Monica, had been dumped by him. Cliff was pleased that the pair of them had found each other, and thought they made a good couple. He had believed that his friend had finally matured and fallen in love, and was making the effort to behave decently with someone who loved him. Perhaps the difference was that to anyone looking from the outside in on their relationship, Paul was more invested than Jennifer. If Paul was going to start messing her around, Cliff had no doubt that Jennifer would walk away. Fast.

Chapter 11

Sunday 20th October 2019, 5.55am

Madeleine awoke with a start, wondering if she had overslept. She always slept well the night before an event, but usually woke up early. She rarely bothered to close her curtains, and although the clear sky outside her window was blue-black before the sun rose, there were no signs of rain clouds. Thank goodness. The last outdoor event they had held at the Woodford Riding Club was destined to go down in Brackenshire HOOFING history as the wettest and muddiest event ever. It would be nice to have decent weather this time. Together with Max, her Patterdale Terrier, Madeleine lived in a tiny cottage on the former farm. The original farmhouse, where the family still lived, was within eyesight but far enough away that Madeleine could enjoy the isolation. She glanced at the big Victorian clock face hanging on the wall to the left of her bed and saw that the time was almost six o'clock. She reached over to her mobile phone on the bedside table to slide the alarm, which was set for half-past six, to off. Max was pretending to be asleep in his bed under the window, but had one eye open watching her carefully as she padded barefoot over the scrubbed and varnished floorboards out of the room and headed for the bathroom next door.

Once showered and dressed, Max fed and let outside for a wee, Madeleine drank a cup of coffee while checking her list for the day's events. Soon she was satisfied she had everyone's official forms, the folders for the volunteers containing their instructions and emergency numbers for the day were comprehensive, and the packed lunches for the volunteers and refreshments for the riders were in hand. She knew she should eat something, but nervous tension about the day ahead meant she couldn't face anything, so she popped a cereal bar into her pocket and together with Max went out to check and feed the horses. If she had time, she would also poo-pick the track.
Alison had also woken early, and while Madeleine was seeing to the riding school and livery horses, Alison was doing the same with the four horses under her care at the veterinary clinic run by her father and sister. Her own two horses, Ernie and Flo, were on livery at the Woodford Riding Club, and so once her official duties were completed and the horses' charts updated on the computer in the office, Alison headed across The Green on her bicycle to help Madeleine. She had told Jennifer she wouldn't need her help after all, enabling her sister to have a little bit longer in bed to rest her tired body. Alison wanted Jennifer to be fresh and alert while they spent several hours together on their allotted tasks that day.
As she cycled into the yard, she could see Madeleine poo-picking the far side of the track, supervised by a string of horses and clearly not needing any more help. Instead, Alison slung her bicycle into Madeleine's truck before collecting the keys and the folder of tickets from the kitchen table. She paused to send a text message letting Madeleine know she was heading out, and set off for an hour and a half of driving to

several suitable spots and cycling along tracks, bridleways, field edges, and through a farmyard, in order to securely fix the laminated A4 tickets where riders should, and should not, find them.
By eight o'clock, Madeleine was back in her kitchen, kettle on, toaster in a permanent toasting state, preparing for the arrival of the volunteers.
'Linda! Hi, thank you so much for stepping in at the last minute,' Madeleine greeted the first one. 'Tea? Coffee? Help yourself to breakfast.'
'No problem,' said Linda Beecham. 'I'm happy to help. It will give me a chance to see what it's like before I have a go,' she said, as she surveyed the work top where Madeleine had laid out a selection of Danish pastries, plates of sliced melon, strawberries, hard boiled eggs, and cold meats. 'Blimey, you HOOFING girls eat well, don't you!'
'Ah, this is for you volunteers. We need you to keep your stamina up! So you are definitely going to enter the next one, the competition next month?'
'Yes, I sent my entry in last week. It will be a fun way to celebrate my birthday.'
Madeleine studied Linda as she handed over the mug of tea. 'Milk and sugar on the table,' she gestured.
Linda's long grey hair was scooped up into a ponytail which fell in attractive loose curls down her back. Her face was clear and tanned, consistent with many hours at outdoor antiques fairs, and her blue-grey eyes were today framed with a dash of black mascara. Madeleine thought she could fall anywhere within the thirty-five to fifty-five-year-old age bracket. She habitually wore jeans, tee-shirts and plain jumpers, so there were no clues to her age in her clothing.
'Is it a special birthday?' Madeleine inquired.

'No, not particularly. I just thought it would be my birthday present to myself. Mmmh, I never eat this well for breakfast,' she beamed up at Madeleine.

The kitchen began to fill up with people and noise as more volunteers arrived, including Caroline Thomas with the box containing the rolls, homemade biscuits and cakes, plenty of fruit, and tubs of salad with her speciality pomegranate topping. In order to both attract and thank the volunteers the club fed and watered them, and there was always plenty of food to sell to the riders while they waited for the prize giving at the end of an event. Fundraising was a permanent activity, and even though they all paid an annual membership fee and entry fees for any competitions or training events, not to mention the cost of keeping a horse and travelling to the event, hungry riders were always ready to dig into their pockets to pay for decent fodder in the form of tasty rolls and delicious cakes. They always brought a lot of food and water for their horses, but usually ran out of time and inclination to pack anything for themselves.

The volunteers were often long-suffering partners of participants, like Paul and Grayson who were currently deep in conversation over a couple of mugs of coffee; riders who were either injured or whose horse was injured; or riders who generously gave up their place in the competition to make sure it could go ahead. Theirs was an active and friendly group, and all of the members committed to helping at a minimum of two events every year, so they were rarely short of helpers. Even though this was only a practice event and not a full competition, the number of volunteers required to ensure problems were minimised was still hefty. In addition to food and drink, the volunteers earned "thank you points" or 'TYPS' which were totalled at the end of the year for the club's annual prize giving. Today's volunteers would all receive ten TYPS for a whole day, much of which would be spent outside. It looked as though they were going to be lucky with the weather, but conditions were not always so pleasant, and for the now infamous event in July when a number of people had to stand out in torrential rain for several hours, the group had decided to give the volunteers an extra ten TYPS just for being heroes. Obviously the riders were out in the same weather, but they were paying for the privilege.

Madeleine checked that each person had their information folder, refreshment pack, and knew where they were going and what they were doing. All of the volunteers had a list of each other's mobile phone numbers and location on the course, and they were set up in a WhatsApp group so they could share the progress of riders as they passed through the checkpoints. Finding suitable locations for checkpoints where there was also adequate mobile signal was tricky in the undulating Brackenshire countryside, but as the chances of a rider needing emergency help in one of the many mobile phone black spots was high, Madeleine had organised more checkpoints than would usually be set up on such a course so that any rider missing for a significant length of time could be quickly located. Grayson was not officially a volunteer, but was usually around at these events because there was always general maintenance to do on-site and he could be close by if someone needed help changing a tyre or jump-starting a lorry. Patricia had tried to sign him up when the Brackenshire HOOFING club first started, but he refused to attend any meetings or stand around in a field with a clip board. None of their children were interested either, so

Patricia had been used to fending for herself. Paul had never attended anything at the Woodford Riding Club before, although Jennifer had been a member for years and had a horse at livery there, and Jennifer hadn't even thought of signing him up as a volunteer when Brackenshire HOOFING came into existence. On a Saturday or Sunday when the majority of their events took place, he was usually out running or working, but as he could not work and had decided to forgo his run that morning, he was glad to have something different to occupy his brain. Usually going for a run was an excellent way to clear his head when he was getting bogged down over a problem at work, but today he was worried that the swamp feeling was too strong and he wouldn't be able to find that happy place where his body pushed through the stages where he wanted to give up and powered out the other side where he felt as though he could run forever. He didn't need another failure. Paul was pleased to see Grayson in Madeleine's kitchen when he arrived, and welcomed his request to help him check the rails and posts of the track for any that needed replacing.

'It will give us a chance to work out the final details for the Woodford Half Marathon,' Grayson said, in his quiet way.

'Yes, it will be a good idea to have a chat. I've hit a bit of a snag with some of the equipment, because it's all locked into the auction house, and the bastard police won't let us have access to it.' Paul was still fuming after a frustrating phone call with Ieuan Davies the previous evening while they were still in the pub. Bolstered by beer, Paul decided to phone him, but the policeman had refused to allow the WSWC boxes to be given to Paul, and neither would he give Paul any indication about when he could have access to his

business premises. A day spent bashing posts into the ground with Grayson Bragg was exactly what Paul needed.
After a quick chat with Linda, who had asked after his well-being, he and Grayson left to start their work, both hoping no one would need their assistance that day.
By half-past eight the kitchen was empty of people, the table cleared of folders although covered in toast crumbs, the draining board crammed with washed up mugs, plates and cutlery, and the compost bin contained several banana skins and tea bags.
When Alison arrived back at the yard a few minutes later, she could see half a dozen or so riders in the lorry park brushing their horses, dashing for a last trip to the toilet, or sorting through the kit they would need for the day. The scene looked so relaxed and attractive that for a moment she wished she was one of them, but Alison preferred traditional competitions and both of her horses, Flo and Ernie, were booked to do a dressage competition the next day where the atmosphere would be very different. Alison's equestrian experience had started from the womb as her mother was a riding instructor and keen competitor in eventing and dressage disciplines. Both she and Jennifer had grown up around horses, and while Jennifer followed their father's footsteps into the world of equine veterinary practice, Alison preferred working alongside her mother running a local riding school. She loved to be the first one on the yard in the morning and see the horses' heads watching her over their stable doors, waiting for her to prepare their breakfast and pop feed bowls through those doorways. She was always a popular instructor, especially with the adults who wanted to be the best in their dressage class or

show jumping round. She was never short of offers of help and vocal support when she competed, and there were always a group of students who travelled to watch whether she was competing in the relative comfort of a dressage test in an indoor school or braving the elements at an outdoor one-day event. It had been a wrench to leave that life behind.
Alison had been living in Woodford for a couple of years, deciding to make the move to assist her father and sister with their equine lameness rehabilitation centre because they were both so enthusiastic, and she was stuck in a rut. She was able to bring both of her horses with her, and with her British Horse Society instructor qualifications had picked up some regular teaching jobs with local riding clubs and private students. She was happy to help at this Brackenshire HOOFING event because a couple of her clients were members and were competing that day, but she wasn't particularly interested in most of their activities. Her world was one of smartly turned out horses and riders, plaited manes and freshly washed tails, with immaculate leather black or brown tack, and beige or cream breeches, and the goal to be the best in their competition class. The scene in front of her was filled with bright colours on both horses and riders, evidence of remnants of a muddy night in the field on horses' legs, and an air of emphasis on performance rather than appearance. To Alison this smacked of low standards and she was not going to lower hers, but she applauded the dedication and commitment of the riders for training in all weathers who turned up so early in the morning for a very long day. She doubted many of the competitors in her classes tomorrow would be able to get their horses down to the start line of today's competition, let alone able to make it safely round the

course. Maybe she should step out of her comfort zone and challenge herself to take part one day. She was sure that Ernie in particular would love the challenges. She left her bicycle in the back of Madeleine's truck and replaced the keys on the hook in the hallway of the cottage before striding back out and across the yard to find her sister with whom she was sharing tack check duties. Alison was combining this role with being on call for any rider who required assistance out on the course, for example, driving with Paul the small lorry emblazoned with the Woodford Riding Club's logo to retrieve a horse if necessary, or talking the rider back onto the course by mobile phone if they had strayed too far and were lost. Jennifer was also doubling up with her volunteer tasks, and was the vet on duty. In the event that both were called away, the tack check would be completed later in the day. Both were expecting not to have to leave their posts, and were looking forward to having some quality sister time. Once all of the competitors had seen them, they were going to drive out to the checkpoints and see if the volunteers needed any additional support. As the last competitors passed through the checkpoint, the sisters would remove the tickets Alison had positioned first thing in the morning, and make sure none of the volunteer checkpoint judges left anything behind after they had packed everything away. With any luck, they would be back on the yard in time for the much anticipated prize giving. Even though this was only a practice competition, the riders were still expecting prizes. It always took at least an hour after the last rider was safely back before the results could be given out, and usually longer, meaning that those who came back first had several hours to wait. The members of the club had fallen into the habit of sharing picnics and tales of that day's adventures while they waited together, cheering as every new person crossed the finishing line. The clapping and cheering for winners, whatever the prize, and thanking the volunteers was guaranteed to encourage even the people who had come last, or worse not even completed for one reason or another and meant the volunteers were properly thanked and willing to help out another day.

Chapter 12

Sunday 20th October 2019, 8.55am

The practice orienteering event was the fourth of four training sessions organised by Madeleine. The first three sessions had taken place without horses at the Woodford Riding Club, and comprised of five groups of six over the previous weeks. Madeleine had originally planned only one group of six to run over four sessions, culminating in today's practical session, but because the take up for the training was so high from the members of the club, rather than limit the numbers who could attend, Madeleine had organised those who wanted to participate into five groups, with their training sessions taking place at convenient times for each group. She had been taken by surprise at the number of riders she knew were experienced TREC competitors who had signed up, but it soon became apparent that a dearth of competitions and trainings in previous years due to bad weather and both equine flu and equine herpes outbreaks meant that people were keen to be involved in anything TREC-related. There were also a number of riders who had recently acquired a new horse and they sensibly wanted to refresh their skills as well as provide the horse with a few quiet non-competitive outings before embarking on the bigger, more serious competitions. This mix of inexperienced and experienced riders had proved to be successful because those who had been there and done that were happy to share their knowledge with the newbies, and this usually came with a funny story. Madeleine was covering the foundations of the sport, and even the most highly decorated riders found they were remembering crucial points they had long forgotten, or were learning something new because rules and regulations had changed in the years since they first started competing in the sport.

The previous sessions had each been two hours long, with the first solely in the classroom where the riders spent their time learning, or refreshing long forgotten memories, about how to read a map, practicing copying a route from one map onto another, and getting to grips with compass work. The second and third sessions were mainly outside, so the groups could practice navigating their way around the site and onto the tracks beyond.

Three of the groups asked to have their trainings on a weekday evening, and they had all made the most of the social opportunity and brought food and drink which meant their sessions ran overtime. In contrast, the two at the weekends both finished early because the participants needed to get home and spend time with their families. Madeleine didn't mind the evening overrun because they had been fun sessions and the riders had also taken charge of evening feeds and final night checks for the livery and riding school ponies. Although she usually relished the peace and quiet of having the place to herself, it had been a welcome change to have her students eagerly helping out and gave her an idea for future camping events. Jumping from one session to five in a week had been quite tricky to organise with her regular clients, but many of

them were also doing the training, or were happy to have a lesson with Alison for a change, or take a break and see their families on a night they would usually be out with the horses.
Today's practice competition was run on a strict five minute starting time interval between riders. At their appointed time, the riders had to be present with all of their compulsory equipment for the ride, including compass and First Aid kit, their horse's tack, and their horse, at one of the four permanent wooden circular corrals which made up a cloverleaf pattern, and where they were met by Alison and Jennifer. The first competitor was a lady who was a very experienced horsewoman and had spent many years enjoying TREC competitions with three different horses. She was popular because she was always ready to help fellow competitors, but never boasted about her own success, and had made several useful contributions to her group's training sessions.
'Hello Amelia,' Jennifer wrote down the time next to Amelia McCann's name on the list secured to her clipboard. 'It is lovely to see that you have brought Rosie out to play today.'
'Hi Jennifer! Hello Alison, thank you both for giving up your day for us. Yes, I thought the old girl would enjoy this event. It's not fair to ask her to be competitive on the pace anymore, but I checked with Madeleine and she thought we'd be able to cope with the distance.'
'How old is she now?' asked Alison, guessing the horse in front of them was about fifteen or sixteen years old.
'She'll be twenty-four this year.'
Everyone was quiet for a minute while Jennifer checked Rosie's heart rate, and then asked Amelia to

run with her up to the water trough a short distance away and back again. Both Alison and Jennifer watched carefully as the horse trotted next to her owner.
'Great' said Jennifer, as she ticked the next few boxes on her list.
'Horse sound; owner lame,' joked Amelia, as she gave her right knee a rub.
Alison checked Amelia's equipment, calling out to Jennifer as she found each item and confirming that emergency contact numbers were clearly visible on both Amelia's arm band and Rosie's saddle. Points were deducted for incorrect equipment, and inevitably someone had forgotten something vital, so the call would go out to fellow competitors for a spare bandage or hoof pick. But Amelia was organised as usual and had everything necessary.
'All done Amelia, you can go to the map room now. We'll see you when you get back here,' said Jennifer, giving Rosie a gentle stroke on her neck.
'Thank you!' said Amelia with a smile.
Amelia left Rosie happily munching grass in one of the round pens and walked with the rest of her equipment, excluding Rosie's tack, into the first checkpoint, the map room. Today it was held in the yard's classroom, and the riders were allowed ten minutes to copy the route from the master map Jennifer had drawn the day before onto a sheet of Ordnance Survey map. Jennifer and Alison were still watching Amelia walking away when they were interrupted.
'Are you ready for me now?' the next competitor barked at them. Diana Smalley had been around for years, long before the Brackenshire HOOFING group were established, and was well known for her impatience. It had been an unpleasant surprise when

Madeleine saw her entry for the training sessions, not just because of her abrasive personality but also because she was one of the few unpopular trainers who taught and examined the officials in the sport. The majority of the trainers were friendly and supportive, but there were one or two who took delight in setting traps for nervous trainees. Madeleine suspected Diana was only signing up so she could spy on the group, and was prepared for trouble. Diana had picked one of the evening groups and confounded Madeleine's fears by bringing homemade coffee and walnut cake to the first session for everyone to eat, hot and tasty sausage rolls (both meat and vegan) to the second, and a moreish Eton mess (both dairy and non-dairy versions) to the third. She had also turned out to be a valuable participant, sharing her experiences and asking pertinent questions. Madeleine decided that even if her motives were sneaky it really didn't matter, because she would welcome Diana into any future training.

The genial sociable Diana had been left at the evening training sessions, and the crabby unpleasant one was bristling with impatience and tension. Jennifer calmly checked her watch, refusing to be hurried.

'We can start with you now, if you are ready, Diana. You do have a couple of minutes spare to continue your preparations,' she warned.

'No, no, I'm ready. Let's not waste any more time,' grumbled Diana.

She fidgeted as Jennifer listened to her horse's heartbeat, and then Alison and Jennifer watched as the skinny woman began to run alongside her huge dark bay warmblood gelding, barely able to keep up with his loose long strides. By the time she reached them her thirty-a-day habit was obvious as she coughed and wheezed to a halt. Alison began to check her

equipment, and couldn't help wrinkling her nose at the ingrained stench of old cigarette smoke.
'Do you have a hoof pick, Diana?' she asked.
'Of course I do. It's in there!'
'Sorry I can't see it. Can you find it for me?'
Alison and Jennifer raised their eyebrows at each other as Diana rummaged through all of the pockets of her saddlebags. The saddlebags were emblazoned with faded and weatherworn Union Jack flags showing off to anyone who cared that Diana had once represented her country in an international TREC competition. The saddle bags were no longer rain proof and had been patched up in places, and it became embarrassingly clear that there was no hoof pick amongst her belongings. Diana poked a finger through one of the holes.
'Damn must have dropped out of here. Never mind, I'll pick one up on my way back.'
'That's fine, I'll leave your sheet open until we see it,' said Jennifer, in as neutral expression as she could manage.
They stood by as she angrily shoved everything back into the bags, watched as she yanked her horse's head around and marched him into one of the pens.
'Bloody well stay there!' was her only comment before turning on her heel and marching off to the map room, leaving her precious saddlebags on the floor next to the pen.
'We'd better say something,' muttered Jennifer.
'Lucky she was early,' agreed Alison. 'Oh, Diana! Don't forget these!'
Every short dyed black hair on her head vibrated with fury as Diana turned and strode back to them, before having to lean on one of the wooden fence posts as yet another attack of coughing overtook her.

As they watched her walk away, Alison said 'Did you see she managed to remember her packet of fags and lighter? I'm not sure if carrying a lighter is allowed in the official rules, but I wasn't going to challenge her.'
Jennifer nodded. 'A good indication of her priorities: forgets the hoof pick for her lovely horse over there; but remembers her cigarettes as well as something to light them with. Did you check her water bottle?'
'Oh yes; it was full.'
'But with what?' asked Jennifer slyly. 'Along with the cigarettes our Diana does love to top up the levels with a strong vodka and tonic.'
'Don't we all!' said Alison. 'Well, the vodka and tonic, not the fags. Although speaking personally, I like a good cherry brandy in my hip flask.'
'Hello ladies. I like a nip of sloe gin in mine,' grinned the next competitor, a tall man in his thirties, his blonde hair flopping over into blue eyes. Charlie Lichmann was one of Jennifer's clients, and ran a business supplying chefs to millionaires when they were on holiday with their family in the UK for a few days.
'I always thought you were more of a campari and soda man, Charlie' teased Jennifer.
'How very dare you,' he laughed. 'We are a bit early; shall I walk him around until it's our time?'
'No, no, let's keep going while we can. You know how these things always end up running late. I'll just check his heart rate,' said Jennifer, as she stepped forward and let the black Friesian gelding carefully inspect the stethoscope. He knew Jennifer, as did many of the horses at the competition today, because she was his usual vet. Madeleine was always grateful when either Jennifer or her father Peter were willing to volunteer at events she was running, because they were very good

with both horses and their owners. This was not always the case with the vets, and unfortunately one bad experience could make a horse difficult and dangerous to manage in the future.
By the time the fourth competitor was ready to be seen, the first competitor, Amelia, had reappeared and was competently putting her tack onto Rosie.
'Good luck Amelia and Rosie!' called Alison.
'Good luck!' echoed Jennifer.
'Thank you ladies!' Amelia said over her shoulder, as she led her horse to the mounting block, mounted easily, and then she and Rosie stood for a moment while she checked that her map case was securely tucked inside her high visibility waistcoat. They strolled away to the start checkpoint on a loose rain, both looking happy and relaxed.

Meanwhile, in the map room, the three volunteers were desperately trying to maintain control and good time keeping. Two of them, a husband and wife team, were experienced at the task and they were helping the third person, seventeen-year old Heather Stanwick, whose parents were both competing together as a pair. The Stanwick family were big supporters of Woodford Riding Club and Brackenshire HOOFING, with Kim Stanwick, the present chair of the group, and her husband, Robin, the organiser for the competition camp the following month. Heather was a keen competitor, but also eager to learn about the organisation of events, and was proving to be a useful and regular volunteer. This was her first time helping in the map room, although she had been in one many times at other events as a competitor. People tended to be nervous when they entered the map room, usually because it heralded the beginning of the competition and was a timed exercise. They had to be quiet and concentrate, which took many people back to their school days, but there were rarely any problems. Today was different, and the couple had already had to tell one of the competitors to put her cigarette out safely as no smoking was allowed anywhere on the premises, and had received a mouthful of abuse as a result. Madeleine was hovering around to provide support to the volunteers as they saw the first few competitors in case there were any kinks she needed to iron out in the procedures she had set them, and had noted Diana Smalley's behaviour. Although Diana had a reputation for being abrupt and rude, this was the first time Madeleine had witnessed it, and it would be the first and last at a Brackenshire HOOFING event. Madeleine waited until Diana had her time studying and copying the map and left the map room, and then took her to one side away from any listening ears and quietly explained that her rude behaviour was unacceptable, it contravened the rules of the club, and she was not allowed to continue in the competition, although if she apologised and promised never to behave in that way again she was welcome to attend another event. They would refund her entry fees in full, and she was to collect her horse and the rest of her tack from the round pens and leave with a minimum of fuss. Clearly furious, but for once lost for words, Diana collected her belongings, packed her beautiful, large and expensive horse lorry with tack and horse, and drove out of the gates of the Woodford Riding Club, watched by a number of people, all assuming her horse had failed the vetting. Although this was not the first time her behaviour had been commented on and she had been reported several times to the governing bodies of various equestrian sports, it was the first time she had been refused permission to continue and was the first time anyone could remember a HOOFING competitor being told to leave a venue. Diana Smalley was popular in a number of organising committees because she regularly sponsored and financially supported events, as well as generously allowing trainings and competitions to be held at her well-equipped equestrian premises, but for several years there had been disquiet among the other riders about her treatment of her fellow competitors and of her horses.

Madeleine's heart was thumping, although she tried to maintain an outwardly calm appearance. No doubt there would be repercussions, but she hoped her fellow members would support her decision. Both the Woodford Riding Club and Brackenshire HOOFING had a reputation for being friendly and supportive environments, and she was not prepared to allow someone who had got away with bad behaviour for years elsewhere to tarnish it.

Fortunately, the practice competition was continuing undisturbed. Once they had completed their ten minutes in the map room, the riders had twenty minutes to finish putting the tack on their horse for riding, and have a little warm up ride if they wished before heading down to the start of the orienteering course. The couple who were running the start checkpoint, Phil Smart and Jimmy Nicholson, were experienced riders and volunteers and enjoyed sending the riders off to begin each adventure. They were used to last minute panics and could soothe and reassure nervous riders with ease and humour. The majority of riders needed little interaction, other than the obligatory countdown from two minutes, one minute, thirty seconds and then ‘five, four, three, two, one, go and have fun!’

‘That woman is such an old bag,’ muttered Jimmy as a particularly querulous and late competitor eventually set off.
Rolling his eyes, Phil said ‘I wouldn't expect anything less from Mrs Bragg. At least she is the only rude person we have seen today. Everyone else has been lovely as usual.’
‘I do love her pony Dougal. Those Highlands make great TREC ponies.’
‘I suppose the way she looks after him and clearly loves him is Patricia's only saving grace.’
‘We’d better be nice; her husband is about to start working on this bit of fencing,’ whispered Jimmy.
‘What a lovely man like that is doing with her I’ll never know. Oh, I think we’re OK, it looks as though he and the other chap are packing up. Look, they’re driving off up the bridleway. Hey, what are you typing? You can't send that!’ Phil grabbed his husband’s phone and quickly deleted the message Jimmy was in the process of typing to the other checkpoint judges on their WhatsApp group. Laughing, Phil replaced the typing with ‘Competitor number 13 The Bragg is on her way.’
Studying it, Jimmy said ‘I'm not sure that is any better.’
A flurry of thumbs up signs appeared, plus a handful of laughing emojis.
‘Hello!’ the next competitor arrived, and the couple checked her number against their list.
‘Hi, what a beautiful horse,’ Phil admired the liver chestnut mare. His own horse was also liver chestnut in colour, and he rarely saw another one. Everyone these days rode orange chestnuts, boring bays, or coloured horses.

‘Thank you,’ beamed the competitor. ‘She is the best-looking horse here.’
The two of them chatted for a minute or two about how gorgeous their horses were, with Phil having to pull out his phone and show her photos of his horse. Jimmy, who had a bay horse and was feeling left out, interrupted them. ‘Okay, you have two minutes to go.’
As she left their checkpoint, the competitor called over her shoulder ‘Thank you for helping!’
‘Now that's more like it,’ said Phil as he politely let the rest of the volunteers know that number 17 was on her way.
With five minutes between each start time, a little bit of time slippage and thirty competitors, it was half-past twelve before the last ones, a jolly pair of ladies who were always dressed head to toe in high visibility fluorescent pink, while their matching grey horses sported the equivalent yellow. More than once they had been likened to two bowls of ice cream as they meandered around the countryside. Phil and Jimmy cheered and waved them goodbye as the ladies cheered and waved back, eager to get out into the Brackenshire countryside.
The route Madeleine had designed was approximately fifteen kilometres long, with a couple of steep undulations, two superb long grassy canter opportunities and a gentle stream to ride in for a short distance. She and Jennifer had started preparing for this practice session twelve months ago. They had each ridden it once a month when possible, although the winter months had made the stream a raging torrent, and fallen trees had blocked the route on more than one occasion. On a good day, like today, they would easily be home in one hour and forty minutes, but that was because they knew the route, wouldn't be held up at

checkpoints, their horses were confident with the water, and their riders knew not to blow them up on the first hill by blasting up it at a gallop. Madeleine estimated it would take even the better riders a minimum of two and a half hours, and could even take some up to four hours to complete the course. If the two pink ladies were coming back last, they should be no later than half-past four, and possibly as early as three o'clock.

The first riders should be arriving back in the yard any minute now.

Madeleine's kitchen had been the temporary headquarters for the organisers of the practice session, with the paper checklists from Alison and Jennifer's equipment check, the map room lists, and the start lists all collated onto Madeleine's laptop every half an hour. Once the two pink ladies had left the map room, it was quickly transformed into the organisers' headquarters and results room, leaving Madeleine's cottage available if they needed an emergency base away from the main action. Alison and Jennifer together with Heather Stanwick had already left to drive out to the five checkpoints and briefly check that the volunteers were happy with what they had to do. Today was a practice for some of the volunteers as well, and Linda Beecham wasn't the only person who was doing it for the first time. Now that their job at the start checkpoint was finished, Phil and Jimmy were sitting together at the laptop with all of the sheets of paper, and were double checking the work Madeleine had been inputting, in between exclaiming at how brave Madeleine was for dispatching Diana Smalley. The couple who had helped Heather in the map room were making tea and coffee for everyone who was left, and were congratulating Madeleine on finally doing what they wished many people before her had done with regards to Diana Smalley, as well as monitoring the WhatsApp feed and informing everyone else of the progress of their competitors. Madeleine decided she would take the opportunity to nip to the toilet while all was relatively quiet.

When she returned to the HQ, she was able to sit down and enjoy a mug of tea and a couple of sandwiches before the clip clop of Charlie Lichmann's Friesian horse Highlander could be heard, and Phil and Jimmy rushed out to do their job of judges at the finish checkpoint.

Over the next hour, the noise of horses and riders returning came in sporadic fits and starts. Sometimes up to twenty minutes would go by giving Madeleine and her team a chance to collate the results and begin to form a list of rider and horse placings, and then in the space of a few minutes one rider after another would stroll into the yard, some officially riding in a pair, some who had paired up on route, and even five horses and riders who assured Phil and Jimmy they had not been riding together until they came in through the gate. All expressed how much they had enjoyed the course as they handed over their score cards, and praised the checkpoint judges for their friendly and helpful attitude.

Jennifer, Alison and Heather had completed their tour of the checkpoints, and were helping Phil and Jimmy to welcome the returning riders. The three of them also set up the refreshments shop in the small wooden lodge, which usually served as the club room for the livery owners and visiting students. The Woodford Riding Club had a strict rule that no horse was to be left tied to the outside of a trailer or lorry without supervision, and so some riders stayed to keep an eye

on several different horses while their owners went and purchased sandwiches, salads and cake. Most people brought their own cold drinks or a flask for hot drinks, or they had portable camping gas cookers and made them fresh, but the kettle in the club room was still on permanent boil and the sound of clinking teaspoons rang out across the yard. The riders congregated around a few lorries and trailers, some with their friends, some making new friends, and in between mouthfuls of food and drink they cheered and congratulated the returning horses and riders.
'There is something funny going on here,' said Madeleine as she input the data from the fourth horse and rider combination in a row who appeared to have missed checkpoint five. 'Has anyone heard from Linda Beecham recently?'

Chapter 13

Sunday 20th October 2019, 1:30pm

Linda wasn't answering her phone, and the last five riders to return to the yard had not had their cards marked off for her checkpoint. When questioned, they all said they had ridden through the checkpoint, clearly marked with coloured cones and a parked car with the card telling them the next section should be ridden at a speed of twelve kilometres an hour, but they couldn't see anyone around. Some had waited for five minutes and written on their score cards accordingly, but others had assumed it was for another competition course and had continued with their ride without stopping. No one had thought it was anything to worry about, and had assumed that as this was only a training practice session there weren't enough volunteers to cover the checkpoint.

'I hope Diana Smalley hasn't gone and nobbled her,' Jimmy muttered to Phil.

'Linda wasn't anywhere near the yard when Diana was sent home. Diana is more likely to have a go at Madeleine,' argued Phil.

'True,' nodded Jimmy. 'I don't really think Diana would do anything like that. She's more of a death by official complaint sort of person.'

‘What are you two chattering about? Do you know where Linda is?’ asked Madeleine feeling like a school teacher telling two naughty boys to share their secrets with the whole class.
‘No idea, sorry. Do you want us to go and see if we can find out?’ Jimmy started patting his pockets for the car key.
‘I think you two are needed here to help get the rest of these results sorted out. We still have riders out on course, and I'd prefer to have as little disruption as possible.’
‘She's probably gone behind a hedge for a wee and her phone battery has gone flat,’ suggested Jennifer. Everyone looked at her. ‘OK, OK, that's not a very likely explanation for why she has been missing from her post for so long. Unless she's tripped and sprained her ankle, or worse, and her phone battery has gone flat.’
‘But no one heard her shouting for help. She can't have also lost her voice, unless she went for a wee, tripped and knocked herself out?’ Alison said.
‘Or she could have been abducted,’ said Heather. ‘A lone woman out in the middle of nowhere.’
It was Heather’s turn to be the centre of attention as she spoke the words everyone was thinking.
‘Yes, well, it's not very likely for something like that to happen around here. This isn't central Manchester. Probably best if we don't scare ourselves with worst case scenarios until we know what has happened. But something serious must have happened for her to have disappeared like this. I don't know her very well, but I don't get the impression that Linda Beecham is the sort of person who just up and disappears for coffee and cake with a friend who happens to be passing while she's meant to be volunteering as a checkpoint judge in

a competition. Even if this is only a practice competition.' Madeleine sounded calm, but inside she was worried about Linda's welfare and was wondering when it was too soon to involve the police.

'Of course, if this was a competition we would have a minimum of two people at each checkpoint,' said Phil, 'for this exact reason. But it has never been necessary for a training session like this. I think we'd struggle to run them in future if we had to rely on twice the number of volunteers. But maybe whatever has happened today means we need to have a rethink about our policy in this area.'

The group spent a few minutes discussing the pros and cons of increasing the number of volunteers for practice and training events until another rider turned up in the yard. While Madeleine, Phil and Jimmy got back to their official roles, Jennifer, Alison and Heather were dispatched to see what had happened to Linda. Madeleine sent a message to the volunteer at the checkpoint before Linda's to warn riders there appeared to be an unmanned checkpoint on course, only to find that the checkpoint judges had already decided amongst themselves to let the riders know and had told them to wait for five minutes at her checkpoint, whether she was there or not.

Meanwhile, more riders were returning and none of them had seen Linda, which meant a significant number of the competitors' times were messed up by the missing checkpoint judge. Phil and Jimmy continued with inputting the data from the riders' score cards, but without their usual noisy banter. The checkpoint judges also ceased posting banter on the WhatsApp group in case an urgent message for or about Linda was shared. Initially, Madeleine had wanted to keep Linda's disappearance secret from the riders while she investigated what was going on, but the other checkpoint judges had taken that decision out of her hands, and she was impressed with the way everyone rallied together. The empty checkpoint was the hot topic of conversation, and the riders were trying to remember what they had seen as they rode through.

Alison drove the 4x4 carefully around the lanes, and all three women cheerfully waved and called out encouragement to the handful of riders they passed, casually checking if they had ridden through an empty checkpoint during their orienteering exercise. Hopes were raised when one pair confirmed that Linda had been in the correct place when they arrived at her checkpoint, but it quickly transpired that the pair had then become hopelessly lost and were probably about an hour and a half later to their present position than they should have been. All seemed to be having a good time, including the pair who were now back on track, and all riders and horses could easily be seen in their brightly coloured high visibility attire.

Alison and Jennifer did not want to transmit their fears about Linda's welfare to the riders or to young Heather in the car with them. They would have preferred to have left Heather behind due to her age, but in the interests of keeping up appearances they agreed with Madeleine that they would include her. She could always be the main telephone contact for emergency services or the yard if necessary, leaving Alison and Jennifer to deal with whatever situation they uncovered.

It took about fifteen minutes to arrive at Linda's checkpoint, and the scene was eerie. The car was parked up as expected, the doors were unlocked, the windows rolled down, and with the speed card prominently displayed. The boot of the estate car was

open, and inside was one of the Brackenshire HOOFING clocks, with which all of the checkpoints were equipped so that accurate time keeping could be guaranteed. Also in the boot was a bag containing a first aid kit, spare record cards, hoofpicks and magnetic compasses, and another containing the remnants of Linda's packed lunch were nestled alongside her personal bag containing keys, tissues, purse and so on.
'She hasn't been mugged,' Alison whispered to Jennifer.
'No sign of a struggle or blood anywhere,' Jennifer whispered as she scanned the immediate area.
The cones and flags were placed correctly to mark the entry, holding area, and exit of the checkpoint. Alison took a couple of photographs just in case there were any clues to what had happened to Linda which weren't immediately obvious to them, and then, as all of the riders had now completed this section of the exercise, she asked Heather to collect the equipment and stack it into the boot of Linda's car.
'You've got your phone with you, haven't you?' she asked.
'Yes, all charged up and I have signal,' Heather confirmed.
'Great. Here's a whistle, and we both have a whistle too. You stay here, while Jennifer and I will have a little scout around the area. We should all be within shouting distance of at least one of us, so don't move from this spot. Jennifer, you go that way,' she indicated along the lane in the opposite direction to the way they had arrived. 'Let's assume if she was walking the other way we'd have seen her. I'm going to walk back along the track into the woods the riders will have come up. We will be no more than five minutes, OK?'

Everyone nodded, and with her heart thumping. Jennifer began to walk along the road, scanning the hedges and gateways for signs of an abduction, but not wanting to see anything. Every gate she came to she opened or climbed over and had a quick check inside the field to the left and the right and a little way towards the middle. The fields with cows or sheep were easy to scan because she was sure that if there was a body in there the animals would be showing signs of distress or curiosity. Also, the grass was much shorter where the animals were than some of the other fields where crops were growing. Those arable fields were perfect for hiding a body, and Jennifer was not keen to find one.
'Linda! Linda!' she called loudly, pausing to hear a response. But the only voice that she could hear was her sister's as she, too, called Linda's name. A few cars passed her in both directions, and in a couple of the fields the farmers were hard at work with tractors. She recognised Bilbo driving one of them and waved to him. Surely if something had happened to Linda in one of those fields, he or the other driver would have seen something?
Alison's heart was also thumping as she walked down the familiar dirt track which was soon enclosed on either side of the woods. She had ridden this route many times in the last year, and was now trying to remember if there were any places that a person could be dragged and hidden. This was a lovely track for a good trot and canter, and she had never paid much attention to the possibility of someone being attacked and concealed. As she walked on, she realised that the possibilities for hiding a body were all around her. She shivered and her voice sounded high as she called out, so she tried to moderate it. It ended up sounding like a

drag act she once saw, and she began to giggle. As she walked and called, Alison began to have a conversation with Linda rather than just calling her name.
'Now look what you are making me do Linda Beecham. Can you hear me? I wonder what my stage name would be. How about 'Alison Stardust'? Yours could be 'Linda Becoming!' It occurred to Alison that there were probably other people in the woods, walkers or horse riders who could hear her strange ramblings and might decide to turn around and retrace their steps, or worse, keep coming towards her to see who was talking to themselves. She blushed, even though she couldn't see anyone, and then almost immediately she felt the colour drain from her face when she realised that, worryingly, someone who had harmed Linda might be listening. Alison decided she had walked far enough, and turned around to retrace her steps, walking quickly with frequent glances over her shoulder.
Although Heather was also concerned about the whereabouts of Linda, she too was familiar with the countryside around them and couldn't imagine anything untoward happening to anyone out here. She carefully gathered up the checkpoint equipment, brushing soil and leaves off the spikes of the little plastic flags before placing them in their bag, and stacking the small domed cones onto the specially designed holder. She could hear Alison and Jennifer and it comforted her. She checked her phone for new messages and tried to ring Linda in case she answered this time. The sound of an old-style Nokia ringtone rang out from the other side of the hedge behind Linda's car. There was no easy way through, so Heather walked a little way down the track in the direction Alison had gone searching, but instead of

staying on the track she veered off through the long grass towards a bramble covered fence. She pressed the buttons to call Linda's mobile again, and frustratingly the sound was further away than when she had been at the car. Heather could see no way through the brambles to reach the fence, so she knew that Linda could not have climbed over this way.
'Jennifer! Alison! I have found Linda's phone!' Heather called out as she turned and ran up the track towards the road.
Alison heard Heather's shout and was already almost out of the woods. She sprinted along the track in time to see Heather disappearing around the corner onto the road. Jennifer couldn't hear Heather over the noise of the working tractor, but happened to glance back and saw her running up the road before suddenly turning off left and clambouring over a gate into a field of cows. Jennifer and Alison both made it to the gate at the same time.
'What's going on?' gasped Alison.
'No idea. Come on she went this way.'
The sisters climbed the gate, and skirting the cows who had congregated near the gate, they raced towards Heather who had finally located the ringing mobile.
'Here! Here! I have found her phone!' she yelled as she held it up. Without speaking, everyone instinctively looked around, at first quickly scanning the area, but then looking more carefully at the ground around them.
There was no sign of Linda.
'Where is she?' Jennifer asked.
Simultaneously all three women shouted 'LINDA!' and waited, straining to hear a response.
'I wish that bloody tractor would shut up,' Jennifer muttered.

‘Oh, great, now there's a helicopter drowning out any chance we might have of hearing Linda,’ Alison threw her hands up in the air in frustration.
‘Hang on a minute’ Heather shushed them both as she looked up, observing the helicopter. ‘It's the air ambulance and it is landing in this field. Look, it's coming down over there around the corner of the woods!’
As one, the three women ran towards the noise of the helicopter.

Chapter 14

Sunday 20th October 2019, 1.50pm

When they rounded the corner Jennifer, Alison and Heather could see two people kneeling next to a prone body on the grass. Together they slowed their steps but continued to move forwards. The scene became clearer as they came closer, and they could see the body was a male, and the long grey ponytail of the person rhythmically pressing down on the man's bare chest belonged to Linda Beecham. The second person, a woman whom they did not recognise, regularly leant forward and tilted the man's head, held his nose and blew into his mouth. Linda and the woman made an incongruous pair: Linda fully dressed in jeans, boots and a long-sleeved shirt; the woman barefoot, and wearing a pretty camisole and short summer skirt.

The air ambulance crew were climbing out of the helicopter with their huge kit bags, so the women stopped and kept their distance, watching as the medics neatly swapped places with Linda and the woman. Heather snapped a few photographs of the scene with her phone, and then rang Madeleine.

'Hi, it's me. We have found Linda and she is safe and well, so you can tell everyone not to worry. We're not sure what has happened, but she had been helping

someone in trouble. Not one of the riders,' Heather added hastily.
'Oh, thank goodness you have found her. I'll let everyone know. Are you making your way back here now?' Madeleine was wavering between concern and annoyance that Linda had left her post, and wanted to hear from her what had happened before she reacted.
'I don't think we'll be too long because the air ambulance has arrived, but we won't leave until Linda is ready to.'
Alison and Jennifer were listening to Heather's side of the conversation, and silently acknowledged to each other that here was a promising young asset to the future of their riding club. They nodded their agreement to her last statement, and continued to watch the scene unfolding in front of them in case they could offer any assistance.
'I've never seen anything like this before. Have you?' Jennifer asked her sister. 'I mean, obviously I have attended a lot of first aid training courses and health and safety veterinary talks, but I have never been involved in a genuine incident which requires an ambulance, let alone an air ambulance.'
'Sadly, I have yes. One of the riding schools where I worked while I was studying for my instructor's exams was a regular visiting place for the local ambulance crew. All of the horses were turned out as much as possible until the first of October, when they kept all the horses in stables regardless of the weather conditions, and no exceptions to the no-turnout rule or a gradual change to the routine. In those first couple of weeks, riders were being trampled or thrown off their horses on an almost daily basis. It was excellent training for my own first aid skills with plenty of broken legs, arms and ribs to deal with, but also head

injuries which I find terrifying. On two occasions we had to call the ambulance for heart attacks, and it was similar to this. I don't know how long Linda has been performing CPR, but I had to do it for seven minutes on a grandmother who had brought her grandson to the yard and collapsed while watching him having a lesson in one of the outdoor schools. It was absolutely exhausting and I was dripping with sweat even though it was a chilly February afternoon, colder than today and without this glorious sunshine. I couldn't believe it had only been seven minutes. It felt more like forty-five. My arms and shoulders ached for days afterwards.'
'Did she survive?' asked Heather.
'Sadly, no. She made it to the hospital and was discharged not long afterwards, but then had a massive heart attack a couple of days later after she had been sent home and died within minutes. It was desperately sad, because she wasn't very old, and was the only person in the family who encouraged the boy to go horse riding. I don't think he was allowed to continue after that, which is a great shame because he thoroughly enjoyed coming to the stables.'
Their eyes turned back to the scene of the collapsed man, who was still being worked on by the medical team. They were preparing his chest for the defibrillator, while continuing with the chest compressions that Linda had been doing when they first found her.
'If this wasn't so vitally important, I'd be really enjoying observing this,' whispered Jennifer. 'Is that wrong?'
'I don't think so. Fortunately it isn't often we get to see these professionals at work,' Alison gestured towards the medical team who were now preparing to jolt the

man's heart back to life. 'Doesn't Linda look calm and competent. I guess the other two are husband and wife?'
'Or at least partners,' agreed Jennifer, looking at the evidence of rugs and plates of food. 'They look as though they came in here for a picnic. Probably making the most of a lovely sunny October day.'
'I think it was probably a bit more than that. Look!' Heather pointed to the discarded clothing and empty bottle of something fizzy.
'Oh!' Jennifer put her hands up to her mouth. 'I assumed they were both half naked because she was trying to save his life!'
'Me too!' Alison was trying not to giggle under the circumstances, and fortunately her embarrassment was saved when a cheer went up from those intent on saving the man's life. The defibrillator had done its job, and the man was breathing on his own again.
Linda had been standing with her arm around the woman, comforting her as she watched while her lover fought for his life. Now Linda turned and came over to join the women with a huge smile on her face.
'Oh, thank goodness! That was a bit too close for comfort. The poor man. His name is Barry, and he and his wife Julia were having a celebratory picnic for their wedding anniversary, but the walk here must have been too much for him and he had a heart attack. He's not very old, I'd guess mid-forties, and looks healthy to me. Poor man.'
All three women decided that now was not the time to spell out to Linda that Julia's pink lacy bra and matching knickers were in a heap next to the empty bottle of fizz, and although Barry's shorts were on his body, his pants were lying in the grass next to his socks and boots. Jennifer quietly went over to Julia and

offered to pack up the picnic and rugs, and gently suggested that Julia disappear into the woods and put her underwear on. Now that she was standing up, the little strappy top she was wearing did nothing to cover her ample bosom, and she was all too aware of this and kept tugging at the fabric. She seemed relieved that someone had given her permission to go and dress herself, and was back in minutes to help Jennifer finish packing everything away.

'I am so grateful to Linda,' Julia said to Jennifer as they folded the rug. 'She said she heard me when I was talking to the 999 operator. I can't remember much about it; I think I was screaming down the phone at him. Linda was here and starting CPR before I realised what was happening. She made me concentrate on saving his life. I thought I was going to lose him.'

Barry was loaded into the helicopter, and the pilot told Julia which hospital they were going to fly him to.

'Where is your car parked?' Alison asked Julia.

'In the car park at this end of the Trailway, not too far away.' Julia said as she prepared to carry their picnic paraphernalia across the field.

'Come with us. Our car is parked just on the other side of the hedge; we'll give you a lift.'

'Mine's there too,' said Linda. 'I'll drive Julia to her car, and then come back to the yard. Oh, I am so sorry. I completely forgot about the competition. You must have come to find me. I am sorry I've lost my phone so couldn't let anyone know I had deserted my post. I stupidly stuck it in the back pocket of these jeans and it must have fallen out as I was running.'

'I found it.' Heather handed it over.

'Don't worry, Linda. Saving someone's life is far more important than checking people in and out of a checkpoint,' Alison reassured her. 'But perhaps one of

us should go with you in your car just in case you are still wearing your superhero cape and get waylaid on the way back?'
Everyone laughed, especially Linda who could feel the shock of events trying to invade her composure. She didn't want to let go just yet; at least not until she had seen Julia safely back to her own car. Julia had far more to cope with than she did.
'I'll go,' volunteered Heather.
'Thank you,' said Linda, thinking that while she was responsible for the teenager she would have to keep her emotions under control.
'I really don't want to put you to any more trouble,' said Julia to Linda. 'I am very grateful you appeared through that hedge. If it wasn't for you, Barry would have died.'
'Never mind that now, it was a team effort and we both kept him alive until the professionals could do the real work. Come on, let's get out of this field.'
Linda led the way until Heather stopped her and said, 'I think you'll find it easier to go through the gate over there, past the cows. How on earth did you get through the hedge?'
'It was a bit tricky,' confessed Linda. 'But I could hear Julia screaming for help, so I just kept going.'
'I'm very glad you did,' said Julia.

Chapter 15

Sunday 20th October 2019, 4.00pm

By the time Linda and Heather drove into the yard of Woodford Riding Club, everyone else was gathered in between the horse lorries and trailers to hear Madeleine as she sat on top of a conveniently placed Land Rover Discovery. Someone had put a horse rug on top of the roof rack so she could sit comfortably, and Madeleine was equipped with the microphone she used for training her clients in the hope that everyone would be able to hear her through the loudspeaker. She was checking she had the correct tally of prizes in the right order according to the list that she, Jimmy, and Phil had carefully compiled in the relative peace and quiet of the HQ and results room. When she was satisfied, she looked up to see if everyone was ready and was greeted with a sea of smiling humans, most wearing more layers now than they had whilst riding, as the Autumnal evening chill began to set in. Many had their hands wrapped around mugs of tea and were enjoying eating pieces of cake, and a large number of happy horses were either tied up outside or were standing inside their trailers and lorries, munching through the contents of their hay nets.

‘Thank you everyone for participating in our four-part training clinic, and congratulations for making it to the end of the fourth session!’

A big cheer spontaneously rang out, and shouts of ‘thank YOU’ could be heard echoing around the yard.

‘Phew!’ thought Madeleine to herself. ‘The general mood seems good, despite all of the upsets we've had today.’

‘You have all been a joy to work with and I hope that today's final practice has been a positive experience for every one of you. We have had some hiccups along the way,’ and a general outbreak of giggles scattered around the volunteers at Madeleine’s understated description of the day’s events ‘but we have made it to the prize giving.

‘I have some prizes to hand out, all generously sponsored by our local tack and feed shop Woodford Equine Supplies, who we all know as WES’ another loud cheer from both the riders and volunteers. ‘But first I would like to thank our amazing volunteers who have given up their Sunday to help this practice session to run as smoothly as possible.’ Madeleine pulled a face, acknowledging it had not gone smoothly, and again everyone laughed. ‘Thank you everyone for staying for the results, and in case you haven't heard the reason one of the checkpoints was unmanned for part of the day was because the volunteer judge was busy trying to save someone's life. Not one of our riders, fortunately, but I'm sure no one will complain if they were inconvenienced by the health emergency.’ Madeleine deliberately looked at a couple of riders who had been alone in their vociferous comments about paying good money for training, only to be let down by shoddy organisation. The two individual

riders had the grace to look embarrassed as everyone else cheered and shouted 'Well done, Linda!'
Satisfied that everyone was now on the right page, Madeleine continued 'I am sorry it has been such a long day, especially for those of you who had a very early start this morning and still have two to three hours ahead of you before you can have a well-deserved hot bath and cold drink. On that note, here is a travel mug for Charlie and a haynet for Highlander, the horse and rider combination who I believe has travelled the furthest distance to be here today, and of course Charlie also travelled over here for the three weekend training sessions too!'
Everyone cheered, and those who had finished their drinks and snacks clapped, as Charlie stepped forward to receive his prizes. He admired the WES and Brackenshire HOOFING logos on his travel mug, and held both prizes up for everyone to see.
'Next, it is my great pleasure to present Katherine and Nova each with a new compass and map case for winning the prize for going so far off course they managed to find a checkpoint for a different competition.'
Katherine and Nova both cheered and clapped themselves as they weaved their way past horses and riders, and when they reached the Land Rover Katherine loudly explained. 'We found a checkpoint for a running race!'
'The joke is the runners were on a longer course and were going faster than us on our horses!' laughed Nova.
'They probably finished before you did!' teased Madeleine as she handed the prizes to the two women, who were both now laughing so hard they had tears pouring down their cheeks.

'Many of you are experienced treccies, including Nova and Katherine, and as usual we have appreciated the help you have given to people who are new to our sport, especially today when things did not go to plan. It can be confusing to turn up to a competition, even a practice one like this, and especially when you have your horse to think about too. But even experienced treccies need help sometimes. As you know, competitors must not help or confer with other competitors during the orienteering phase unless they are in an official pair, when they can chat away to each other as much as they like. But today was not a competition, and although we would like you to practice every aspect of a true competition, there are times when an exception to the rule can make the difference between someone being scared and put off from the sport and someone learning how to correct a mistake and having a positive learning experience. There is one competitor who demonstrated this perfectly today, and they have been nominated anonymously, and indeed she may not even know what she did. But the person who put your name forward was very grateful for your instinctive act of kindness and took the time to come and tell us about it. As a thank you, the person has donated the money for one of our beautiful high visibility pink waterproof jackets which has the Brackenshire HOOFING logo in fluorescent silver on the back, and the WES logo down the sleeves. When we told them about it, the lovely people at WES have also donated a set of four high visibility yellow leg bands. Amelia, please step forward and collect the prizes for you and Rosie!'
Amelia was another popular winner, and the cheers and clapping became louder as she looked as though she was going to hide rather than come up to receive

her prize. Eventually, blushing furiously, she walked quickly up to Madeleine, who jumped down and gave her a hug, taking the opportunity to whisper in her ear the reason she was receiving such generous prizes. With an 'Oh!' Amelia cast her embarrassment aside and held her prizes up for everyone to see, just as Charlie had done with his, and was now sporting a huge grin on her face.

'I am sure I didn't do anything more than anyone else would do in that situation, and I certainly didn't do it to be recognised in this way, but thank you. I love this sport. Indeed, I love this group, and have always appreciated the help I have received, so I am only too pleased to give some back.'

Everybody wanted to know what she had done and who had put her name forward, but Amelia simply smiled and nodded as she made her way back to her horse van and Rosie.

Madeleine climbed back up onto the top of the Land Rover and settled down on the rug. 'Now to the results of the competition. The first thing to say is that everyone who signed up, attended and completed each of the four sessions is a winner, and you'll go home with one of these!' she held up a turquoise and navy blue double tiered rosette. 'Brackenshire HOOFING' was stamped in silver on the navy blue disc in the middle, and 'Woodford Riding Club POR Training 2019' with the rider and horse's name handwritten on the back by Heather, who loved every opportunity to use her calligraphy set. The riders loudly cheered at their own successes.

'Obviously when it came to tallying up your results we had the challenge of what to do about the vanishing checkpoint. Some of you were judged correctly as you came through; some of you took the initiative to judge yourselves when you realised no one was there to do it for you; and some of you didn't realise it was part of the competition. Today is a practice session, so whichever category you fall into, congratulations, you have had some practice and we have all learned something from this unexpected challenge. We decided to take you all on trust, and if you were honest about not waiting there for five minutes, we added that time onto your final score.'

There was an uncomfortable silence while riders wondered if anyone had not owned up to riding straight through the checkpoint, but all of the volunteers had looked at the timings and final scores and didn't think the results would have been dramatically affected by anyone who was cheating. Madeleine raised the mood again by holding up the next rosette and prize. 'In sixth place were Charlie and Highlander!'

Yet again, Charlie walked up to collect his prizes, this time a purple Brackenshire HOOFING rosette and a folding hoof pick, and also his finisher rosette. Madeleine called out the rest of the winners, all of whom received the same prize but a different colour rosette appropriate to their placing, until she was left with first place, a red rosette and a fifty pound voucher for the Woodford Equine Supplies shop. 'First place goes to Patricia and Dougal!'

The volunteers were already primed to make sure Patricia's unpopularity did not detract from her achievement, and they clapped and cheered loudly, with Heather throwing in a few wolf whistles. Encouraged by the noise, after a few seconds delay all of the riders joined in, and Patricia walked up to collect her prizes with a look of pure joy on her face. Madeleine didn't think she had ever seen her look so happy, and knew that despite all of the trials and challenges of the day the whole team of riders and volunteers had been successful.

Chapter 16

Monday 21st October 2019, 5:55am

‘Oh god why did I agree to this?’ groaned Jennifer, as the sound of her alarm woke her up. ‘It's still dark outside!’
She had laid out her running gear the night before and stepped out of bed and dressed quickly before heading into the en-suite bathroom for a wee. She hurried down the stairs, putting on her running shoes and out of the front door with her greyhound, Lucy, at her heels. She zipped the front door key and her phone into the pocket of her running shorts, which nestled comfortably just below the small of her back and walked through the alley towards the green. Madeleine, with Max and Alison with Woody were already there waiting by the bench agreed, as well as a third person, Rebecca Martin. All three women were clearly visible in a mixture of reflective strips and coloured light against the black backdrop of The Green behind them. The other women looked horribly perky to Jennifer.
‘We were just debating whether to give you a call,’ grinned Alison.
‘I'm here; I'm not late,’ grumbled Jennifer as she fiddled with her head torch to make sure she didn't shine it directly into her friends’ eyes. ‘Hello Rebecca, you’re a glutton for punishment too are you?’

‘Madeleine persuaded me to join you,’ said Rebecca, who managed to look casually glamorous even at this time of the morning.
‘That’s a good idea. I should think a bit of routine and exercise, as well as a giggle, will help you at the moment. It’s lovely to see you here, even if it is stupid o’clock,’ said Jennifer.
‘Come on sis, you’re the expert runner here after your epic twelve kilometres at the weekend. You can lead the way!’ teased Alison.
Jennifer narrowed her eyes. ‘I’m going to challenge you to a five kilometre race at the end of this.’
‘Let's get started,’ said Madeleine, keen to put a stop to a sisterly squabble before they could get started on their run. ‘Do you have your phone, Jennifer?’
‘Yes,’ she huffed as she unzipped the pocket and pulled it out.
The four women took a few moments to open their Couch to 5K app. They had all downloaded it independently the day before, and chosen their virtual running coaches. As Sarah Millican's voice rang out from four different phones, with a slight delay, the women laughed.
‘I didn't know you'd all chosen her!’ said Madeleine.
‘Great minds think alike,’ said Jennifer. ‘We only need to hear her once though. I'll keep mine on and you three can mute your phones. Is that okay?’
‘Yes, that's fine. We’ll keep them recording though, so we can keep track of our own progress.’ Madeleine put hers back into her navy blue bum bag emblazoned with Brackenshire HOOFING in sparkly pink letters. ‘Does anyone mind if Max stays off the lead for this run? If he's a nuisance I'll clip him on, but I've ordered a proper running harness and lead and it hasn't arrived yet.’

‘I'm sure he'll be fine. After all, he's always very good when he comes out with the horses,’ said Alison, ‘and he is well lit up with that flashing collar.’
‘I didn't think to bring a lead for Lucy, I'm sorry, she's normally so good at being nearby it didn't occur to me she could trip any of us up. I didn't take her on the run last Friday because she's not keen on long distances, but this should suit her. I'll bring one for her on Wednesday if that's OK,’ said Jennifer. ‘Tell me more about this harness, Madeleine?’
They set off in a walk on their planned route, starting from The Green along a quiet Brackendon road to the entrance to the trailway.
‘Well done for yesterday,’ Alison said to Madeleine. ‘I have never seen the work that goes into an event like that from the organiser’s perspective. Obviously, I have helped as a fence judge at cross country competitions, and have written for numerous dressage judges over the years, but normally I'm competing, and although we all know a lot of work goes into running those events, it's the first time I've seen how one of the numerous emergencies to be planned for actually works in practice.’
‘Yes, I agree,’ nodded her sister. ‘Your ability to stay calm and delegate ensured that a drama did not turn into a crisis, Madeleine.’
Madeleine was blushing as she walked along beside her friends. ‘Oh, days like yesterday are only successful if everyone pulls together as a team, and thank goodness the volunteers and competitors did just that. You know all about it, don’t you Rebecca?’
Rebecca nodded ‘Oh yes. After all these years running the Woodford Summer Fete, I appreciate the team players and try to avoid everyone else. What is all this about; did something happen yesterday?’

'I don't know how you do it, year after year,' wondered Madeleine. 'Yesterday we had a bit of an incident, which wasn't actually related to our event, but one of our volunteers got caught up in it. It worked out well in the end, but if we had been running an official competition then things could have had serious repercussions. Fortunately I had Jennifer and Alison on my side, who found the missing checkpoint judge, Linda Beecham. Linda helped to save a person's life; the rest of the checkpoint judges worked together to ensure the competitors knew what to do at the vacant checkpoint; Phil and Jimmy kept things running smoothly back at headquarters. When you think about it, there wasn't anything that actually went wrong other than a missing checkpoint judge.'
Alison laughed. 'Believe me, I've seen events fall apart over much less. All it takes is for one person to stir up trouble and everyone loses faith in the organiser and all start doing their own thing. I was competing in one dressage competition run by a riding club when the person adding up the scores decided that the judge wasn't making the correct decisions, and actually ran after the winner of the class shouting that the scores had been corrupted and wouldn't count in the regional, let alone the national league. The competitor was mortified, thinking that she had erroneously been awarded first place and had denied a more deserving winner, and ended up feeling responsible for the whole thing. All of the joy at winning the red rosette with her mare, whom she was planning to retire on a high, was destroyed. Everyone took sides, mostly with the judge because the scorer was a well-known troublemaker, but sadly the scorer had supporters in high places and that judge was never asked back. In a matter of months the club had lost members and volunteers, then a new club

was started by a few of those who didn't want to be associated with the original club, and it was quickly flooded with members and volunteers, and although the original club still had some kudos at a national level, it never recovered.'

'Blimey,' said Madeleine. 'That story has made me even more nervous about volunteering to organise anything ever again!'

'Don't forget you handled Diana Smalley very well too. She is someone who could potentially bring down the club,' said Jennifer.

'Oh, good,' said Madeleine. 'That's not helping either. What if she goes to national level to make a complaint about me? They're all friends of hers and are bound to take her side.'

'Oh, I don't know,' said Jennifer. 'I think you are forgetting that the National HOOFING Board are more realistic about things than some other organisations we know. I think the general mood of the Brackenshire HOOFING members is that you did the right thing, and it was about time somebody did. If the Board members do not agree, they will have to deal with an uprising from their members. However, I believe they are more in touch than you give them credit for.'

At that point Sarah Millican's voice interjected and encouraged them to start running, putting an end to their discussion. The surface of the trailway was easy under foot, and together they walked and jogged according to Sarah Millican's instructions, with the dogs exploring and sniffing together, keeping well away from human legs. It soon became clear that Woody had no intention of running at the speed everyone else wanted to, but preferred to sprint on ahead. Alison was glad that Madeleine had brought a twenty-two foot rope with her, and she allowed Woody to trot to the end of its length, by which time Sarah Millican was usually telling them it was time to walk again and she could reel Woody back in. It was the first time Alison had used such a rope. She was used to flat webbed lunge lines of about thirty feet long, and short lead ropes of about six feet long, but had never used this type of rope before.

At the halfway point, everyone obediently turned around and continued to follow the programme of several short running intervals interspersed with walking for a couple of minutes, as they headed back to The Green. Three of the humans collapsed onto the bench and the dogs lay down panting underneath it, and Woody stuck his head down to eat grass, but Rebecca looked ready to run again.

'Thank you everyone, I really needed that,' she said as she bounced on the spot. 'I hadn't realised how tight my neck and shoulders had become over the last few days. They feel free!' She wildly windmilled her arms around. 'I can't wait until we go again on Wednesday!'

'Oh my God, I'm not doing that again,' groaned Alison. 'Why on earth did I think it would be a good idea to bring Woody along? My arms and shoulders are killing me.'

'I think we were running too slowly for him. It's hard work for them to trot at that pace.' Madeleine was disappointed because she had liked Alison's idea and thought it would give Woody the enrichment he so obviously craved. 'He clearly enjoyed himself, but I think it will be too hard for you to continue doing this three times a week with him. We'll have to think of something else to occupy his brain.'

'That wasn't as bad as I thought it was going to be,' said Jennifer. 'In fact, I really enjoyed it and could go and do session two right now! I wish I'd started with

this app rather than trying to keep up with the Streakers last week. My legs are still aching from going out with them on Saturday.' She stretched out her legs and flexed her feet, grimacing as she found a couple of sore spots.
'Talk of the devils,' Rebecca pointed along the Brackendon Road where a small group of runners including Cliff, Paul, and Caroline were running with two Staffordshire Bull Terriers in the morning sunshine.
'Morning runners!' yelled Caroline, before peeling away from the others and taking the dogs into her aunt's house.
'*Runners*' preened Alison, all negative thoughts vanishing at the compliment. 'We are actual runners.'
Paul and Cliff jogged over to the bench, waving goodbye to the rest of their group.
'You'll be running with us in no time,' said Cliff, sweat dripping into his eyes as he peered at his watch. 'Not bad, not bad. That pace was better than I expected. Where did you run to?'
'We went down to the trailway and back,' said Alison.
'That was a good choice. It is relatively flat down there and a nice surface which shouldn't get too boggy when it rains. Once you start to run for longer distances there are a few tracks you can pick up from there which bring you back here.'
'Have you heard any more from the police?' Madeleine asked Paul.
Paul pulled a face. 'Nothing useful. You know they won't let us have the WSWC boxes?'
'Yes, you told us on Saturday,' said Madeleine. 'But I have asked around, and one of the Brackenshire HOOFING members can print your running club race numbers for you by Thursday, if you need him to. He

runs his own printing business, and probably did your original ones. He's going to have a look and see if he has your original order, and if so he'll do it free of charge.'
'That's brilliant, thank you Madeleine!' said Cliff. 'Hannah will be pleased. We've been working to a tight budget as we don't want to make a profit, but do want to raise money for the charities.'
'Yes, thank you Madeleine, that's a great weight off my mind. Hannah did the original order, so she'll know who she used. I'll text her now,' said Paul. 'They should have been here two weeks ago and posted out to the competitors. Perhaps it wouldn't be a bad idea to ask your contact how they feel about printing our race souvenirs too, Madeleine?'
'I'll ask,' said Madeleine, 'but I know when we've ordered clothing for the riding clubs it takes weeks to get the order processed. What are the race souvenirs?'
'Thinking about it, I don't think it's going to be practical. Every finisher and volunteer gets a wooden medal, which are going to be impossible to make in the time we have left, so worst case scenario, everyone will just have to wait for their Finishers prize,' said Cliff gloomily. 'We have also had a load of t-shirts and hoodies made, which could be re-printed in time if someone already has stock, but as they are printed and in boxes in the auction house there is no point re-printing them because they are unique to this race. It's not a great start to our first race, if we can't hand out prizes to people who have put the effort in to train and race.'
'Neither is it the end of the world,' snapped Jennifer. She had every confidence that Paul would find solutions for the difficulties he was facing, and his intelligence and resilience were qualities she loved

about him. But after a weekend of hearing him go round and round over the same ground her patience was worn out. In her work as a veterinary surgeon she regularly had to make life or death decisions, and although she appreciated how serious the police investigation was and how it was affecting Paul's business, she couldn't face hearing yet again about how the runners weren't going to be able to have their t-shirts and crisps. 'Look, I don't think we're going to get much done standing around out here. I'm starting to get cold, and want to get home and have a hot shower. You've talked through all the possibilities a thousand times.'

But Paul needed to talk to the others in the hope one of them would come up with something he hadn't thought of. He had never been in the position where he couldn't come up with a workable solution, and did not enjoy it. 'I don't know how I'm going to pay the staff at the end of the month if this continues. I don't know if I should be encouraging them to look for other jobs. I don't know what to do. The bills for that place,' he nodded to the auction house on the other side of the road, 'are still rolling in. But as both my business and personal bank accounts are frozen, I'm going to have a problem paying them. It's a nightmare.'

'That's awful, Paul. I'm so sorry I can't help. What can you do?' Alison asked.

Paul spread out his hands. 'I just don't know. I'm helpless. I have never been in this situation before. I've checked my insurance policy, but it doesn't seem to cover a situation like this.'

'Insurance never covers the things you want it to cover,' muttered Madeleine.

Jennifer, who regularly received pay outs from insurance companies for injured horses, decided to

keep quiet. She and her father, together with Alison's help, had recently set up an equine veterinary hospital and the majority of their patients were paid for by insurance companies. She had also heard this particular complaint from Paul several times since he discovered the omission from the insurance documents on Saturday morning.
Cliff said 'I suppose the only thing you can do with our help is find out who, if anyone, was money laundering through your auction, and make sure the police catch them and prove your innocence that way. I was talking to Rebecca last night and she wants to help too, don't you love?'
Rebecca had been standing quietly, listening to everyone throwing out ideas and solutions, as well as admitting defeat over some things. She was the sort of person who liked to have all of the facts before coming up with ideas, and had managed to avoid becoming too involved with the WSWC organisation in spite of being Paul's personal assistant. Fortunately Hannah McClure was very good at organising, and had not delegated anything to Paul, or Rebecca would have probably been the one doing the work. But she had been giving a lot of thought to the problems with the auction business, and because of the police's actions had the time to do it. Now she spoke 'I have been doing some digging around, Paul, and believe it is going to be up to us to find out what, if anything, is going on.'
'But how can I do any detective work like that when I have no access to my computers or filing cabinets?' Paul was overwhelmed, and could feel the euphoria from the run draining away to despair.
Rebecca smiled 'I know a way around some of that. Yes, it is frustrating not being allowed access to the

tools of our business in the auction house, but Jennifer is right, and we're not going to get anything done while we're all dressed in very little for the time of year on The Green.'
Cliff could see that Paul was about to argue, and intervened. 'Jennifer and Rebecca are right; we all need to get home. You are in a real bind being locked out of your business premises, and I can't imagine what I'd do if the same thing happened to me. Thank goodness all of the admin for this race is going to Hannah, or we'd probably have to cancel it. Your hands really would be tied if you couldn't access anything, but Rebecca has found a small way around some of it. Why don't you call all the staff together, listen to their ideas and their worries, and talk to them about it. Find out what they think about the situation. Someone may have thought of something which has not occurred to you. From what I see as a customer, you all work well as a team when things are good. And everyone is committed to the success of the business. There is no reason why your staff would not do the same when you hit a sticky patch. If you gather them into one place, like The Ship Inn or The Woodford Tearooms, or if you want a private neutral place you could use my flat at the antiques centre, you might be able to move forward. It could be that some of them have already started looking elsewhere for work, in which case you won't have any more responsibility for them. Don't forget, you and your staff hold a lot of information about the business in your head, and it may be that dodgy behaviour is witnessed rather than recorded onto a computer.'
Jennifer saw a smile cross Paul's face for the first time since the previous Saturday. 'Good idea, Cliff' he said. 'Thank you.'

‘Thank you, Cliff,’ said Rebecca. ‘I think that’s a great idea. I’ll contact the others, and we’ll meet up face-to-face. Thanks for the run ladies; same time Wednesday morning?’
To a chorus of ‘Yes, we’ll be here!’ Rebecca waved goodbye, and walked to her car which was parked in The Ship Inn’s car park.
‘I had better get home and showered, and put my thinking cap on,’ said Paul, as he made to start the short walk home.
‘Hang on a minute! I need that shower more than you do. I have to be at work in less than two hours, and I have more hair to dry than you,’ said Jennifer cheekily, as she leapt off the bench and started power walking across the road with Lucy close behind. Paul walked after her, keeping pace. She broke into a jog. So did he. The pair of them began to race. It was Jennifer who reached the entrance to the alleyway first, and their laughter and the sound of them arguing as they disappeared from sight.
‘It's good to hear him laughing’ observed Cliff.
‘He must be so worried. I can't imagine what it must be like to be in his shoes,’ said Alison as she stood up more slowly than her sister had. ‘I'd better get home too. Thanks for the run, Madeleine, and for bringing Woody with you too. I’ll try and think of something else to do with him, but I don’t think taking him running with me is going to work out well for either of us. Max, on the other hand, was great. You needn’t worry about that harness just yet. I'm going to have to get a dog so I can fit in with you and Jennifer.’
‘Careful what you say,’ teased Madeleine. ‘I'm always being offered dogs and horses.’
‘Me too,’ said Cliff. ‘I mean, I'm always being offered dogs, not horses. And cats and parrots. That's the

trouble with doing house clearances. Too often the original owner has died, leaving behind a pet who no one else in the family wants.'

'Not quite as sparkly as a diamond necklace, I suppose,' sniffed Alison. Turning to Madeleine, she said. 'I'll be over later for my lesson at two o'clock this afternoon.'

'Yes, you're in the diary. Good luck with their dressage tests this morning. I believe you will be teaching Patricia Bragg and Dougal to passage around the indoor school this afternoon.'

Alison laughed. 'Is that what she's been saying? I like teaching Patricia because she is honest about her abilities, and Dougal's, and she also has goals and wants to progress. Thanks for organising us to run this morning. I'd better get a move on and plait my ponies' manes before I go for a shower. I'll see you later, Madeleine.'

'I'll walk with you, Alison,' said Cliff. 'I need to get a move on so I can grab some breakfast at the tea rooms before I open up the antique centre. Bye Madeleine.'

Madeleine watched as they walked across The Green, chatting easily together, as they headed towards their respective homes: off to the right to the flat above Williamson Antiques for Cliff; Alison was heading straight ahead to the old farmhouse within the grounds of the equine veterinary hospital. Smiling, and wondering if she was witnessing the fledgling stage of a relationship, she encouraged Woody to leave his grass-mowing job, and together with Max they started the ten minute walk back to the yard.

Chapter 17

Monday 21st October 2019, 11.45am

'Hello Paul, I've set you up in the snug. You should be able to have a peaceful meeting in there without too many people overhearing,' Tom Higston greeted Paul as he walked through the front door of The Ship Inn. His personal and friendly welcome was one of the reasons many of the locals supported the pub, and at a time like this Paul appreciated it.

Rebecca had been as good as her word, and had rung around the full-time staff as soon as she was home. Paul was pleased to see them already sitting around the table which Tom had positioned in the middle of the small room, and there was an array of food and drinks spread out over it. He had wondered if he should provide the food as this was a work-related lunch, but he wasn't sure how he could pay for it while his personal and business bank accounts were frozen. Fortunately, it looked as though the Black's Auction House staff had taken that dilemma into their own hands by ordering and paying for a selection of salad bowls, cold meats, and freshly baked bread. The Ship Inn's chef, Amanda, was renowned throughout Brackenshire for her food. Paul could feel a huge lump in his throat and his eyes blurred with tears. Seeing his boss's predicament, Daniel Bartlett, one of his

employees, a tall, dark haired, blue eyed young man in his early twenties, jumped up and ushered Paul into a nearby chair. 'Here you go, Paul. As you can see the first meeting of Save Our Auction House has started as we mean to go on, with plenty of Scooby snacks.'
Everyone laughed and Paul looked around the table, still feeling overwhelmed by his staff's enthusiasm to help him. He had been feeling the weight of responsibility for the company's situation for days, and yet here were his four employees already established in a meeting. Rebecca was sitting with a glass of ginger beer and a plate of mozzarella cheese, tomatoes and avocado in front of her, a laptop open to one side and her notebook with one page already full of notes on the other. To her left was Richard, a quiet, tall skinny man in his late thirties with lank greasy brown hair and green eyes who rarely spoke but could be relied on to make clearing a house easy. He was good at lifting heavy furniture and carefully wrapping exquisite glass ornaments. He had opted for half a pint of the local beer and was tucking into a plate of couscous. On Rebecca's other side was Doug, a musclebound former soldier with tattoos everywhere, shaved grey hair and startling blue eyes. It was obvious to even a casual observer that he thought Rebecca was very attractive and was always hanging around the office when she was in there. It didn't surprise Paul that he was sitting next to her, nor that he had a half-drunk pint of Guinness and an almost empty plate containing the remnants of a pork pie and Scotch egg. His capacity for eating and drinking enormous amounts was legendary.
'What would you like to drink, Paul?' Tom appeared in the doorway behind him.
'Oh, I'll have a coffee, please Tom.'

‘I can recommend the Scotch eggs,’ Daniel put an empty dinner plate in front of him and leaned over to pick up the bowl of Scotch eggs, another of green salad and a jar of green tomato chutney.
‘These pork pies are good. The pork is from Higston's Farm and Amanda has made the pastry very tasty as usual.’ Doug passed the plates to Paul and continued tucking into his own food.
By the time Tom brought his coffee, Paul had recovered his composure and was enjoying the feast his employees had chosen, while listening to their discussion. Rebecca had given him a quick run-down on the areas they had already covered, and he was impressed. Although Rebecca had told him they were meeting at the pub at midday, the staff had agreed to meet as soon as the door to The Ship Inn opened at eleven o'clock so they could have a discussion in Paul’s absence. Paul was highly regarded by his staff, and they wanted to be able to support him as best they could. Between them, Rebecca and Daniel had updated the other two on what had happened as they understood it. Daniel was Jennifer’s step-brother, and it was all the family had been talking about since Saturday morning.
Rebecca was officially Paul’s personal assistant, but in reality her task encompassed almost every aspect of running a busy auction business and house clearance company. Although while she had been married to Cliff he had discouraged her from being involved in his business, and she had been happy to put her time and energy into raising their three children at the time, she had gleaned a lot of information about the ebb and flow of the antiques world during their eighteen years together. An auction house is a different beast to an antiques centre, but the people and objects are similar

and so her knowledge of the antiques world combined with a practical and logical brain and friendly interpersonal skills made her an essential part of the business. They worked closely together, and Paul trusted her with every aspect of his business. After Rebecca had explained their actions that morning, Paul was not surprised when it was Rebecca who began to sum up their discussions so far, although it was clear that they had all been keen to bring their ideas to the table.

Referring to her notebook, Rebecca said 'Firstly, Paul, we'd like you to know that none of us believe you are laundering money through Black's Auction House. All of us have an intimate knowledge of some workings of the business, and between us we are confident we would know if you were operating in that way.'

She paused, holding his gaze with her dark brown eyes. He blinked first and looked away, afraid he was going to start tearing up again. When did he start getting so emotional?

'As Rebecca says,' piped up Daniel 'none of us have seen any evidence that you are laundering money, and none of us believe you would do it anyway.'

Both Doug and Richard were nodding with sombre looks on their faces.

'Thank you,' said Paul, quietly. He let out a deep breath, feeling his shoulders drop several inches from his ears. 'I appreciate your faith in me. It means a lot.'

'We also think it is important to state that none of us are involved either,' said Rebecca, looking at her fellow staff members for confirmation.

A chorus of 'No, no we're not!' echoed around the table.

Paul's eyes widened. He hadn't even thought of that. 'Well, that's good!' he said, a more jovial tone creeping

in. 'We can be confident that we're all on the same side.'
'However,' Rebecca's voice brought the proceedings back to a serious level, 'we have individually been giving the police's suspicions a lot of thought since Friday, and we have all come to the same conclusion. It is possible that one or more of our customers are pushing goods through our auctions at unexpected prices. All of us can think of at least three people who have had some surprising results in the last couple of years, and these three' she gestured to Richard, Doug and Daniel 'can think of many more instances going back even further.'
'It's tricky because the very nature of an auction means that sometimes something worth one hundred pounds sells for five hundred, and vice versa,' said Doug. 'But there are some of our clients who regularly have a lucky streak, and I've made a note of them here.'
Paul looked at him in surprise as he leaned forward to accept the piece of paper Doug was holding out to him. Doug was usually a man of few words, who could be relied upon to deal with the customers quickly and quietly without engaging in banter or discussion. He followed orders and instructions, drove the company's vans efficiently and carefully, turned up for work on the dot, and was through the gates on or before his finishing time. It had never occurred to Paul that Doug paid attention to anything other than his job sheet for the day. Certainly he could be relied upon to think on his feet and resolve any problems which cropped up, such as an address which had been written down incorrectly, or the infamous time when they were clearing a house in Woodford after the old lady had moved into the nearby nursing home only to find her wandering in through back door and starting to scream

that they were murdering thieves and someone should call the police. Doug had calmed her down in seconds, taking her kindly by the arm and led her back down the streets to her new home.
Looking at the names in front of him, Paul knew he had underestimated Doug's investment in the business. He too had made a list of names and they exactly matched the ones Doug had written down.
'I've made a list too, but they're all on Doug's list,' volunteered Richard. 'I didn't have as many as he did.'
'Same here,' said Rebecca. 'I'm feeling a bit inadequate because I hadn't thought of a couple of them, but looking back through the records, Doug is right about them. Perhaps we should swap jobs' she laughed.
Doug allowed a small smile to soften his usual hard expression.
Paul's head had snapped up at Rebecca's mention of records. 'What do you mean?' he asked. 'What records? The police have prevented us from accessing our computers. Cliff said you had worked out a way of getting round the problem. What is it?'
Now it was Rebecca's turn to smile. 'They can't stop me from accessing the backups from home. Ever since I started working for you, I have been backing up all of our computer files every night, so that if the worst came to the worst, the most we would lose would be one day's work. Of course, I was thinking in terms of fire or theft. It didn't occur to me we'd be raided by the police and refused access to our own hardware. I asked your permission at the time, don't you remember?'
Paul had a vague memory of Rebecca giving him login and password details for online back-ups, but to his embarrassment now he remembered he had been too busy gloating over the fact he had recently employed

his best friend's estranged wife and was planning to add her to his list of sexual conquests. He hadn't paid any attention to the system, and had never had reason to access it. He could feel the colour rising in his cheeks as he thought back to what an idiot he had been towards her, and that she could possibly have saved his company. Fortunately, at the time because she knew him of old and was aware of his pathetic behaviours, Rebecca had firmly quashed any ideas of a romantic entanglement, and he had long forgotten that she was anything other than a valued friend and an integral part of his business.

'I had completely forgotten about all of that,' he admitted. 'But thank goodness you did. It will make our task a little easier.'

'Excuse me,' Linda Beecham, in her usual uniform of t-shirt and jeans, with her hair scooped back in a loose low pony tail, popped her head through the doorway of the snug, closely followed by Hazel Wilkinson. 'I'm really sorry, we weren't trying to eavesdrop on your conversation, but we think you are trying to work out if one of your customers has been money laundering through your business, as the police suspect. Would it be OK if I give my five pennorth worth? Tell me to butt out if I'm intruding too much, please.'

Paul cast a quick glance around his staff, and seeing their acceptance gave her a nod and beckoned them both in. Hazel hung back, and it was evident that Linda was going to be the one doing the talking.

'I'm sorry for gate-crashing your lunch, but from what I heard, and I promise we really weren't trying to listen, I think you may have misunderstood how money laundering works.'

'To be honest, I don't have a clue,' agreed Rebecca. Doug had been looking a little resistant to being told he

was wrong, but as soon as Rebecca gave Linda her trust, he immediately followed her lead.
'I'm not sure either,' he admitted.
'There is no reason why you should,' said Linda. 'But I do, and Hazel and I have been talking about it. The people you are looking for are going to be more interested in paying their illegitimately earned cash into the auction house, and taking clean money out through their bank account, than raising unexpectedly high prices for goods. If you can think of anyone who regularly pays for their items in cash combined with someone who always wants to be paid out through their bank account, then those are possibly going to be the people involved.'
Paul felt like such a dunce. Of course he knew that was how money laundering worked, but he had been so stunned by being accused of involvement in it that he had lost all common sense about the matter.
'Thank you Linda, and Hazel, of course you are right. It might make it easier for us to pinpoint who the culprits are,' he said to his staff. 'We only accept cash payments up to five thousand pounds as a rule, although we can go to ten thousand for trusted customers, so Rebecca if you can have a check through the records we may be able to see a pattern.'
Rebecca nodded, and asked 'That will narrow the parameters down by quite a lot, thank you Linda. But I don't see how you can prove you are not involved, Paul?'
Linda explained 'The police must think that Paul has a personal connection with one or more of the people doing this, always assuming money laundering has been operating through the business.'
Everyone looked at Paul, who shrugged. 'This could be quite tricky to prove I am innocent, since the family

firm has been going for many years, and I am friends with a lot of our clients. The majority live in the area, and of course I bump into them in the pub, as we are now' he gestured to Linda and Hazel 'or through my children at school or at clubs they go to, or when I'm out running.'
They sat quietly as they thought about all of the people they came across in their daily lives, and wondered how to prove they were innocent encounters.
'It's a little more specific than just regularly bumping into someone,' qualified Hazel, stepping forward for the first time, and today wearing a long, flowing pink and purple top and skirt combination. 'It's occasions when you have accepted entries into the auction when you've been walking round an antiques fair, for example, or have met up with someone in a layby or carpark on their way through the county.'
'I do that sometimes,' admitted Paul. 'But obviously only people I know and trust.'
'And there's your potential problem,' said Hazel. 'If you do have a close relationship with someone who is money laundering, then you are in trouble. Anyway, we've taken up too much of your time already. So sorry for the intrusion, but we only want to help.'
'Yes, yes, thank you, you have,' said Paul, as the two women ducked back out of the snug.
Paul had been feeling encouraged by his staff's enthusiasm for solving the mystery, and together they were motivated to put the effort in to tracking down the culprits. The potential crisis he was responsible for currently looming over the inaugural Woodford half marathon also seemed to have been averted, thanks to the kind efforts of the people around him pulling together and producing magic rabbits out of hats. But now he was feeling as though saving his business was

a lost cause. If they did manage to work out who, if anyone, was laundering money, then it was likely to be someone he counted on as a friend, and that was a hard thing to deal with. Paul wondered if anything could ever be the same again.

He had always loved his work, and counted many business associates as friends. Indeed, his work/life balance was tilted heavily to the work side, because he loved it so much.

Jennifer was a truly bright spot separate from his work because she had no interest in antiques or auctions. She provided him with an alternative perspective to many things because their business worlds were so different, and yet they were similar in their dedication to their jobs. Now that his daughter was also working in the antiques trade, and his son had shown signs of wanting to be an auctioneer when he left school, after many years of estrangement he was finally allowing his children into his life too. He had never been a family man, never been a good father, or partner to the various women in his life, but with Jennifer by his side Paul had been feeling content, no longer causing chaos by cheating with another woman, or avoiding time spent with his children because it took him away from the fun of his work or the adventure of the latest female in his life. For a fleeting moment he wondered if it was Jennifer who was laundering money, but immediately realised how stupid that idea was. Jennifer didn't have the first clue about antiques, and certainly didn't have the lifestyle of someone who was illegally making hundreds of thousands of pounds.

His thoughts turned to his best friend, Cliff Williamson. Cliff knew how to use antiques to illegally make money, but he rarely put anything through Black's Auction House, and when he did Paul usually

knew the provenance of the item. No, it couldn't be Cliff, he wasn't the type.
Linda Beecham? What had she been doing, hovering outside the snug, eavesdropping on their conversation? He had known her for years, without really knowing her. She had always been a fixture in the auction room, and a regular stallholder at nearby Drayton Flea Market. He knew nothing about her life, other than she owned her own horse and lived with her mother. Did that sound like someone who was a successful money launderer?
Hazel Wilkinson? Another dealer who kept popping up at the moment. A retired school teacher, married to a retired vet. Certainly they were well-off, but neither profession tended to attract master criminals.
And what about Gray? He certainly seemed to have pots of money, and put items into the auction. But he also ran a highly successful property development company which explained the money, and was always hard at work getting his hands dirty lugging wooden posts around to build fencing, or on a building site with his employees as they took down the dilapidated buildings and put up quality ones in their place. Was organising something like money laundering antiques as opposed to designing and building a new country residence something Gray could do, even if he had the time?
Paul listened vaguely as his staff talked through their plan of action, with Rebecca leading the discussion. Rebecca? No, Paul couldn't even countenance that suggestion. She was his rock, his confidant, and if Jennifer and Cliff hadn't got there first, she would be his best friend. If it turned out that it was Rebecca who was ruining his business, his reputation, his life, he would have no faith in the human race.

Who was he missing? Surely it had to be someone else. The stench of the swamp was fading as he found his way back to being able to plan and problem-solve, even if the answers were still out of reach.

Chapter 18

Wednesday 23rd October 2019, 6.00am

‘Good morning!’ Rebecca called to Jennifer, who had been the first one to the bench at The Green with Lucy. She could see the pair of them enjoying a few minutes of the early morning peace and quiet, and sat down next to Jennifer. Rebecca was excited about this next run and keen to get going, but matched Jennifer’s silence, and soon found herself relaxing into the atmospheric stillness of their environment.

In an instant the peace was shattered, as Madeleine's dog Max came running over ahead of her, and he and Lucy engaged in a quick game of zoomies while the humans watched and laughed, before the dogs settled down to sniffs and wees.

‘Morning,’ Madeleine managed to say as she slumped down on the bench. ‘I think I am having a delayed reaction to the weekend. I'm exhausted! Unlike you two, who are clearly feeling energetic.’

Jennifer grinned. ‘I am! I think I must have finally recovered from Saturday's run with the Streakers.’

‘I am!’ echoed Rebecca. ‘I really enjoyed our first run on Monday.’

‘How are you, Madeleine?’ Jennifer asked. ‘I'm not surprised you're tired. That was a big exercise you organised on Sunday, not to mention the additional

drama of worrying about what had happened to Linda Beecham. Thank goodness it all worked out well in the end and everyone had a great time.
'Except for Diana Smalley,' said Madeleine. 'I still haven't heard from her, or from the national HOOFING office. Whatever complaint she's putting in must be a serious one.'
Jennifer shrugged 'I think it's more likely that she went home with her tail between her legs and is laying low for a while. Surely anyone she speaks to is not going to support a complaint against you. You did the right thing, and from the sound of it, it's a shame no one acted earlier, because then perhaps things would not have got to the stage they did on Sunday.'
'It all happens at your horsey events,' said Rebecca. 'I have heard about Linda's heroism, but not about this Diana Smalley.'
'Oh, she was very rude to a number of people at our event on Sunday, and I had to be the one to pick her up on it.'
'Oh, I hate it when that happens,' nodded Rebecca. 'Why can't people just be nice to each other?'
'Exactly,' sighed Jennifer. 'Are you still going to have the wrap-up dinner tonight at The Ship Inn, Madeleine? You're not thinking of putting it off?'
'No, I'm not cancelling. I'm not that tired.'
'Ah, here's my sister,' Jennifer waved as Alison jogged towards them from the equine hospital.
'Morning ladies!' she called. 'Sorry to keep you all waiting. I lost track of the time. I was up early with loads of time to spare and decided to quickly check on the rehabs. The next thing I know it's five to six and I'm late!' She brushed some white horse hairs off her lime green running top.

Jennifer laughed. ‘I know what you've been doing. You've been cuddling Shandy.’
‘Of course I have. He's so gorgeous. Those Irish Draught horses are like big Labradors.’
‘I know,’ grinned Jennifer, whose own horse Jasper, was a grey Irish Draught gelding. ‘Come on, now that you're here let's get going.’
‘Are you alright?’ Alison was watching Madeleine with concern as she pulled herself off the bench, groaning with the exertion.
‘Delayed exhaustion from the weekend,’ Jennifer explained for her.
Madeleine shook herself to try and summon up some energy and said ‘Right come on, let's go.’
She strode across the road with Rebecca, and Alison and Jennifer found themselves lagging behind. They had to jog to catch up as Madeleine led the way along the Brackendon Road, towards the entrance to the trailway. The four of them started the running app on their phones, with Jennifer’s the only one issuing Sarah Millican’s commands, made sure their dogs were with them and together they ran and walked the prescribed training session for week one day two.
It was a beautiful autumnal morning with enough chill in the air without being unpleasant, and the promise of bright sunshine for the remainder of the day. Their running shoes walked and jogged over crispy fallen leaves, and Lucy and Max ran backwards and forwards trying to catch the squirrels who danced and jumped across the branches overhead. As the women ran, they chatted about the organisation for the next Brackenshire HOOFING event to be held at the Woodford Riding Club, a full TREC competition. Rebecca was happy to listen to the others brainstorm, enjoying the freedom that for once she was not the one

organising other people. She was a bit concerned though when she heard them discussing camping arrangements.
'Oh good grief, you're not tell me you are mad enough to sleep under canvas at this time of year?'
'Not under canvas, no,' Madeleine corrected her. 'Although there are usually a couple of people who have super-duper tents and sleeping bags which claim to protect you from the elements in minus two hundred and seventy degrees centigrade and fifty gale force winds.'
'Most people sleep in their trailers and lorries, inside a pop-up tent with many layers of blankets, sleeping bags and duvets,' explained Jennifer.
'The really savvy ones bring a living hot water bottle in the form of a dog with them,' laughed Madeleine.
'Well I have never heard of that. I thought you only ran your camps in the summer.'
Madeleine was struggling to talk while running, but she was determined to explain to her sister 'Unlike the national organisations, our local riding clubs can continue to run overnight camps and events throughout the winter months where safe and sensible accommodation for horses and humans is available. The UK's winter weather conditions mean that there aren't many places around the country where it is sensible to hold outdoor equestrian orienteering competitions, but if you think about it, the area around Woodford has enough quiet lanes and off-road tracks which don't become impassable due to flooding or bogs, so the fun can take place twelve months of the year.'
'Fun!' laughed Rebecca. 'What's wrong with an evening in the snug of The Ship Inn with food, drink and friends? In the warm and dry! Surely it can't be

safe to be out with horses when we have strong winds or thunderstorms?'

Jennifer took over from Madeleine 'Obviously there are occasions when we have to postpone, for example severe gales could mean that travelling a horse trailer or lorry is dangerous, or trees do fall across the planned riding routes, and if the conditions are icy then even the healthiest bare hooves cannot manage without slipping and sliding. But the members of the club know the challenges the organisers face, and only those prepared and able to be flexible compete. It isn't unusual for national competitions to have to be postponed, or in some cases cancelled, during supposedly more suitable summer months due to high winds or flooding, or both.'

'Yes, I can see that. We've had a few horrific so-called summer fetes where everything is soaked before we've even opened, and the children's sports days have had to be cancelled when the forecast has been terrible in June and July.'

Their chatter made the time pass quickly, and the women and dogs arrived back at the bench on The Green elated with their running achievements and excited about the upcoming equestrian competition. Even Rebecca was looking forward to hearing all about it when they met up on the Monday afterwards for the third week of the nine week running course. Jennifer was entering the competition with her grey horse, Jasper, and Madeleine was able to compete with her Welsh Section D Gelding Sonny, who was also grey, thanks to other club members taking over the main responsibilities for the event. It was rare for her to enter any event at the Woodford Riding Club because it was usually Madeleine who was organising them. As usual, all club members who were competing also

volunteered in some capacity, and there were strict rules safeguarding everyone from accusations of score tampering. For example, no competitors were allowed prior information about the route that was planned for the orienteering, but everyone would be helping to set up the obstacle course. All competitors received a diagram of it several days in advance, and the course designer always offered a course walk detailing the specifications of the scoring system prior to the start of the competition. It was Madeleine's job to ensure all of the required equipment belonging to the Woodford Riding Club was ready for use, so she had to be informed well in advance of the event. Again, Alison was helping to lay out the tickets as she did for the practice event at the weekend, and this time she had persuaded her dad to man one of the checkpoints with her. She had not been involved in a full competition before and wondered how it would differ from the practice events she had previously volunteered at.
The four of them congratulated each other on their running effort that morning, high fiving each other for completing day two of the twenty-seven day programme, and went their separate ways with smiles on their faces. Even Madeleine felt energised after spending half an hour exercising and chatting with her friends, and was ready to tackle the tasks of the day. However, the spectre of Diana Smalley still loomed large.

Chapter 19

Wednesday 23rd October 2019, 6.00pm

The two Brackenshire HOOFING organising committees filled the garden room of The Ship Inn. This evening was a combination of the final meeting for the team who ran the training event at the weekend and the first full meeting of the team who were organising the camping competition in November, with a number of members overlapping the two. Although the club was only two years old, the majority of the sixty-two members were seasoned equestrians, bringing a range of experience from dressage, eventing, liberty, TREC, nutrition and plenty more aspects of horsemanship. Camps such as the one they were discussing had become a regular feature for the club, and this would be the fifth that year, and the third to be held at the Woodford Riding Club. It was to be the fourth full TREC competition since the club started, although this event was not affiliated to any national league and was only open to Brackenshire HOOFING members, meaning that many of the competitors would be familiar with the routes set for the orienteering test, and with the obstacle course. This provided them with an opportunity to practise under competition conditions, build confidence in both horse and rider, and provide the volunteers with more

experience in judging, setting up and running an event under competition rules.
The weather conditions in November were probably going to be something to be endured rather than enjoyed.
The club chair was Kim Stanwick, who along with her husband and two children, was an active participant in all Brackenshire HOOFING activities. The club attracted members who were active with horses and from a variety of management systems. In Kim's case, her family were fortunate to have their own land where they had developed a track and field system, enabling their horses to live out twenty-four/seven, and they managed their horses barefoot, as did many of the other members.
The club had established a constitution in which no post was held by the same person for more than a year, and each of the responsibilities such as Chair, Safety and Scoring had two deputies, one of whom was the outgoing post holder, and the other was the potential incoming post holder. All members were required to volunteer in some capacity throughout the year, although in these early stages of the club's development the posts for crucial responsibilities such as these were held by people with established credentials from other organisations. The rules were designed to deter cliques of people who could take over the direction of the club, and no one could sit on the side lines and snipe about decisions being made because at some time they could find themselves in charge. This wasn't the way all of the HOOFING clubs around the country were run, but it was the way in which the majority were set up, and it was a formula which had a successful track record. Kim's two deputies were Zoe Sherrett, a local Zumba instructor

who was in training to be elected as chair after Kim's term in office was over, and she loved competing in cross country events with her Thoroughbred retired racehorse Jack, and Madeleine who had been Brackenshire HOOFING's first chair during its inaugural year.

The meetings usually started relatively early by equestrian standards at six o'clock, which meant that in some cases people had to call on friends and family to see to their horses, as there was no time between finishing work and getting to the meeting on time. Those who kept their horses living out twenty-four/seven were always the smug people who arrived with freshly washed hair and clean clothes, makeup and sometimes, as in Kim's case today, even wearing a skirt. Her short blonde hair was neatly styled rather than its normal appearance of sticking up after she had taken off her riding hat and had run her fingers through it, and her slim figure was encased in a long navy-blue dress which skimmed her body in all the right places and managed to ignore those she was self-conscious about. Since she spent most of the summer in short shorts or tight riding breeches and strappy vest tops, nobody could have suspected she had body issues. But for some reason out of her horsey uniform, she became self-conscious. Other members arrived directly from mucking out and feeding their horses, and left their boots at the door, probably noticing the hole in their left sock where their big toe was poking out for the first time when they sat down.

The majority of members were women, many of whom enrolled male family and friends into volunteer status, and so the gender mix in the room was probably two-thirds female. Non-riding members paid a reduced membership fee, which some people outside the club

felt was cheeky since they were effectively paying to volunteer for the club. But the members were keen to ensure that there were benefits for all members, regardless of whether they rode horses, kept their feet on the ground when working with horses, or simply had a desire to support the club. Training was free or with minimal entry fees and was open to all members on a variety of subjects. So far these had included trailer towing and maintenance, fitness for the unfit, the art of photography with horses, and a very popular session, how to create exciting and nutritional food to fit into pockets of horse-riding clothing. The club had started with fifteen members at its inaugural meeting in March 2018, and doubled that number within the first year. Now that they were halfway through their second year, the membership had increased with only three people deciding not to renew their membership due to moving too far out of the area to be actively involved.
The club tried to match up the volunteers in nearby locations with the event, meaning that almost everyone in the room was relatively local to Woodford, and the atmosphere was friendly with dressage divas mixing with happy hackers, and three-day eventers chatting with liberty specialists. Kim surveyed the room with a smile on her face. The role of chair was a time consuming and demanding job, but the enthusiasm and commitment demonstrated by the members made it a pleasure.
She stood up, and instantly the noisy hubbub of friends catching up with the horsey updates was replaced with silence. 'Hello everyone and thank you for coming,' she beamed at the thirty or so faces looking back at her, who all smiled back. 'I have received no apologies and I don't think anyone is missing presumed late?'

A general agreement rippled through the group as heads turned in an effort to check all who should be present were comfortably seated at the tables. 'Good, then I will hand over to Madeleine for the first item on the agenda: the four-week orienteering training event, which I may say was a fantastic success and congratulations and thank you to Madeleine for your time and effort.'

Kim sat down and Madeleine stood up as the room erupted into loud applause and calls of 'Well done, Madeleine!'

Blushing furiously, she kept her eyes down at her notes while she composed herself. Equilibrium restored, she smiled, raised her eyes and joined in with the clapping as she gestured to everyone else in the room. 'Thank you everyone, we all did a good job!'

As the noise died down, she began her report. 'This is the first time we have offered a training series, rather than our usual one-off sessions, and it proved to be very popular. In order to accommodate the demand, we ran the first three sessions in four groups, with some at the weekend and others in the evening to suit those who wanted to attend. I thought this would prove popular with the newcomers and wasn't expecting the numbers of experienced treccies who replied, so I hope that all of the sessions proved useful to everyone.'

There was a general note and murmurs of approval from those present who had attended the training sessions.

'A useful and unintended consequence of the large numbers of experienced competitors in the groups meant that they were all more than willing to pass on their top tips and exchange good practice. Personally, I liked the way all of the sessions across the groups evolved, where I presented the formal lesson, so-to-

speak, and the participants felt able to discuss and share what had worked for them. And what did not work.'
Laughter throughout the room as people recalled their own mistakes and mishaps.
'The feedback I have received since those classroom training sessions has all been positive, both for the format of the session and for the timing of them. They did take up a big chunk of my time and in future if we are going to have this level of interest, then we need to look at having a group of coaches who could either see one group through the whole four weeks, or one or more trainers for each week.'
'I would be happy to run one or more of the sessions,' volunteered one person.
'Me too,' said another.
Kim made a note of their names, and said 'Yes, I think we can formalise that with the training group in future,' she nodded to the head of the group.
Madeleine continued 'I think the good standard of competition we saw in the final training session on Sunday, as well as the excellent attitudes displayed on the day by the vast majority, both while things were running as expected and when they didn't, demonstrated not only that the previous training, and by that I mean both the series we are now discussing and the one-off events we have previously run, are achieving their purpose.'
She took a deep breath before continuing, glancing around the room and at Kim, before looking back at her notes. 'There were two incidents on Sunday which we do need to address.'
Kim stood up and motioned for Madeleine to stay standing. They had already discussed how they were going to present the next item, and Madeleine was

relieved that Kim wanted to be the one to speak to the group.
'Unfortunately, we have received a complaint as a result of actions taken by Madeleine on Sunday. Brackenshire HOOFING committee have already investigated and completed their review of this complaint, we have dismissed it, and we commend Madeleine for her actions in the matter.' More mutterings and small cheers could be clearly heard, so Kim put her hand up to request silence. 'We will not tolerate bullying of any description, and that includes actions which could be deemed as bullying towards the complainant in this case.'
The room was silent. A number of people had not thought about it in those terms before, and were digesting what Kim had said.
She continued. 'Although at the time I think that only those involved in the incident in the map room were aware of it, it is obvious that since the results for the final training event of the series, the orienteering phase on Sunday, were published, gossip and mis-information has spread about Diana Smalley's mark of E for elimination. The details are not important, other than to say that the complaint was not made by Diana. Indeed, Diana has written a personal apology to those involved in the original incident, and we are very pleased that she will remain as a member of Brackenshire HOOFING.'
The expressions on the faces of those members who were not on the main committee was a picture, and Madeleine struggled not to allow a smile to cross her face. She knew that someone sitting in the room had worked very hard to discredit her, and had completely re-written the incident, whether deliberately or not she wasn't sure but it seemed likely it was a personal

attack. A quiet Diana had turned up at the yard that afternoon, and Madeleine had been brought to tears by the hand-drawn card depicting her horse Sonny, and had enjoyed both eating and sharing the homemade chocolate brownies which accompanied the card. The two of them had spent half an hour in Madeleine's kitchen chatting over a cup of tea, and the friendly person Madeleine had seen during the classroom training sessions was the Diana she could see now. Heather Stanwick and the couple who had been running the map room had all also received a card offering her apologies, and home-made brownies, and as far as the three of them were concerned Diana's apology was accepted and they had no grudges to bear. Kim had also received an apology from Diana, this time in the form of a phone call, in which she admitted she was struggling with alcohol, and was going to take some time away from committees and competing, but was hoping she would be allowed to retain her membership of Brackenshire HOOFING, and come back to the group in a more positive capacity than she had left. Kim chose not to reveal Diana's problems with alcohol to the committee, knowing that when the time was right and if that time ever came, Diana could tell whomever she wished. But she did have to bring the complaint about Madeleine's handling of the incident made by another member to the committee, and allow everyone to debate the issue. They all voted unanimously in Madeleine's favour, and felt the complaint had been malicious. The committee members were aware of the identity of the complainant, however, they had all agreed to keep that person's identity a secret unless or until that person chose to reveal themselves. It was generally felt that

nothing positive could come from naming them at this stage.
Satisfied that the general mood in the room was relatively calm, Kim handed back to Madeleine and sat down.
'Thank you Kim, and thank you to the members of the committee.' Another outbreak of applause and congratulatory murmurings broke out, but rather than let it run on, Madeleine continued speaking. 'Another issue which arose during the practise orienteering competition was our usual system of using only one checkpoint judge rather than the minimum of two we use on competition day. Linda Beecham is a recent member of Brackenshire HOOFING, and I was very happy to allow her to practice how to run a checkpoint on her own on Sunday, and for the time she was there she did a very good job as did all of our checkpoint judges. It is also worth noting for our annual awards event that Linda was an integral part of the team who saved a man's life.'
Again, the members broke out into applause, many seeking to catch Linda's eye as they did so, and this time Madeleine waited until it came to a natural close. Linda nodded and smiled, her face burning furiously with the unexpected attention. She felt and then saw a hard stare from one of the members who was clapping, and looked away. She knew what that was about and made a mental note to make the others aware. She turned her attention back to Madeleine, who was speaking again.
'I appreciate that volunteer numbers are precious, and we don't want to ever get into a situation where we have so called professional checkpoint judges or control of paces judges and so on. We all have experience of events where it works very well to have

someone who knows the role inside and out, but from the start of this club we pledged to ensure that everyone has a working knowledge of all aspects of our activities. Therefore, I propose that for checkpoints away from the venue, but probably not including the start and finish checkpoints or any others which are located within sight of another checkpoint or the main event, we always have a minimum of two judges.'

'I second that,' called out Alison Isaac.

'I third,' said Charlie Lichmann.

'Any objections?' asked Kim.

Patricia Bragg put her hand up. 'Can I ask, would it have been possible to run Sunday's event with this proposed new rule in place?'

Madeleine shrugged. 'With the number of volunteers I had on the day? No. But then I didn't ask for more volunteers because we had enough under our current rules from those who put themselves forward. So I suppose the answer is that I don't know what would happen under the new rule, if we accept it.'

Patricia nodded and didn't add anything else.

Charlie raised his hand 'Roughly how many volunteers are required?'

Madeleine answered 'With this new rule in place, we would have needed to fill eighteen posts. But one person can fill more than one of some of these, for example a first aider can also be a scorer, and the secretary can also be the checkpoint judge at the finish. For next month's camping competition we will need approximately twenty-six posts to be filled, but again some can be doubled up over the weekend. This proposal is only calling for three additional volunteers to the ones we had on Sunday. However, as we know, if we don't have the volunteers then we won't run the event.'

Kim looked around the room. 'Any more comments or questions, either for or against the proposal?'
'It's a shame to have to bring this into the equation,' said Linda, 'but I do think it is safer for there to be at least two people in some places in our countryside. I know we all like to think that Brackenshire is a safe county to live in, but something like an organised event when notifications will be available on social media far in advance of the date, may alert someone with evil intent. I don't want to spread fear when there is no evidence to support such measures in this area, but I do think it is worth highlighting.'
'True,' nodded Alison. 'Also, the checkpoint judge may not see any competitors for up to three-quarters of an hour if there is a problem en-route, and having a second person on hand in case of that judge having a health emergency is a good idea. Some of those flying insects we get around here can be evil with their stings, for example!'
'It only takes a matter of minutes for someone to become incapacitated from a stroke or a heart attack, as I saw on Sunday,' agreed Linda.
'All good points,' said Kim. 'Although if any of these medical emergencies happened to a rider, they could be in trouble for a long time before anyone was able to assist them.'
'As riders that is a risk we must be prepared to take,' said Madeleine. 'With certain mobile phones and watches they have an alert which can automatically raise the alarm with a designated contact. Perhaps we should also have a rethink about the equipment we are willing to be allowed in our events.'
'So long as the phones are in a sealed envelope, I don't see why they shouldn't be allowed,' said Charlie. 'I'm not sure what we can do about some of these high-tech

sports watches which have functions that would constitute cheating if used.'

'I like the fact we use paper maps, and not GPS systems,' commented Patricia. 'I would hate to see our sport change irrevocably. As you say Linda, there are no incidents of people being attacked in our countryside, and I feel that all of this may be fear-mongering.'

A few people nodded their heads in agreement with Patricia, but many more clearly didn't agree.

'Let's discuss the use of mobile phones and sports watches at our next full members' meeting, and move to a vote on the proposal for a minimum of two checkpoint judges at our forthcoming camp now as a trial, and take the formal proposal to the next members' meeting along with the conclusions from the trial,' Kim drew the wider discussions to a close. 'Are there any more points to be made about this specific proposal?'

Heads were shaking as people looked at each other to see if anyone else had more to say on that subject.

'No? In that case let's go to a vote. Please may I have a show of hands for the proposal to have a minimum of two judges at practice training events where the checkpoint is away from the venue.'

Everyone except Patricia put their hands up. Seeing that she was out-numbered, she quickly put hers up too.

Nodding, Kim said 'Motion carried.'

'Excuse me, can we bring the food in now?' Tom Higston was standing in the doorway.

A general chorus of 'Ooh yes please!' spread around the room, and the meals everyone had ordered when they arrived at the pub were duly delivered to the hungry members.

The meeting resumed while desserts and coffees were served, and Robin Stanwick replaced Madeleine in leading the discussions. He and his team for the camping weekend were very well-prepared, and with no more tricky subjects or controversial proposals, business was concluded by eight o'clock. A few people chose to stay and continue to socialise, but most people were keen to get home, or to see to their horses, or both.

By the time Madeleine left it was very late, but for the first time in days she felt relaxed, and knew she would have a good sleep that night.

Chapter 20

Saturday 26th October 2019, 5.00am

'Is the kettle on yet?' Paul asked Caroline through the wide hatch of her catering van.
'The urn is boiling away, if that's what you mean,' grinned Caroline. 'You're in luck, the coffee machine is also hot. Do you want one?'
'Yes please. Any chance of a bacon butty too?' he asked, eyeing up the sizzling rashers on one of the hot griddles.
'Any minute now. It's looking good,' Caroline nodded across The Green at the race day structures which had been set-up the day before. Even in the dark cold October morning, the gantry Gray had designed and put together, and the two marquees the Brackenshire HOOFING team had put up, together with the welcoming signs advising where food could be bought and where the toilets were located, made the place look alive and exciting.
Paul, who had slept very little that night and had been on site since four o'clock, barely took it in. To him the scene was broken up into sections of problems which had been resolved. The police had consistently refused to allow the WSWC members access to their equipment which was still securely locked away in the auction house, and Paul felt the weight of the

responsibility of making all of their hard work redundant. He also felt terrible that so many people from outside of the running club had given up their time, expertise, and in many cases money to help out. What had started as a fun adventure cooked up over a curry and a few pints in The Ship Inn with Cliff, had turned into a major nightmare.
'Hello, hello,' Cliff appeared, wearing a woolly hat, thick parka, and gloves. 'I could smell the bacon while I was lying in bed, so I've come down for a sandwich.'
Caroline's van was parked outside The Woodford Tearooms on The Green, and Cliff's bedroom was in the flat above Williamson Antiques next door. He was used to cooking smells pervading his flat from the tearooms, but to be woken this early by the mouth-watering aroma of sizzling bacon was a novelty, and one he didn't mind at all.
Caroline poured two cups of coffee, and deftly made two bacon rolls, handing them over to the men who took them gratefully. She made a note on the pad, where a tally of food and drink for race organisers and volunteers was made for settling up at the end of the day. She and her mum had an agreement with the WSWC in which they would donate a percentage of their takings to the club in the form of food and drink, in return for being the sole caterers at the event which was due to be finished by midday, although packing away and clearing up would take the organisers late into the afternoon. With the number of competitors and supporters, the event was due to be lucrative for all parties. Tom and Sarah at The Ship Inn had agreed to open their toilets to the competitors, and the football club had also agreed to open their carpark, toilets and showers for competitors, many of whom were also members of the WSWC. Both The Ship Inn and the

football club were going to be open from midday onwards as usual, and were hoping to supply competitors and their supporters with food and drink late into the evening. What had started out as a little race organised for a few members of the WSWC had turned into a major town event.
The original plan had been for volunteers to meet at Black's Auction House, but with the gates padlocked by the police their rendez-vous was moved to Williamson Antiques where Cliff had a small parking area at the back of the shop for his stall holders to unload antiques and collectables for their stalls inside. The volunteers weren't due to meet until six o'clock, but already there was a group of about twenty people, obviously local enough to walk to the venue, converging from various points across The Green and appearing out of the dark with head torches lighting their way.
'This is a good butty,' said Paul, who was surprised to find he had an appetite. He could feel a sense of calm wash over him as he watched the volunteers walking towards them, and a couple of cars appeared around the corner from the High Street heading to their parking place. There was nothing more he could do now. Whatever was going to happen was beyond his control.
The club had chosen to raise money for the local air ambulance charity, and all profits once the basic expenses had been taken out were going to them. With so many people donating their time and facilities, plus the sale of race tickets which included the cost of the finishers' medals and t-shirts, and collection boxes all over the town, it was hoped the money raised would off-set the inevitable bad-feeling from a minority of residents who objected to having their Saturday

morning affected by other people coming together. Without exception all of the competitors had waived the club's offer of a partial refund because the finishers' medals and t-shirts were not available on the day, and many had ordered and paid for the last-minute offer of t-shirts emblazoned with 'I ran the Woodford Streakers Wearing Clothes Half Marathon, even though the police had my t-shirt'. The town's jury was still out as to whether or not Paul was guilty of money laundering through his auction, but public opinion seemed to be that if he was then it was a perk of the job. Paul was torn between wanting to vehemently deny that he would ever be involved in anything illegal like that, and getting overcome with emotion that so many people had faith in him.

The state of The Green with numerous pairs of running shoes tramping over it was a concern for everyone, particularly at this time of year. So far the race organisers had been lucky with the weather, the ground was firm and dry to start with, and they had carefully laid out six starting lanes for a maximum of fifteen competitors in each to try to minimise the damage.

Although the race had been the brain-child of Cliff and Paul, neither of them had the necessary experience of organising such an event, and the Race Director was Hannah McClure, a local fitness instructor, a founding member of WSWC, and wife of the local policeman Ian McClure. Hannah was embedded in the race headquarters, which was in the back store of Cliff's Williamson Antiques, and Paul took a coffee and a breakfast roll from Caroline over to her.

The big doors were open, and as he walked through his sense of calm was enhanced as he saw Hannah and several other people sharing a joke. All of the hard work preparing for the race had been done, and there

was a brief spell of peace before the race marshalls needed to be sent out to their checkpoints, and the competitors began to arrive. The club hoped that this would be the first of many races they organised, and plans for another half marathon at Easter 2020, followed by a fifty kilometre race the following October were fully formed. By offering three races a year, it was hoped there would be enough people to swap around the roles so that all members could enter at least one of their choice, but they needed this first one to be successful before they could move forward with the plans for the others.
By seven o'clock the marshalls' briefing had finished, and in the weak light of the emerging sunrise those who were manning the two checkpoints out on route at the only two main road crossings, and five other points where changes of direction were needed, drove away to their destinations, while everyone else walked onto The Green and began to take up their positions. There were already a number of competitors milling around, even though the first start time, number one of the twelve runners with their dogs known as canicross entries, wasn't until eight o'clock.
All four 'Couch to 5k' runners, Jennifer, Rebecca, Alison and Madeleine, had volunteered, and Hannah had assigned each of them to partner an experienced runner. Madeleine had expressed an interest in the canicross, and she was working with Hannah who was starting each cohort of runners as the Race Director. Madeleine was dressed in her warmest equestrian clothing, and the owners had to battle to keep control of their dogs who thought she smelled marvellous. Jennifer had agreed that the canicross entries could park in the veterinary hospital car park at the bottom of The Green so that each pair could leave their car one at

a time and have a rolling start of two minutes between them, in an attempt to reduce the dogs' excitement.
Madeleine enjoyed meeting the owners, who all left their dogs in their vehicles while they checked in and received their race numbers. When it was their time, one by one the owners and their dogs walked up to Lane One, which with hindsight Hannah wished she hadn't placed in front of Caroline's catering van as the delicious smells certainly did not help to keep any of the twelve dogs calm. Madeleine was astonished at the variety of breeds as a dalmation, several staffy-types, a couple of pointers, a German Shepherd, three border terriers, and two she couldn't even begin to work out their origins, came to the start line with their owners, who also came in various shapes and sizes. One by one at Hannah's signal each pair raced off across The Green, over the crossing point on the Brackendon Road, and onto the Trailway where they had five miles of relatively flat hardcore track to run along, before turning right across the land belonging to the Higston family for six miles. There they would be running through woodland, crossing horse fields, a section of golf course, and along one side of the fishing lakes. Next came their second road crossing, which was further along the Brackendon Road, up the steep field Jennifer had struggled with on her first run out with the WSWC, and then a hilly but gentle run down the country lane which came into the far end of The Green where a small section of tarmac formed a public car park, but which the town council had allowed the club to utilise as the Finish for the race, again attempting to reduce excessive wear and tear to the grass.
Once all of the dogs and their owners were clear, it was time for the so-called elite runners to start. There were only three women in this group of fifteen, and they

were all runners who expected to complete the course in under an hour and a half. About half of these runners were WSWC members, including Tom Higston, Bilbo, and Hannah's husband Ian McClure, with some of the others travelling from all over the country, including two men who had travelled down from Cromarty, in Scotland. Hannah fervently hoped that the course they had laid out was going to justify the time and expense these runners had put into their entry. At her signal they all set off from Lane Two, with one in particular racing away from the pack.

'He won't last the course,' Hannah murmured to Madeleine.

Lane Three was filling up with another fifteen runners, who also hoped to run the course in an hour and a half, but Madeleine could see that they were less focused and more hopeful than the first cohort. She recognised the local paramedic Krista Tennison, who was a regular volunteer at events Madeleine organised, and Zoe Sherret, who was Hannah McClure's business partner in their fitness company and a member of Brackenshire HOOFING. She shouted her encouragement as they all set off at a fast but steady pace, and they were still all running together by the time the last ones were disappearing from view onto the Trailway.

Lane Four was full of eager runners in a variety of shapes and sizes, ages and genders. Madeleine could see a flamingo, two dinosaurs, a unicorn, several gladiators, and a team of firemen in full firefighting kit. This group had the largest, and noisiest, group of supporters, and as they set off several of their supporters ran alongside them cheering encouragement. The flamingo had lost his head before he'd crossed the Brackendon Road.

Lane Five was filling up with nervous-looking people, many in club t-shirts from neighbouring running groups. Hannah got them all shouting the countdown from ten, and Madeleine could see the tension lessen as they did so. They all shouted 'ONE, GO!' and set off at a more sedate pace than the previous runners, and in clear groups of twos and threes.

'This time next year, that's where I'll be,' Madeleine said to Hannah.

Finally, Lane Six had a small number of people who had stated on their entry form they wanted to finish in under two and a half hours.

'Surely everyone should be home long before then?' queried Madeleine.

'Don't underestimate the difference between walking just over thirteen miles, and trying to run it,' warned Hannah. 'That chap who set off at a fast pace from Lane Two is not going to be able to keep that pace up, and when his legs rebel at the final steep hill his brain will have a meltdown.'

'But surely he knows that?'

Hannah shrugged. 'He will do after this race! Possibly he has run half marathon distances on roads, and isn't a trail runner.'

'Are you talking about the competitor who shot off at a rate of knots?' asked Paul who had walked over with two cups of tea for them. 'Here you go.'

'Yes,' said Hannah. 'Thank you very much!'

'Cliff knows him. You're right. He usually runs in road races, so I don't know why he has chosen to run our trail half marathon. This could be his first and last attempt. The sweepers will pick him up and carry him home, I expect.'

'The sweepers?' asked Madeleine.

‘That’s right,’ Hannah explained. ‘We have two runners who will leave in about an hour to check for any struggling competitors, and collect up all our signs to give to the volunteers out on course. So long as the last competitor has gone past them, they are released from their posts, so that no one is abandoned out on course. Any runners the sweepers come across on their way round the course, they will support them all the way back to the Finish.’
Paul continued ‘The WSWC think that three-and-a-half hours should be the cut-off point for this race, because most people could walk the course in that time, but in reality the sweepers will support anyone still out on course who thinks they can finish. Hannah has decided that so long as someone is still able to walk unaided, and has a clear possibility of finishing, they could keep going. We want to encourage people to run, not put them off by making them feel useless as is the case with some famous races.’
‘I think there could be as many as five from that last group who are going to struggle,’ warned Hannah. ‘We need to be prepared to rescue anyone who needs it.’

Chapter 21

Saturday 26th October 2019, 9.29am

‘Whoop whoop’
‘Yay, well done!’
‘Congratulations, you’re first across the line!’
Hannah, Paul, Cliff, Madeleine and anyone else around were clapping and cheering the first canicross pair to run under the Finish gantry, a WSWC member and his large German Shepherd named Max.
‘Phew! That was brilliant fun!’ he said, as Hannah gave him a big hug and handed him the version of the official WSWC Canicross 2020 Half Marathon t-shirt which had been quickly made, and arrived with the rest of the order on Thursday. It read “I ran the WSWC Canicross 2020 Half Marathon, but the RD’s dog ate my t-shirt, so she gave me this one instead”.
‘We’ll have to have a big presentation of the medals and your official t-shirt when the police finally release them,’ she said apologetically. ‘And yes, there’s a medal for you too,’ as she gave Max a rub on the head.
‘No problem at all,’ said the winner. ‘This t-shirt is brilliant, and a great reminder of what we have been through. I’m just glad we were able to put the event on. The route was great. It was a treat to be able to run across the Higston land. I had no idea how much they had on there for horses and golfers! I’d better get him

back to the car for a drink. Thank you everyone for giving up your place in the race this morning.'

'Here comes number two!' called Madeleine, as the next pair ran towards them, this time the runner was accompanied by a border terrier.

In quick succession more runners and their dogs appeared in the car park for The Green, running under the gantry to cheers and clapping as more people came to congratulate the finishers. Hannah and Cliff were keeping a record of their finishing times, and without exception everyone was more than happy to wait for a presentation ceremony for their medals.

It wasn't long before the first competitors from the elite group began to appear, running in a long strung-out formation along the lane which led to the car park, except for the two at the front who were within strides of each other. First one was in front, then the other was alongside and slipped into the lead, then the first one would speed up.

'Look, Bilbo's in the lead!' shouted Paul. 'Come on Bilbo!'

'Sssh,' hissed Hannah. 'We're meant to be impartial!'

'Come on everyone!' shouted Paul.

'You record the other chap's finishing time; I'll record Bilbo's' Hannah said to Cliff, as they checked their stopwatches were primed. Hannah stood one side of the gantry and Cliff stood the other, as Bilbo and another runner raced each other across the line to ear-shattering cheers and whistles from the large crowd now gathered nearby. The two men shook hands and clapped each other's shoulders as they panted from their exertions. Hannah and Cliff conferred, before Hannah was able to declare that Bilbo was the winner, and the other runner was second. So many people had taken photos of the finish with their phones, there wouldn't be a shortage of footage if there was a complaint, but only the official photographer's picture would be taken into account. As it was there was a clear 1.4 second difference between the two men, and the second placed runner knew that Bilbo had won.

There was no time to dwell on the result or the congratulations because the rest of the elite group came through one after another, and then they were closely followed by some from the second group, and in no time at all runners from the first four groups were coming in together, and mingling around the two marquees and Caroline's catering van. The flamingo and the post box were deep in conversation, and the firemen were stripping off their firefighting equipment as fast as they usually put it on. Collecting buckets for the various charities were clinking as locals and supporters put their hands in their pockets, and applauded the competitors' efforts. Krista Tennison had come first in the women's race, and Tom Higston was teasing Bilbo that he had let him win. Tom was a faster runner than Bilbo, and everyone had expected him to be the first WSWC member home, but he was in seventh place having pushed too hard at the start and then been over-taken by several people on the last steep hill, including Grayson Bragg much to his delight. Grayson was a good thirty years older than Tom, and was starting to feel his age when running with the younger men. Tom had managed to make up a few places on the run back down the lane, but not enough to beat Bilbo. The pair had a bet that the loser would buy the drinks for a week. Tom had not expected to lose, and Bilbo had not planned to go to the pub on Tom's nights off. The pair of them laughed and joshed, with Tom agreeing to buy Bilbo a burger

from Caroline and a pint for Grayson next time he was in the pub.
Hannah's phone had been pinging with messages from a couple of the volunteers out on course who were reporting that a group of four runners appeared to have followed the route in reverse.
'How?' asked Hannah.
A series of laughing emojis appeared from the volunteers at what was officially the last road crossing across the Brackendon Road. 'Apparently they saw the Finishers gantry from the back and thought it was the official Start. They were laughing that everyone else from their Lane had gone the wrong way until they came to me.'
'But that must have been quite a while ago,' typed Hannah. 'Why didn't you let me know?'
'Oh they're alright. They're happy to keep going and follow the route anti-clockwise.'
'But it is going to cause a problem for the sweepers if they don't come back in good time,' Hannah muttered. She typed 'OK, it's done now. Any other anomalies?'
'Nope, all good. Happy runners, some grumpy drivers.'
'Hope they're not too grumpy. Thank you!' She turned to Cliff and said 'We may have a problem with four runners who are running the route anti-clockwise. Apparently they mistook the gantry for the start.'
Cliff frowned. 'I don't think that's right; we'd have seen them. It's more likely they haven't officially entered and thought they'd take advantage of our permission to run across non-public routes.'
'Well then they are not a problem,' said Hannah. 'They should be prevented from going onto the fishing lakes by the marshalls there. I'll give them a ring and find out if they've had any problems.'

Cliff listened to Hannah's side of the short conversation. It was clear that four runners had indeed tried to pass through the gates, but the marshall who was there with Rebecca had refused them entry because they were not wearing the hastily made WSWC race numbers which were bright yellow because that was the colour the printer had spare, and instead had made their own fakes in white.
'Good job, thank you.' Hannah smiled. 'Honestly, some people will try anything to avoid a twenty pound entry fee. Ah, here are some more of our lovely legitimate runners.'
The next wave of finishers were clearly very tired, and some were walking. Paul joined them and encouraged them to summon up a last bit of energy to jog across the finish line, and was rewarded with beaming smiles and exhausted 'Thank yous.'
Madeleine re-joined them, and reported that the two sports therapists in one of the marquees were treating the two men who had dressed as dinosaurs. The body of the creatures had reached to just above their knees, and the men's legs and backs were protesting at the restricted movement.
'Moral of the story is to always train in your costume!' laughed Paul.
'Or, to not wear one at all,' observed Madeleine.
'Ah, here he comes,' said Paul, and went to coax the runner who had taken off from lane two at such a fast pace. 'Come on mate, you can lift those knees a little higher and try for a flying feet pose for the photographer.'
As if he was a robot and Paul had said the correct command, the runner obediently began to run towards the gantry.

'I'm such an idiot,' he said, as Hannah stepped forward to congratulate him. 'I had no idea that trail running was so different from road running.'
'You've done well to finish in this time,' she said.
'Your terrain here is completely different to the parks I've been training in. All that mud; I swear it drained the life out of my legs. And as for that last hill, it was a killer. I'm such an idiot!' he repeated.
'It's an error you will never repeat, but hey, you've finished, congratulations!' said Paul. 'Come with me and you can collect your t-shirt from that marquee over there.'
'Is there really such a difference?' asked Madeleine. 'Surely if you can run a half marathon on the road you can run it across country.'
'You have only just started on your couch to 5k programme, and you're running it on the relatively even surface of the Trailway. Once you start running for longer distances, over poached or muddy fields, up and down the hills, you'll understand,' explained Cliff. 'The route isn't too muddy at the moment. Wait until December, January and February, and some of those tracks he is complaining about will only be suitable for wading through. From the sound of it he's been running laps around his local park, which isn't anywhere near here. He's right, he is an idiot, but he's an idiot who is humble enough to recognise it which makes him a proper runner.'
'We only have three more runners still out on course,' said Hannah, checking her phone. 'They have passed the last road crossing, and our marshalls should be returning. The sweepers haven't picked them up yet, so maybe I was wrong about some of those competitors in the final group.'

As she spoke a pack of three runners could be seen jogging along the lane towards them. It became clear as they ran closer that they were aiming to run through the Finishers' gantry together, so Hannah and Cliff nodded and made sure they recorded the same times for them.
'Really well done,' Hannah congratulated them as they gasped and hugged.
'I can't believe I've done it!' said one, a woman who looked to be in her fifties. 'That's my first half marathon. I'm so happy.'
'It's my first one too. We did it!' beamed the second, a plump young man.
'It's my fifth,' gasped another woman who was probably ten years younger than the first woman. 'Oh my god, they don't get any easier, do they,' she laughed.
'We've never met before,' the young man explained to Hannah, 'but we were struggling up that bastard hill, and promised we would finish together.'
'Thank you both,' said the five-time half marathon finisher. 'That hill was trying to defeat me.'
'You conquered it,' said Hannah. 'I'm so pleased for you all! Head over to that marquee and collect your t-shirts, and make sure you have something to eat and drink too please.'
'Well done,' Cliff said to her. 'You've done it. You are no longer a Race Director virgin, and you've made your first half marathon a blinder. Everyone has finished, and is happy, the course was just the right level of testing and doable, and after all the last-minute hitches there are a lot of people who wanted this to succeed and they are happy too.'
'Phew!' laughed Hannah. 'I'm just glad everyone finished and we didn't have any casualties. Thank you

very much for your help. Our club can be very pleased with itself. Right, enough of all this congratulating. I still have mountains of work to do over the next few hours. No doubt there will be a few complaints about the signage or the scoring or the way a cow looked at someone.'

Chapter 22

Saturday 26th October 2019, 5.00pm

Paul, Cliff, Bilbo, Grayson and Tom were sitting together in the snug.
'Cheers'
'Cheers'
'Cheers'
'Cheers'
'Cheers'
They all clinked glasses across the table, and took a sip or a gulp.
'Well done, Bilbo. You ran an awesome race, I have to admit.' said Tom.
'Cheers mate,' said Bilbo, raising his glass to Tom before drinking deeply.
'You'll be needing another one of those in a minute,' observed Grayson as Bilbo's glass rapidly emptied down his throat.
'Hannah did a great job organising everything this time. Do you think there's a chance she'll agree to be the RD if we make this half marathon an annual event,' asked Bilbo.
Cliff nodded 'She did, and she has said she will. So long as she can run the ultra races, she's happy to help to organise or RD for these shorter ones.'

‘Here’s to Hannah,’ said Grayson raising his glass in a toast which everyone joined in.
‘I thought I’d find you in here,’ said Linda Beecham as she stuck her head around the curtain which separated the snug from the rest of the pub. ‘Congratulations Bilbo. There’s a drink at the bar for you when you’re ready.’
‘Cheers Linda,’ grinned Bilbo.
‘Well done everyone,’ she said including the rest of them. ‘I gather the day was a great success, and lots of money was raised for the various charities. It almost makes me want to take up running.’
You’re very welcome to join us,’ said Cliff. ‘You know there is an informal beginners’ running group don’t you? Rebecca is part of it.’
Linda laughed ‘I said almost! Sorry, I’d rather stick to four legs for getting around the countryside. I won’t disturb you any longer, I just wanted to pass on my congratulations. See you tomorrow Paul?’
‘Yes, see you in the morning.’
Bilbo put his glass down on the table with a sigh. Linda took the hint. ‘I’ll get you that pint now.’
‘Good woman, thank you,’ he said. ‘It’s thirsty work on two legs.’
‘The Green doesn’t look too bad,’ said Tom. ‘I think we did a good job of spreading everyone out so that there are not too many damaged areas of grass. Setting your gantry up on the car park was a good idea, Gray.’
‘Yes, we were lucky the town council allowed us to take over the car park like that. They’re not keen on closing it off to the public.’
‘Rebecca has never managed to persuade them to let her use it for the Summer Fete,’ agreed Cliff. ‘It would make sense to use it as the entry and exit point, and the same for the car boot sales.’

'I wonder why they agreed to let WSWC use it?' pondered Paul.
'No idea,' said Tom. 'I thought the whole thing worked really well. Caroline's food van was a hit, we've taken a good amount since we opened at lunchtime, and the sports club are very pleased with their sales too. The sports massage therapists were busy in their marquee, and the Brackenshire HOOFING lot had to wait an extra hour before they could take it down. They didn't seem to mind though.'
'I'm relieved everyone was so good about the lack of medals and finishers' t-shirts,' Paul said quietly.
'I saw loads of our WSWC "the police have my t-shirt" tops' laughed Tom, proudly displaying his. 'It will be a running theme throughout all of our events now, I think. We'll have to have the official finishers' t-shirt and the alternative one.'
Cliff joined in 'I loved the canicross "The WSWC RD's dog ate my t-shirt". '
'Next year we could have "WSWC finishers' t-shirt lost in transit" ' laughed Bilbo.
'What about "I'm wearing my WSWC finishers' t-shirt over the top of this one". We could have a whole collection!' said Tom.
'My stomach thinks my throat's been cut,' said Bilbo pointedly to Tom.
Tom raised his eyes to the ceiling. 'Alright, alright, I'll get you another one. Anyone else?'
Everyone looked at their almost-empty pint glasses and nodded.
'We'd probably better order some food,' said Cliff, 'especially you, Bilbo.'
When Tom came back from ordering Amanda's special pheasant curry for everyone, and with a tray of drinks, he said to Paul 'Any news on your situation?'

‘If there is the police aren’t telling me,’ Paul shrugged.
‘They still think you’re guilty of money laundering?’ asked Bilbo.
‘I reckon so,’ nodded Paul as he gazed into the bottom of his glass.
‘Do you think someone has been pushing things through your auction?’ asked Grayson.
‘You’d know if they had, surely?’ said Bilbo.
Paul spread his hands out ‘I can honestly say if they have been I had no idea. We go through all the checks and balances we have to as an auction house, and no one has stuck out as blatantly laundering through us,’ he lied. Paul and his team now had a strong idea of who was the guilty party thanks to the information Rebecca collated during her search of the backup files, but they weren’t going to show their hand too early. The police had refused to share information with them, and so they were keeping their knowledge to themselves, but they did have a rough plan of how to expose the culprits. No one outside of their group was aware they even had suspicions, not even Cliff. Paul certainly wasn’t going to start blabbing in the pub and allow the people who were ruining his life to cover their tracks.
‘That’s rough,’ said Tom. ‘Sarah and I were talking about what we’d do if for some reason the pub was suddenly closed down because of something out of our control.’
‘What did you decide you would do?’ asked Cliff.
Tom shook his head, ‘We didn’t know. Obviously I could claim nepotism and find a position somewhere in the family businesses, and Sarah doesn’t need to work for financial reasons, and she’d be perfectly happy buying and selling portrait miniatures. But we’d miss this life, and all of you, and it would be terrible to be

so helpless. Of course, you have got an idea of what it's like,' he said, referring to a vendetta someone had carried out against Cliff a few years ago.
Cliff nodded, 'I do. You certainly find out who your friends are when anything like this happens.'
'Friends and family,' Grayson raised his pint in another toast. 'Can't live with 'em, can't live without 'em.'

Chapter 23

Tuesday 29th October 2019, 9.00am

‘Thank you everyone for coming here today,’ said Paul to his employees, who were all sitting around his kitchen table. He checked that everyone had a steaming mug of tea or coffee in front of them, and that the plate of pastries he had ordered from Caroline was disappearing at a satisfactory rate. ‘I thought this would be a safer place than the pub. We don’t want someone like Linda Beecham eavesdropping on us again.’

‘I agree, although she has been very helpful,’ said Rebecca.

‘Anything we can do, boss, to get the company back up and running,’ said Daniel Bartlett, to a chorus of agreement. ‘But I’m afraid that I have nothing useful to report. I’ve been asking around and no one seems to have anything on him.’

Paul sat down and nodded to Doug. ‘Doug has some more information on our suspect.’

Doug drained his coffee, placed the mug carefully on the coaster decorated with a gavel, and said ‘I’ve had a chat with my mate down at the marina, and he’s managed to check their records. The boat is not registered in our suspect’s name after all.’

This time a chorus of groans rippled around the table.

‘I can’t believe it,’ said Rebecca. ‘We were so sure he was the one.’
Doug held his hand up, enjoying his moment in the limelight ‘But, my mate says that our suspect and the other three all claim ownership of the boat even though it is not in any of their names, all of the invoices are always paid for in cash, as is his tab in the club house, and the person whose name is on the documentation is never seen from one year to the next.’
There was a glum silence, before Richard spoke. ‘Does any of that help us? That does not sound like the evidence we need, is it?’
‘No, it isn’t, or at least it is not the evidence we thought we were going to get,’ said Rebecca, ‘but if we can keep building this list of his behaviours it should be enough to give to Ieuan Davies and persuade him to investigate.’
‘I don’t know,’ said Paul. ‘It all sounds a bit hopeless to me. I was so sure we’d have him with the boat; I’ve always understood it was his, or at least that he had a share in it. I’m sure he said he owned it when he took me out on it.’
‘When was that?’ asked Doug.
Paul rubbed his chin as he thought. ‘It was a long time ago. Must have been ten years?’
Doug gave a small smile. ‘According to my mate, he has been involved with five boats in the past seven years, none of which have had his name on the paperwork. The one you went out on may have belonged to him, but that’s probably long gone. If he’s as successful as we think he is, then he’s going to be good at covering his tracks. It was probably naïve of us to think we could find the evidence so easily.’
‘Perhaps the buying and selling of boats is also part of the money laundering,’ suggested Daniel. ‘He buys

them for cash, no paperwork with his name on it, sells them on for more than he paid with the money going into someone else's account.'
'But where is all this cash coming from in the first place?' asked Richard. 'I don't understand how this works.'
'It's usually drugs or prostitution, or both,' explained Doug.
'He doesn't seem the type to be involved in either of those things,' said Daniel.
'Oh, I think he does,' said Rebecca.
Everyone looked at her in surprise.
'What do you mean? He's a nice bloke, always willing to help anyone, works hard, loves his kids. He gives those daughters anything they want for their horses, and he has the patience of a saint with his wife,' Paul jumped to his defence.
'That's true,' nodded Doug. 'I'd have chucked her out years ago.'
'Don't you think he has a creepy vibe about him?' asked Rebecca. 'He's always standing a bit too close.'
Paul looked at her sharply. 'Is he? To women, you mean? He's been bothering you?'
'He's never said or done anything to me,' Rebecca reassured the four men who were looking appalled. 'Other than he can't come into the office and just pay his bill without coming around to my side of the desk and touching my arm, and breathing that evil cigarette-breath into my face.'
'Does he?' Paul looked shocked. 'But I always thought he was very respectful around women; if anything he is quite shy, and keeps himself apart from everyone else in a group.'
'Not when he's on his own with me,' Rebecca shrugged. 'I've been asking around, and Madeleine

says the same. She's worked out a system of always having a list of jobs for him to do which she writes on the white-board in the clubhouse at the riding stables. When she first moved there she welcomed him into her kitchen for a coffee so they could discuss what needed to be done around the place, and he did that standing too close thing to her too. He didn't do anything, or suggest anything, but she didn't like it. After that she only invited him in if there were other people around too, and she tries not to get into a situation where they are alone out on the yard. It's difficult, because there are so many places she could get trapped with all those higgledy-piggledy stables, and as she says, out in the fields no one would hear her scream.'
Rebecca looked at the faces of her colleagues and could see that none of them had ever experienced that kind of daily concern. She continued 'Sarah Handley said that when her husband Mike was still alive, Gray tried to sell him a crate of wine he said he'd brought back from France on his boat. The Ship Inn is not tied to a brewery, and Sarah and Mike could buy from whomever they wanted, but there are strict tax regulations on alcohol, as well as the obvious safety checks for anything we imbibe, and Mike told him firmly that no, that was not how they did business. Apparently he was fine about it, and nothing else was ever said.'
Paul sighed 'It's a shame Mike is not alive to tell anyone this now.'
'Do you think it would make a difference?' asked Daniel. 'It's not much to go on, is it.'
'No it's not, but it builds up a picture. I'm certainly looking at the man with different eyes after this morning's revelations,' said Paul, looking at Rebecca with concern. 'I am really sorry you have been made to

feel uncomfortable at work, Rebecca. Please don't keep anything like that to yourself in future.' The other men murmured their agreement.
Rebecca laughed, kindly, 'Thank you boys, but if I voiced my concerns every time someone alerted my spidey-senses we'd never get any work done and have no customers left.'
'I hope that's not true,' said Paul, seriously.
Doug spoke tentatively 'None of us make you feel like that, do we?' He was suddenly aware that his behaviour towards her might have been unwelcome. He didn't think anyone else knew how he felt about Rebecca, but he wanted to be sure he didn't make her feel uncomfortable in his presence. He hated to think she might be cringing every time he came into the room.
'Absolutely not,' she said. 'I don't want you to all start treating me and any other woman who comes into the auction house as though we're going to have a fit of the vapours if you so much as look at us. Just keep being respectful of personal space, don't make personal comments, be friendly and polite. Just keep doing what you have all been doing. We're getting a little off topic here.'
'No, we're not,' said Paul. 'This is a valuable discussion. The way customers treat us is as important as the way we treat customers. Someone, or some people, have chosen to put our livelihood in jeopardy by carelessly using and abusing our business. Whether it is someone behaving inappropriately towards an individual, or someone breaking the law, it affects all of us. Unfortunately, we do need proof that Gray Bragg is laundering money through our business, before we can resolve this ghastly situation. Ensuring he never steps foot in the office again is easy to do.

Until we heard from you today, Rebecca, I was still hoping that he was not going to be the person who is bringing down my business, but now I hope he is, and that we destroy him.'

'Is it worth going to Ieuan with what little we have?' asked Rebecca.

Paul looked at his watch and pulled a face. 'It's too late now to make that decision. I asked him to join us.'

On cue, there was a knock at the door. Paul went and let their visitor in.

'Hello everyone,' Ian McClure said as he came into the room first. 'Ieuan asked me to come along too, in case some local knowledge was needed.'

Ieuan followed behind Ian, and everyone made their introductions while Paul put the kettle onto boil and made another round of hot drinks.

'Thank you for inviting me to talk with you,' Ieuan said, once everyone was seated again. 'I understand you have some suggestions for us to investigate.'

'Do you have any news for us?' asked Rebecca.

'Only that Mr Black here is no longer a suspect in our enquiry. I cannot tell you anything more,' he said in his soft Welsh accent. Today he was dressed again in blue jeans, and wore a pale grey jumper which accentuated the blue in his eyes. His blond hair had a slight curl to it, and there was a few days' growth of soft stubble on his face. Rebecca caught herself staring, and mindful of the conversation she had just been having with her work colleagues, she blushed.

'That's good news,' said Daniel looking at Paul. 'Why didn't you tell us?'

'I have asked Mr Black to keep it quiet for a few more days, while we continue with our investigations,' said Ieuan. 'All of the time the criminals think our focus is elsewhere should make it easier for us to gather more

evidence against them. Now, what was it you wanted to tell us?'
'Wait a minute,' said Doug. 'Does that mean we're all back in a job?'
'Yes and no,' said Paul. 'My personal bank accounts have now been released back to me, because I am no longer a suspect, but the police are keeping the business closed to preserve the evidence. The sooner we can re-open the better for all of us, and I have been assured that it will be very soon.'
'But until it happens, we have to keep being vigilant,' Rebecca finished for him.
'Exactly,' said Paul. 'You will definitely get your wages as usual this month, and next. I guarantee you that. If the police can formally charge their suspects before then, the auction house will re-open immediately.'
'That sounds hopeful,' said Daniel, who had been picking up a few shifts in the family tearooms and, although he was enjoying being at work and the change of scene from his usual involvement with antiques and collectables, didn't want to keep serving teas and coffee and cooked breakfasts for months on end. His aunt, Lisa, was making the most of her nephew's situation after a busy few years while her business partner and sister, Daniel's mother Gemma, juggled a new-born baby who rapidly grew into a toddler, with co-running the tearooms. Lisa and Gemma were fortunate that Lisa's daughter Caroline had embraced the family business and had been only too pleased to step into Gemma's shoes during those early years of maternity and nappies. Gemma's daughter was now old enough to be attending a local nursery, and Gemma's husband Peter Isaac, Jennifer and Alison's father, was stepping back a little from the

equine veterinary practice he and Jennifer ran while his daughters took on some of his duties. Caroline was finally able to pursue her dream of catering for parties and mass events, while still working some shifts in the tearooms. Daniel was longing to return to work at the auction house, and get away from his increasingly large family.
Paul addressed Ieuan and Ian across the table. 'Your raid on my auction house came as a complete surprise to all of us. It doesn't matter whether or not you believe me, but that is the truth. None of us had any idea that money was being laundered through the auctions, but now it has been brought to our attention we can see a clear pattern of transactions involving four people over a period of eighteen months.'
All five staff members of Black's Auction House looked intently at Ieuan and Ian to see if they were giving away any clues that this was the timeframe that was being looked into. The two policemen kept an inscrutable look on their faces.
'Go on,' prompted Ian.
'If we are wrong,' said Rebecca, 'then we have nothing else to offer.'
Doug nodded, and said 'Like Paul mentioned earlier, I was hoping we were wrong, but now I just want this to be over, and am sure we are right. But I don't think we have any evidence for you.'
'I'm here to listen to anything you have,' encouraged Ieuan.
Paul, who had been studying his notes, spoke out 'We believe that two of our regular clients, Grayson Bragg and William Borange, have been regularly putting items into our sales which have sold for hammer prices far exceeding my valuations and others' expectations. Every single one of these items have been paid for in

cash, ostensibly by several different people but on deeper investigation we believe the same four people, including Gray and Bilbo, have been behind the purchases using the names of their relatives, and sometimes their own. On every occasion they have been paid out by Black's Auction House via the online banking system. Rebecca has a spreadsheet of the transactions we have identified.'
Rebecca said to Ieuan 'Here's a paper copy, but I can email it to you as an attachment.'
'Yes please, and thank you for this,' he said as he and Ian studied the paperwork Rebecca had printed for them. Giving nothing away, he looked up and asked 'Do you have anything else?'
'Not really,' Paul shook his head. 'Just hearsay about boats and building companies.'
'Go on,' prompted Ieuan.
'Ian probably knows all of this; it's just gossip really,' said Paul 'but we've been trying to work out the truth about Gray's fishing boat. For many years he and his wife have given the impression that they own or have a share in a small luxury cruiser which Gray and a few friends use to go fishing in the Channel, and make trips over to the Channel Islands and France, but now it appears it doesn't belong to Gray. I also think it is too posh to be used by a group of hobby fishermen.'
'You've been on it?' asked Ieuan.
Remembering Linda Beecham's warning about being friends with the criminals, Paul hastily explained 'Oh, many years ago Gray and his wife invited me and my ex-wife Monica out for an evening to watch the fireworks in Poole Harbour. He doesn't have that boat anymore, but at the time we commented on how pristine it was, and Monica was particularly impressed

with the two bathrooms. Our house only had one, and there were four of us living there full-time.'
'Anything else?' asked Ieuan.
Paul checked with his staff 'No, I think that's it. I am sorry, it sounds a bit pathetic now.'
Everyone looked crestfallen. They had all been convinced they had cracked the evidence the police would need, but hearing Paul lay it all out in front of the policemen, they realised it was paltry and insubstantial.
'Thank you for your time and information,' said Ieuan, signalling to Ian that they should go. 'You all know how to get hold of Ian if you have anything else you can tell us. Thank you.'
The Black's Auction House staff stayed sitting around the table as the two policemen let themselves out of Paul's house.
'Well, that's that,' said Rebecca. 'I suppose we just have to sit and wait for them to do their job.'

Chapter 24

Friday 1st November 2019, 4.00pm

'Welcome, welcome!' Phil Smart greeted the new arrival as she drove through the electric gates into the familiar setting of the Woodford Riding Club. Phil was one of the Brackenshire HOOFING competitors who was also volunteering to help out at the camp, and he and his husband Jimmy had arrived with their horses in time for lunch. Along with Linda Beecham and Patricia Bragg, they had already set up camp and were now meeting and greeting and directing the arriving competitors to their allocated spots, using their own setups of lorry and trailer parking and corrals as an example for others to follow.

Amelia McCann waved to Phil through the window of her ancient Hilux and followed his signalled directions over to Linda Beecham, who sent her up a hardcore track towards another volunteer in the distance. Linda could see Amelia's experienced competition horse, Blackstone Silver Ring, or Blackie, as he was better known, continue to munch contentedly at his haynet as the trailer bounced and rolled over the ground. Madeleine had designed the camping ground so that the mix of towing vehicles, trailers and horse vans and lorries could park on a section of the hardcore track system which ran around the edge of the field, and the

horses could be corralled on the other side of the fence to their human's vehicle. Most people drove 4x4 vehicles, which could have coped with the ground in the field but they would have messed it up and taken months to recover, which was not ideal as they headed into winter. As she drove closer, Amelia could see that the third volunteer was Patricia Bragg, who unusually greeted her with a happy smile. Amelia was used to Patricia only ever talking to her when she had some gripe to make about a fellow competitor, but today's attitude was a pleasant surprise. Patricia had been tasked with ensuring that everyone had a sensible amount of room between them without spreading out too much, and from what Amelia could see she was doing a good job. She wondered if that welcoming smile would still be there in three hours' time when the last of the thirty-two competitors rolled up.
'Thank you, Patricia!' Amelia said as she pulled on the handbrake and switched the engine off.
'You can set your corral up anywhere level from the front of your vehicle to the back of your trailer, and as far out into the field as you want to make it,' Patricia pointed. This was Amelia's third camp at the Woodford Riding Club and she was familiar with the organisation of them, but she patiently allowed Patricia to run through her spiel, knowing it was Patricia's first time volunteering in this capacity.
Patricia rushed off to organise the next person driving up the track, and Amelia took a moment to lean on the wooden rail, separating the track from the field and gaze around her. She loved to see everyone setting up their little area of the site. Horses being unloaded from the various modes of transport, and then exploring their corrals; exclamations, as people discovered they had forgotten their water bucket, or that their electric

fencer wasn't working as it should; and the familiar sight of mugs in hands and smiles on faces.
Once she had set up the corral for Blackie with tape and posts she had brought with her, checked he had enough water, and securely fixed the label stating her name and mobile number on one of the posts in case of an emergency, Amelia wandered over to check-in with the camp secretary, who was based in the indoor school. For this weekend, Zoe Sherrett had volunteered to be secretary, and for the past year had been working closely with the director of the camp in preparation for the weekend. The director of the camp was Robin Stanwick, who was married to Kim, the chair of Brackenshire HOOFING. He had never been solely in charge of running a camp before, and Zoe kept teasing him about death-by-list. He made lists for everything, often in duplicate, so that she had a copy too, and he ticked things off only to create a new list of things which hadn't been ticked off, or which had been completed. He was a lawyer and was used to preparing thoroughly for cases. Zoe appreciated how thorough he was being, even if at times she felt he was being overzealous. She was grateful for the dedication now as one after another, the competitors arrived in quick succession and she was able to point to the wall, where Robin had carefully detailed a map of the site explaining where the obstacle course was to be laid out and at what time the next day the course walk would be held, where the toilets were, and the showers, although most people made their own arrangements in their trailers and lorries. Most importantly was the information about where and what time the evening meals were being held. From their perspective, the competitors appreciated being greeted by Zoe, who many knew either as their local Zumba instructor or as

a very good eventer and treccie. Her mass of blonde curls were rarely allowed their freedom, usually either being firmly plaited under a riding hat or held back behind wide, brightly coloured sweat bands. Many people had to look twice to see who was checking they had the correct standard of equipment as they handed over hats and body protectors. Robin's tall thin frame suddenly appeared to fill the indoor school as he came to check that Zoe had everything she needed. She imagined that he had a strong presence in a court of law and would be fairly intimidating, but today he was his usual charming and friendly self, mucking in with finding items to fill in the gaps of a competitor's kit where they had accidentally left things behind, and checking that the pizzas ordered for this evening's meal were going to be delivered on time from the local Italian restaurant, Amore.

At eight o'clock sharp everyone was already seated in the indoor school with their own chairs and shared tables, wearing plenty of warm layers and with notebooks and pens in hand.

'Welcome everyone!' Robin raised his hands up to attract attention and included both competitors and volunteers in his address.

'Hello!' the assorted group called back, everyone in good spirits.

Robin spent the next few minutes explaining the do's and don'ts for the weekend, aware that the majority were experienced at this type of event, but also that some were newcomers and wanting to ensure that everyone was included and knew who to ask for help if they felt out of their depth. A few people had pertinent questions about how the weekend was going to run, and then there was a big cheer as the pizzas arrived. Bottles of lager and wine were opened, flasks of tea were poured into mugs, and the indoor school quickly filled with the smell of onion and garlic. By ten o'clock most people had checked their horses and then snuggled down in their sleeping bags, warmly wrapped in blankets inside their trailers and lorries, but there were a few hardy souls who were chatting inside lorries big enough to accommodate a small group of people. By midnight Robin, who was restlessly patrolling the corrals to check that all of the horses had water and none appeared to have colic, could breathe a sigh of relief as the last torches had been switched off and the giggling had stopped. The majority of people were over fifty, but the scene along the track reminded Robin of sleepovers he'd had as a child. Quietly, he said ‘Goodnight everyone,’ and walked back to the horse trailer he was sharing with his family, content that all humans and horses were safely settled in for the rest of the night.

Chapter 25

Saturday 2nd November 2019, 7.00am

Seven o'clock on the morning of the orienteering competition. Although not properly daylight yet, the beginnings of the day could be discerned if one looked carefully around the countryside. Robin and his wife Kim, together with their daughter Heather, had spent the night in their horse trailer, which was a tight squeeze for three adults but meant that they were all warm enough to sleep relatively well. Robin had slept in a pair of thermal tights and tracksuit bottoms in case he had to leap out of bed in an emergency, and he was so warm and cosy he was reluctant to change out of them, fearing the bracing hit of the cold air. Heather persuaded him to get changed in his sleeping bag, so he had clean warm nightwear to put back on that evening without having to get cold in the process. Wriggling and muttering, he managed to peel the layers down his legs, but decided against trying to put his trousers on inside the sleeping bag and managed to disentangle himself from it and quickly pull on the fleece lined outdoor trousers he favoured in the winter. His wife and daughter were creased up with laughter at the fuss he was making, while they stayed safely zipped into their own sleeping bags, and when he finally emerged from the groom's door of the trailer

there were a group of people outside, most of them with mugs of coffee or tea in their hands, laughing too, having heard the kerfuffle and squeals of laughter. He gave a low sweeping bow and called ‘Good morning!’ before heading over to the classroom.
The first competitors were due in the map room at half-past eight. The classroom was again being used as this first checkpoint for the competition, and it didn't take long to set up the finishing touches. The three volunteers were already there when Robin walked in and he was pleased to see that everything looked organised and ready for the first competitors. He checked that they had both his mobile number and one walkie talkie between them, wished them good luck, and set off across the yard to check on Zoe where she was stationed as the secretary in the indoor school. In theory, no one should have needed to see her after the previous evening, but there were always little issues which cropped up, and to have someone manning a safe space was invaluable in ensuring that the weekend ran smoothly. As it was, she had been able to reassure one competitor that their last minute order for food from the local fish and chip shop had been accepted, and contact the local farrier for two competitors whose horses had both lost shoes during the night. When Robin arrived, Zoe was busy rejigging the starting order with orienteering course designer Debbie Tolstoy to accommodate the farrier's shoeing schedule.
Fortunately, it looked likely that both competitors would be able to start after all.
Officially, this was the farrier’s weekend off, but he was always willing to help out at Woodford Riding Club events because both he and his wife kept their horses on livery with Madeleine. So far neither had joined Brackenshire HOOFING club, but Zoe

suspected that part of his enthusiasm to re-shoe the horses, despite receiving a text before half-past seven in the morning, was because he wanted to see what it was all about.
Debbie was a woman of indeterminate age, small and wizened, and she could have been anywhere between late fifties or early eighties. She had ridden the byeways and bridleways of Brackenshire for as long as anyone could remember on a variety of chestnut arab horses, none of whom she could stop. Her input into the Brackenshire HOOFING events was immeasurable, combining her local knowledge and her enthusiasm for horse riding. She had devised a route which could be chopped and changed at a moment's notice depending on weather and ground conditions and the inevitable fallen trees. The October weather in the preceding two weeks had been kind, and when Debbie rode the route for the final time on Friday morning she was satisfied that the river levels were where they should be, all of the gates could be opened from horseback, no bulls had suddenly appeared in fields they shouldn't be in, and the tracks were clear and passable. She and Robin had sat down together on Friday afternoon and finalised the master map from which the competitors would copy the route onto their own maps. They also had quite a discussion about pace from one checkpoint to another as Debbie's ideas were always a lot faster than most people could manage. However, although this was a fun weekend and not part of a national competition, it was the final one of the year for Brackenshire HOOFING, and both Kim and Robin wanted everyone to feel that they had achieved their finishing rosette and not just had them handed out as a sort of end of year celebration. There was the Christmas party to look forward to for that sort of thing.

‘Hello hello,’ Krista Tennison bounced into the indoor school, a tall slim thirty-something with shining long dark hair and a smattering of freckles. She was employed as a paramedic with Brackenshire Air Ambulance, and had volunteered her medical services for the weekend. Like Alison, she was a Dressage Diva who preferred competing in shiny long black boots rather than scruffy ankle boots which doubled as walking boots, and dressing her huge German warmblood dark bay horse in a white saddle pad rather than flourescent colours. Zoe suspected that here was another horsey person who was curious about the popularity and enthusiasm for their group after seeing numerous photos and write ups on social media.
‘Krista, hello!’ Robin crossed over to her in three easy strides and gave her a hug. ‘Thank you very much for giving up your weekend. Hopefully you won't be needed and we can keep you supplied with food and drink without you rushing off on a first aid emergency and leaving it to go cold. Come this way and I'll show you the facilities.’
As Robin led Krista away, the checkpoint judges came in as a group. Robin and Debbie had briefed them the night before and they knew where they had to be, and at what time. Zoe and Debbie double checked that they had their boxes containing the necessary scoring paperwork and pens, cones and flags to designate their checkpoint, a clock, two stopwatches, one walkie talkie per checkpoint, at least one fully charged mobile phone between them, and their packed lunches. Except for Alison Isaac's father, Peter, and Patricia Bragg, everyone had been a checkpoint judge before, and they all had their own stopwatches and food and drink provisions in addition to the delicious lunch supplied by Caroline Thomas. Peter was paired with Alison,

who was confident she knew what she was doing, and Patricia was paired with a seasoned checkpoint judge Charlie Lichmann. Charlie was not looking forward to spending the day with Patricia and her constant bitching about the riders as they came through their checkpoint, but he had been assured by Robin that he would never have to do it again if he did it just this once. With his usual good grace, Charlie agreed and resolved to smile and wave if she posed any problems, and would try to find a good side to the lady.

With a field of thirty-two competitors, half of whom were in pairs, and a twenty-two kilometre course with three checkpoints expected to take an easy four hours, in theory all of the checkpoint judges should be back at the Woodford Riding Club by three o'clock. Debbie was planning to visit every checkpoint at least once, and was going to be bringing everyone's second flasks recently filled with just-boiled water to ensure that no one suffered too much in the November temperatures. Toileting arrangements were alfresco, which was always easier for the men than the women. Toilet roll, trowels, and hand cleanser were also vital pieces of kit for the checkpoint judge, especially in chilly conditions when imbibing lots of warm drinks.

The sun was shining brightly when the first two competitors, Jimmy and Phil riding out as a pair, walked into the map room, and everyone had a good feeling about the day ahead.

Chapter 26

Saturday 2nd November 2019, 3.00pm

Robin was daring to hope that the most difficult part of the weekend was almost over. Just one more competitor out on course, and then everyone would be home safe and sound. The checkpoint judges had returned to the Woodford Riding Club and reported good things about the riders and horses, with no one falling off and no lame horses. Everyone had been in a cheerful mood, and even Charlie reported positively on Patricia's attitude, saying that he had been pleasantly surprised at how friendly she had been both to him and to the competitors. Indeed, her friendliness had been commented upon by several of the riders when they thanked Robin and Debbie for their hard work, and also asked for their thanks to be passed on to all of the checkpoint judges without exception. Patricia had been handing out delicious homemade dairy free and gluten free chocolate brownies to everyone who passed through their checkpoint, and these had gone down very well. Charlie even commented to Robin that he'd been wrong to make such a fuss about being paired with her for the day, and was happy to be partnered with her at a future event. Robin wondered if she'd put something illegal in the brownies.

Phil and Jimmy had been the first pair out and were the first competitors back. They quickly sorted their horses out with a warm water sponge bath and tucking them both into drying and warming sweat rugs. After a quick toilet visit, and a mug of tea by their sides, they got stuck into the scoring for the competition. They were a good team, and Robin knew he could leave them to it. Debbie had already been out and visited all of the checkpoints by the time Jimmy and Phil arrived just after midday, and she had collected the score sheets completed so far, so Phil and Jimmy had a few they could start to enter before the next competitors arrived back with their personal score cards. By three o'clock all except one competitor's scores had been entered and checked against both the judges' score sheets and the personal score cards.
'Where's Linda then?' Jimmy asked Robin.
'It's like déjà vu!' laughed Phil.
No one was very concerned. They were treating Linda's absence as a joke.
'Did anyone check to see if she was wearing her underpants on the outside of her riding breeches when she left?' asked Jimmy.
'No, but she could have been wearing a cape,' chuckled Phil.
Laughing at them, Robin shrugged. 'She came through Charlie and Patricia's checkpoint without a problem and they were the last one before the finish checkpoint here as you both know, so presumably she's got lost between there and here. She was the last to start the course after having had her time delayed so her horse could be seen by the farrier. I'm wondering if perhaps her horse has lost a shoe again, or perhaps he's gone lame. This is the first time she's competed at this level, so we'll give her another twenty minutes before we

start looking for her. Can I get you chaps another cup of tea?'
'Don't worry, I'll go and make us one,' said Phil. 'Would you like one Robin?'
Robin shook his head, and being careful to maintain a smile he walked over to the indoor school. Although Robin was giving a calm performance, inside he was worried. He kept checking his phone in case Linda or someone else had activated the emergency number. He went to find Zoe and discovered her deep in conversation with Debbie and Krista.
'Hi Robin,' she greeted him. 'We were saying that maybe Debbie and Krista should pop out and have a quick scout around just in case Linda's horse has gone lame and her mobile isn't working.'
'She's not terribly late for our original timings,' said Debbie, 'but compared to everyone else, she is very late.'
Robin nodded, relieved that the others were feeling as concerned as he was.
'Yes please, that would be great if you two could drive out. Do you want to take the horse lorry just in case?'
Debbie shook her head. 'No, we'll go in my 4x4 because I can think of a couple of places where she might have gone off the route and where we will be able to see her from a distance if we drive in that. If the horse is lame then I'll come back for the lorry.'
Robin waved them out of the electric gates, checked that Phil and Jimmy were happy to take over the finish checkpoint in case Linda turned up under her own steam and they could finalise the scoring. He walked over to the obstacle course with the original finish checkpoint judge to where all of the available volunteers and competitors were hard at work setting out the obstacles for the next day's competition. As

well as the orienteering course, Debbie had also designed this obstacle course, so keen was she to have a go at such a fabulous setting and knowing the standard of equipment was high. As a competitor, she had been riding the courses Madeleine had designed for the previous two years, and was eager to have a play with the layout and obstacles. Although she was now out looking for Linda with Krista, her presence on site wasn't necessary because, like Robin, she was very good at lists and diagrams, and the course was clearly laid out on several pieces of laminated A4 paper. Debbie had made use of one of her granddaughters to do the designing on a computer, and together they had spent a happy evening moving obstacles around and typing in dimensions until both were satisfied with the result. Robin could see several groups of people around the three fields laying out poles and placing flags, and in one case setting up what looked like a market stall.

Debbie had designed the sixteen obstacles to be positioned in groups of five or six, so that the competitors would have a lovely canter or gallop if they chose to around one section, and a controlled trot through the wooded area at the far end of the land. After the distance and terrain of the orienteering course, it wasn't fair to ask too much of the horses the following day, but it was a good thing to have a moving recovery session before they travelled back home. At least the ground in the field was comfortable for their hooves and joints, after some of the rough tracks they had covered, and they would have all spent the night turned out in their corrals allowing freedom of movement and a good lie down and roll if required. By keeping the obstacles in groups, Debbie was able to make good use of her judges, and three volunteers

could easily manage a cluster of five or six obstacles between them. The course flowed easily on paper and covered approximately three kilometres, but Debbie was keen to see how it would ride the next day. She had put three very technical obstacles in there using related distances, and another two which also required very good communication skills between horse and rider, so she wasn't expecting any but those at the top of their game to get high marks. There were also three humorous obstacles, with a nod to the local town, including: a food stall sponsored by Caroline, where riders had to pick up an item of food and eat it without their horse first sticking his or her muzzle in it; a pop-up-bar complete with beer pump which poured ginger beer, and another which poured water, provided by The Ship Inn, although the task for the riders was to pour a glass of fizzy water from a plastic bottle designed for festival-goers, into a plastic champagne flute without spilling any, and carry the flute from the bar to a table set-up nearby; and an auctioneer's desk with gavel, which the rider had to bang on the wooden block.
Robin looked anxiously at his watch. Officially, the course walk with Debbie was due to start at six o'clock and would take at least an hour, with fish and chips for all booked to be delivered at eight o'clock. The riders always enjoyed these course walks because it gave them a chance to stretch their legs, and for many to walk their dogs who would have been sleeping in their vehicles for most of the day. The lack of daylight hours was one of the tricky parts of organising a competition at this time of year, but everyone was used to working with a head torch, and by setting up the course together at least everyone saw it in daylight too. Next year, the group planned to run an obstacle course on a moonlit night during one of their summer camps. Night-time

orienteering was something they were used to doing, and the numbers on the waiting list for the planned summer camp was already high.
The loss of daylight hours was also a factor in needing to find out what was happening with Linda Beecham as soon as possible.

Chapter 27

Saturday 2nd November 2019, 4.22pm

Robin's mobile started to ring, making him jump. He'd been checking it and was slipping it into his pocket when it rang. For a moment he thought he was hearing sirens, but then he realised that he could hear both noises. When he saw the name on the screen, he felt a lurch in his stomach.

'Krista, any news on Linda?' he asked, unable to keep a note of fear from his voice.

'Robin, we have really terrible news. I am so sorry but yes, we have found Linda and I'm afraid she is dead. Debbie is coming back now for the lorry to collect her horse. Could you ask Madeleine to drive her, please? We have both had a terrible shock and I think Debbie could do with some help.'

'Yes, yes, of course I'll ask her to go and meet Debbie when she arrives. What happened? Did she fall? Is her horse alright? Are you okay?'

'Her horse is absolutely fine. No, we don't think she fell off, we're not really sure what has happened. I've called for an ambulance and I think the police are coming too. Oh, here they are. Sorry Robin, I've got to go. Debbie should be there soon.'

Robin stood with the phone to his ear for quite a while after Krista hung up, trying to absorb the news. A rider death, or a horse death, were the worst thing that could happen. Despite all of the risk assessments and worst-case scenarios he had been required to prepare for, he had never truly believed that Linda would be dead. Obviously, everyone involved with horses knew that it was a dangerous sport and the risk of permanent injury, let alone death, was something all horse riders knew was possible, but rarely had to face. The outside noises of horses and humans seeped back into his consciousness, and he glanced around to see if anyone had overheard his conversation. Fortunately those nearest and within earshot were busy constructing and measuring a series of concentric circles for the led immobility obstacle.

'Does anyone know if Madeleine is out here?' Robin asked the group, hoping his voice did not reveal the deep shock he was feeling.

'I think that's her over there with her truck,' someone pointed in the direction of another group setting up the three local obstacles in the far field.

Robin decided it was too far to walk in the time he had available and rang her instead.

'Hi Madeleine,' he said in what he hoped was a breezy, nothing to worry about tone. 'Could you leave what you are doing and pop over to collect Linda's horse for Debbie please? Linda's had a bit of a tumble, but her horse is fine. Debbie should be pulling into the yard in a minute, and she can show you where the horse is out on the course.'

'No problem,' said Madeleine, as he knew she would. 'Does Linda need to be picked up too?'

'No, Debbie is sending her off in an ambulance as a precaution,' he lied. There would be time enough to tell Madeleine the truth of the situation, and while they

were both standing in separate fields, surrounded by happy campers, was not that time.
In the distance he could see a figure which must have been Madeleine leave the others and climb into the truck. Turning around he could just about see the electric entrance gates opening, and then Debbie's vehicle driving carefully up to the Woodford Riding Club horse lorry. Robin walked quickly up to the yard and arrived just as Madeleine drove in.
Debbie had retrieved the keys from the hook inside front door of Madeleine's cottage, and was already starting up the lorry by the time Robin went around to the driver's window. 'Stop a moment please, Debbie. Madeleine will drive. I am so sorry you had to find her like that.' He could see that Debbie was in full capability mode, and the shock of finding Linda had not set in yet. She looked as though she was about to argue, but then she nodded and shuffled across to the passenger side. Looking puzzled, Madeleine started to climb up into the vacated seat.
'Just turn the engine off a moment, please Madeleine,' Robin said gravely. 'I have something to tell you.'
Looking across at Debbie's face and back to Robin, Madeleine said 'There is clearly something seriously wrong. I think you'd better tell me what has really happened to Linda's horse.'
'Haven't you told her?' Debbie said in an accusing tone to Robin. He shook his head and was about to speak when Debbie interrupted him, her voice strong and clear. 'I am very sorry to tell you that Krista and I found Linda just past the entrance for Madam's Copse on the road before you turn into Broom Lane. None of the riders who came along after her will have seen her because she was the other side of the entrance around the corner.'

Madeleine nodded, 'Yes, I know where you mean. That's only about twenty minutes from here. What happened? Did her horse lose a shoe again? Robin said that Linda is going for a check-up at Swanwick Hospital, so I assume she's injured.'
Gently, Debbie said 'I'm afraid she was dead when we found her.'
Madeleine gasped, and covered her mouth with both hands. Of the two of them, Robin thought that Debbie looked better able to drive the lorry than Madeleine at that moment. He supposed Debbie had had longer to take in what happened, despite being the one to have found Linda's dead body.
'Had she fallen?' he asked.
Debbie shook her head, her tone more gentle than when she last addressed him. 'We don't think so. It looked as though she'd got off to be sick. Her horse was grazing nearby, the reins safely looped through those ties on the D-rings of the saddle, and there were several piles of vomit around where Linda lay on the verge at the side of the road. She looked to us as though she'd had a seizure or allergic reaction to something. Her face was horribly swollen … you don't need the details. Krista checked her for signs of life, but there was no pulse. She thinks that Linda must have been dead for a while. Perhaps she was already feeling unwell and planned to ride straight back here along the road, instead of following Debbie's route through the Broom Lane bridleway.'
Robin tried to remember if Linda had put anything on her health and safety forms about epilepsy or similar. He then thought back to the pizzas they had eaten the previous night and briefly wondered how much Linda had been drinking. Just as quickly he discarded that train of thought. No one who was capable of riding

their horse for over twenty kilometres was going to die from a hangover. Could it have been food poisoning? He hadn't heard about anyone else being taken ill, and with the shared facilities on site he was sure someone would have mentioned it.
Absentmindedly he said 'She was approximately an hour and a half late by the time you two went to search for her. I do hope it was quick, and she wasn't lying there suffering for all of that time.'
Madeleine had partially recovered from the shock of the news, and said with determination 'Right, we'd better get a move on and bring her horse back here until we can contact someone to look after him.'
Debbie nodded in agreement, and Madeleine started up the lorry, looking much stronger than she had a few minutes earlier. Robin watched as the two grim-faced women drove away, grateful that he was surrounded by people who were able to be practical in the face of tragedy.
There was no precedent for a death at a Brackenshire HOOFING event, and Robin went to find Zoe to discuss how best to break up the camp. There was no sign of her at the secretary's base in the indoor school, so he went to the next place he thought she could be, and sure enough, she was in the classroom which Phil and Jimmy had again transformed from the map room into the scoring headquarters. As soon as the three of them saw the look on Robin's face as he entered the room, they knew something bad had happened.
'What is it? Is it news about Linda?' asked Phil, all jokes about her repeated absences forgotten.
Robin nodded, and lowered himself down onto a chair just inside the door. 'I'm afraid that poor Krista and Debbie have just found Linda, dead by the side of the road. It doesn't appear that she or her horse were in an

accident, but they think that the evidence points to her being taken severely ill, and died shortly afterwards. I have not spoken to anyone in authority and can only relate to you what both Krista and Debbie have told me. Krista stayed at the scene with Linda's body and her horse, and Debbie is now on her way back with Madeleine to collect the horse and bring him back here.'

Everyone sat silently for a moment, as they tried to comprehend the news Robin had brought them. None of them knew Linda very well, as she had only recently joined the Brackenshire HOOFING club and was not one of Zoe's Zumba clients. But nevertheless it was a shock that someone had died during one of their events. Zoe was probably the person who knew the most about her, because Linda's mother was a regular at her classes, but until Linda had volunteered to be a checkpoint judge at the training event the previous month, the two had never met.

Robin slapped his hands on his knees, and said 'Zoe, please can you dig out Linda's details for me, and I will contact her next of kin. Possibly the police may have already spoken to them, but I think it would be the right thing to do to speak to them too. Also, on a practical level, we need to find out if they are capable of taking care of her horse.'

Zoe nodded, and disappeared from the room without a word. For once Phil and Jimmy were also silent. Robin regarded them for a moment before saying 'I'm going to have to close down the camp and send everyone home. In case there is no time to say this later, thank you both very much for everything you have done to try to make this weekend a success. Volunteering and competing is not an easy thing to do, and I have appreciated your input very much indeed.'

The two men nodded, appreciating his words but feeling helpless to support him.
‘You can leave all of this’ Robin gave a vague sweep of his arm at all of the paperwork in front of them. ‘I don't suppose anyone is going to be interested now.’
Jimmy found his voice ‘Don't you worry about any of this Robin. We will finish up, and tally the scores the best we can. After all, the competitors did complete the course, and something positive should still come out of this tragic weekend. I am so sorry this is happened on your first event. Obviously, anything more we can do to help just let us know.’
Phil joined in ‘Yes, I agree with everything that Jimmy said. We're here for you and we won't leave the site until you're ready to go. If you need someone to talk to or a shoulder to lean on, or even a cup of tea, we’re both here for you.’
For the first time since he’d heard the tragic news from Krista, Robin could feel tears falling from his eyes. He had been so busy thinking about Linda, Krista, Debbie and Madeleine that he hadn't thought about the fact that he might need support too.
‘Thanks guys,’ he said as he stood up, giving them a watery smile as he left to find Zoe again, and prepare himself for a phone call he did not want to make.
As he walked towards the indoor school where Zoe had everyone's details in an ancient briefcase of his which they kept securely locked, he could see the people out in the fields where the obstacle course had taken shape. It looked as though they were organising themselves into their own course walk while there was still some daylight, and he decided to leave them to it while the logistics of dealing with Linda’s death could be moved a bit further along. Having to handle almost fifty upset volunteers and competitors, and their horses

and vehicles moving around the yard as everyone packed up and left, wasn't going to make things any easier.
'Hi Robin, how are you coping?" asked Zoe as he walked in.
'I'm fine,' he said. 'It's just so sad, isn't it? Are you OK?'
'Not really, but I will be. I've checked Linda's forms, and they don't say anything about any allergies. I've got the details of her next of kin here. Would you like me to phone? It's Linda's mother, who I know from our Zumba classes.'
For a brief moment, Robin wondered if it would be kinder to her mother to hear the news from someone she knew, but then common sense kicked in and he knew it had to be him who made that phone call.
'Thank you very much for the offer, Zoe, but no, it needs to come from me. Then maybe you can be there to support her without her always thinking of your voice on the phone, breaking the terrible news about her daughter's death. I'll just give Krista a quick call and see if she has any more news before I do, just in case. She may have the number of someone Linda's mum can phone for information about her body or something.'
Zoe nodded. 'Have you told anyone else? Kim, for example?'
Robin shook his head. 'No, I haven't told anyone else, not yet.'
'Would you like me to tell her? You're going to need some help to close the camp down, and Kim could do that while you concentrate on dealing with the logistics of Linda's death.'
'Thank you, Zoe. That's a good idea. I last saw her out on the obstacle course where it looked as though

everyone had just finished setting it up. I think we'll leave it all out for now and organise a working party to come back and dismantle it tomorrow or Monday. The sooner everyone can leave the better.'
'OK, I'll tell her. Good luck,' Zoe put her hands on his shoulders in a gesture of support. 'I'll leave you in peace to make that phone call.'

Chapter 28

Saturday 2nd November 2019, 5:30pm

Linda's mother wasn't answering her phone, so Robin left a brief message asking her to call him as soon as she was able, saying simply that unfortunately Linda had been in an accident and was unable to bring her horse back home. He had no idea how elderly her mother was or if she lived alone, and although he knew that the future of Linda's horse wasn't the most important issue, because he could clearly be looked after by Madeleine for the time being, he didn't want to break the tragic news over an answer phone message. Madeleine, Debbie and Krista all arrived back at the yard together with Madeleine and Krista in the horse lorry with Linda's horse, and Debbie driving her own car behind them. They had no more news about what had happened to Linda, other than to say she had been taken to the morgue at Swanwick Hospital, and Krista had given his contact details to the police.

'Do they want me to contact them?' he asked, wondering what the protocol was in these situations.

'No, they'll get in touch if they need to. Linda had her ICE contacts on her, so I don't think we're needed anymore,' she said. 'I knew the ambulance drivers who collected her body, and I'll check in with them later just in case they have any news on exactly how she died. What a horrible way to go.'

They could hear the sound of several feet tramping across the yard and in trooped the volunteers and competitors. Robin drew himself up, preparing to address the group. He'd made a few written notes to thank everyone and reassure them he would let them know the outcome of Linda's death, just in case he forgot anything in the emotion of the moment. Zoe broke free from the group and came to his side, facing away from everyone else.

'I know you were expecting everyone to go home, but I think they have other ideas,' she murmured.

He looked askance at his wife, who was clearly the spokesperson for the group. Kim could see that he was still in shock, and came up and gave him a big hug. At the feel of her familiar comforting body he struggled to hold back the tears, and held onto her until he was sure he wasn't going to break down.

Kim stepped away, not attempting to hide her own distress, as she said 'Zoe has told us about the terrible events of this afternoon. Poor, poor Linda.'

The group as one all quietly agreed.

'Do we know anymore?' Kim asked.

Krista spoke up. 'No, only that she had already died by the time Debbie and I found her. She didn't appear to have been in an accident and had obviously been taken ill while she was riding. It looks as though she dismounted, made her horse safe, and then her condition must have worsened. She had her phone with her, but whether or not she telephoned for help we don't know.'

'I haven't received any calls from her,' Robin said.

'No, neither did I,' said Krista, whose mobile number was the second one the competitors had been given in

their information pack, to ring in case of an emergency.
'I'm glad we did manage to find her before too long. I'm just sorry it wasn't in time to help her,' said Debbie.
'I should think it all happened fairly quickly considering the time frame,' said Krista.
'Obviously we'll have to review our systems once we know more,' said Debbie, 'but I think for now we need to accept this is a tragic death unrelated to the competition.'
Krista nodded her agreement.
Seeing that Robin was about to speak, Kim said quickly 'We've all had a chat and would like to continue with the weekend as planned.'
This was a shock to Robin, who had not considered continuing. Linda's death weighed heavily on his mind, and he couldn't imagine anyone being able to concentrate on inconsequential details, like how to tackle the auctioneer's gavel obstacle, or enjoying themselves in any situation. He scanned the faces in front of him and could see that they all appeared to agree with Kim's proposal.
Hesitantly, he said 'Wouldn't that be disrespectful?'
Patricia Bragg spoke up 'We were thinking more in terms of continuing with this weekend in Linda's honour. She was relatively new to the sport and clearly enjoyed her short time with us.'
'It would be different if we knew she had died from falling while riding out on the obstacle course, or being hit by some reckless motorist during the orienteering,' said Kim. 'From what we know, she was taken ill and very sadly died. It just so happens that it was while she was competing. It sounds as though it was the sort of thing which could have happened at any time.'

Charlie Lichmann said 'If it had been me, I do hope you would all continue as planned.'
A general agreement of 'Yes, me too,' echoed around the indoor school.
Robin wondered if he was the only one who thought it was wrong to continue. 'I'm not sure' he said suddenly feeling a bit shaky and looked around for something to sit on.
Kim guided him to the chair Zoe had been using behind her desk, and helped him to sit down. He looked very pale.
'Darling, I appreciate that this is a lot of responsibility for you. No doubt there will need to be phone calls and emails, forms to fill in and questions to answer. You have put so much work into this weekend that we don't really need you now.'
'We have all your lists,' Zoe gently teased him and was rewarded with a faint smile.
Madeleine stepped forward. 'You can sleep in my cottage tonight. I'm sleeping in my lorry anyway as a show of solidarity with the rest of my competitors, so you'll have some peace and quiet and a comfy bed. The spare room is already made up in case we needed it as a sick bay, and we still have my bedroom in case we really do need a sick bay.'
Robin groaned 'Please, no more problems to deal with.'
Patricia spoke again. 'Zoe is perfectly capable of acting on your behalf for the rest of the weekend. I'd like to volunteer to work with her in the role she was doing. I'm one of the control of paces judges tomorrow, and as there are five of us I'm sure that should something happen and I need to be called away, the other four can manage without me.' She looked

around at the four volunteers who all nodded enthusiastically.
'There you are,' said Kim. 'I'm not fussed about competing tomorrow, so I can be on hand to help you out with anything official. I think it would be much nicer for everyone if we can continue as planned. Saying that, we all know that Linda's death is always going to be our main memory of this weekend, but this way it won't be our only memory.'
'Isn't it a bit callous?' asked Robin.
Phil said, 'I must admit I thought we'd all be packing up now. But hearing how keen everyone is to continue, I don't think it is callous. I'd like to award a prize for the most improved combination on the orienteering course today. This was Linda's first attempt at orienteering, and from what I've seen of the scores which have come in, she did very well indeed. As Kim said, none of us is ever going to forget that one of us has died during an event, and it doesn't sound as though it was an accident but probably a sudden illness, although we won't know for sure until there has been a postmortem. So, if everyone really does want to carry on, let's try to make the best of it. As Charlie said, if it was me, I'd like you all to continue. Except for you, Jimmy. I'd like you to be distraught with grief and never ride a horse again.'
'Oh, goes without saying. Same for you,' agreed Jimmy.
Unexpected laughter broke out through the group as the couple played the fool with crossed fingers behind their backs, and silently mouthing 'No way.'
'Thank you, Phil. That is a very generous thought,' said Robin. 'Well, it certainly looks as though everyone is in agreement, but I'm going to come and speak to all of you individually, and if anyone else has

reservations, anyone at all, please tell me. Our conversation will be private, and I promise I will not tell anyone what you have said. I still think the right thing to do is to cancel the remainder of the weekend, but you have all convinced me that it may be possible to continue. So,' he checked his watch 'we have another couple of hours before the food is due to arrive. If it's OK with Debbie, I suggest you all grab your torches if you don't already have them with you, and do a quick course walk of the obstacles. Please can everyone be back at their own camp by seven o'clock and I'll come and speak to each one of you there.'

Chapter 29

Saturday 2nd November 2019, 8.00pm

‘A toast to Linda Beecham,’ Charlie stood with a glass of Malbec in his hand, and soon everyone in the indoor school was toasting Linda's memory with glasses and cups of wine, cans of lager or bitter, or with steaming mugs of tea or hot chocolate.

Robin had been surprised to discover that the competitors and volunteers were unanimous in their determination to continue with the weekend. However, after the initial enthusiasm and fervent reassurances to Robin that it was the right thing to go ahead, those who had been riding out on the orienteering course that day, followed by the hard work of setting up the obstacles and then the chilly coursework in the dark, were remembering how arduous these weekends could be. Particularly in winter. The mood was sombre, and the delicious fish and chips were eaten in silence.

Spirits lifted a little when Robin called for everyone's attention, so he could give out the interim results. He had managed to speak to Linda’s mother, who had already been informed by the police that her daughter was dead. She telephoned him to thank him for trying to contact her, and to ask if Linda’s horse could remain at the Woodford Riding Club until she could collect him in the next few days. Although clearly distressed by her daughter's death, she had been composed, and had somehow managed to end the phone conversation by making Robin feel that he had been the one at the receiving end of her condolences. They had not discussed the continuation of the event, but hearing her speak with clarity had helped to ease Robin's conscience. PC Ian McClure had also spoken to Robin, and reassured him that there was unlikely to be anything further they needed from him in relation to the running of the event.

His misgivings partially assuaged, Robin was determined to make sure that the remainder of the weekend was a good experience for everyone. With a cheery note in his voice, he said 'Thank you to Phil and Jimmy for beavering away on the scores!'

Everyone enthusiastically called 'Thank you to Phil and Jimmy!' The two men nodded their thanks and waited for Robin to continue.

'Everything I say is with the caveat that a person died today and I do not want anyone to think I have forgotten that. We cannot forget, but we have all agreed to keep going, so let's continue to do our best.'

He waited until the subdued cheers had died down. 'I have only heard excellent reports from the checkpoint judges about the competitors. Everyone was friendly, nobody complained, nobody was rude, and although Debbie's course did test some people's skills to the extreme edge of their ability, and both horses and riders found their fitness was pushed if they wanted to keep within the times she set, everyone has passed and is through to tomorrow's tests.'

A small cheer ran through the competitors, and the volunteers clapped them.

'I would also like to say that we have had super feedback about today's judges. I am very grateful to them for volunteering on such a chilly day and for being able to keep their smiles on their faces, and efficiently running the checkpoints.'

This time the roles were reversed, and it was the competitors who were clapping the volunteers.

'Phil has very kindly offered to donate a prize to the most improved combination in Linda Beecham's memory. The result is surprising to us because his intention was for a fairly novice horse and rider, but the recipients are Amelia and Blackie who have beaten their personal best by one hundred points.'

Amelia looked embarrassed to have won a prize so clearly designed for someone relatively new to the sport, but Phil was enthusiastically clapping and cheering, so she went forwards to collect the fifty pound voucher he had managed to organise from the WES manager before the shop closed that evening.

Shortly afterwards the rubbish was collected, the tables and chairs packed away, and the competitors, volunteers and organisers made their way to their beds. Tomorrow was another day.

Chapter 30

Sunday 3rd November 2019, 8.00am

The atmosphere in the camp the next morning was subdued, unlike the weather which had earlier produced an amazingly bright sun rising to create a spectacular red, pink and yellow sky. Robin was standing on top of a man-made hillock which had not been used in the course in case heavy rain turned it's carefully maintained sides into avalanches of mud after several four-legged half ton animals had cantered over it. From his vantage point in the furthest field, he cast his gaze towards the vehicles and corrals near the yard, and reflected that the second day of competition was often quieter as two nights of sleeping in trailers or lorries took their toll. His misgivings about continuing with the weekend had disappeared over night, entirely due to the determination to make the weekend a success from every competitor and volunteer he encountered. Phil's considerate donation of a prize which he committed to sponsoring for the next ten years had ensured that Linda's memory could be celebrated as well as mourned. PC Ian McClure had made a brief appearance late the evening before to speak to Robin. He wanted to make sure they had the contact details of everyone present, and to let Robin know that the coroner had requested a post-mortem for

Linda to take place as soon as possible. Robin decided not to pass on this information to the rest of the camp, choosing instead to let everyone try to concentrate on the day ahead. He prayed that no one would have an accident.
Kim and Heather were both competing that day, and because he had declined Madeleine's offer of her spare room their alarm had woken him at half-past six, all set to give them a chance to give their horses a good brush after yesterday's exertions, and themselves another chance to walk the course. From where Robin was standing it looked as though all of the competitors had the same idea, and there were small groups of people spread throughout the three fields. The Woodford Riding Club was a popular venue for people with dogs because each field was securely fenced, meaning that Robin could also see a variety of spaniels, lurchers and collies racing around together. The sight of the happy dogs brought a smile to his face, and he resolved to put the heavy sadness of yesterday's tragic events to one side until the end of the day. In the distance he could see Zoe talking to someone on the yard, presumably the local photographer who had agreed to spend the November day in one of three fields trying to capture the thrills and spills of the happy campers and their horses. These days with the capabilities of mobile phones there were always plenty of good photographs available to share on social media, but there was still something about a professional photograph which spoke of quality in the image. He stayed where he was as Zoe loaded the photographer and a couple of assistants into Madeleine's truck, and drove them across the field towards him.
'Hello!' he called as they emerged, carrying several different shaped bags.

‘We thought this might be a good place to stand’ explained Zoe.
The photographer and her assistants stood looking over the obstacle course, and Robin tried to see it through their eyes. The atmosphere was picking up now that the competitors were concentrating on how many strides to this and what gait they should be in for that. Everywhere he could see mostly middle-aged women wearing navy blue jackets and gillets with pink sparkling writing on the back, and/ or woolly hats with pink sparkling pompoms. The few male competitors were wearing black jackets with Brackenshire HOOFING in reflective strips instead of sparkling pink. The division of the genders was obvious, and he was surprised there were no black jackets being worn by women. He had expected his daughter Heather to shy away from the pink sparkly adornment, but she now had quite a collection of clothing decorated this way.
He could see a group of eight women in their early twenties earnestly discussing the obstacle sponsored by Black’s Auction House; over in the field where the corrals were set up, half a dozen volunteers were checking the control of paces obstacle with measuring wheel and numerous brightly coloured pimple cones; a lone competitor was pacing the related distance between three obstacles; and there were several people in deep conversation close to the obstacles in and around the water.
‘This is brilliant’ murmured the photographer, who was turning her camera from one group to another, while the two assistants were studying a laptop where the photographs were downloading. A folding table and three chairs had magically appeared while he was

looking the other way, and the three of them were already focused on their work.
Zoe said to Robin 'I have explained the course layout, and where the most likely places for a good canter photograph, or possible bloopers at the bending poles through the water, might be.'
One of the assistants said 'I'm going to be based over there' pointing to the three local obstacles, and then gesturing to one of her assistants 'and he's going to start at the control of paces test before coming back here to sort and edit our photographs.'
Now that Robin looked more closely he could see that the two assistants were probably the photographer's son and daughter. Satisfied that they were happy, he made sure they had his mobile number in case of any queries, and left them to continue planning where the light was going to work in their favour throughout the day.
The first competitor wasn't due to start the control of paces until ten o'clock, and then straight onto the obstacle course where for each horse and rider combination Debbie had set a generous course time of twenty-eight minutes and a penalty time of twenty-five minutes and below, because the ground on parts of the course was very hard if not frozen, and they did not want anyone to push their horse too much. Robin knew that these dodgy areas were one of the reasons so many people were thoroughly checking the course on foot.
Robin headed over to Madeleine's kitchen, where he found all of the volunteers now congregated around the kitchen table, and a welcoming smell of sausages and bacon as Caroline cooked breakfast rolls for those who wanted them. The volunteers were buzzing, and Robin welcomed the rise in energy. He basked in it while drinking a coffee Patricia passed to him. He was

pleased to see that she seemed to have settled in with the other judges for the control of paces obstacle.
Charlie Lichmann and Paul Black were taking over the scoring responsibilities from Phil and Jimmy, and the four of them were now in a huddle as Jimmy explained the scoring from the day before and how to work out the time scores from the overall time the competitors spent out on the obstacle course. Charlie was used to the scoring system from a competitor's point of view, but it was all new to Paul, who wished he had paid more attention when Jennifer had been celebrating or complaining about her scores over the years. Fortunately his aptitude for numbers, combined with Jimmy's clear explanation, enabled him to pick it up quickly. Although the time limit for penalties was twenty-eight minutes, in the case of tie-breaks over points scored on the obstacles, the start to finish time of the competitors would come into play, and was where controversy was most likely to arise. It was imperative that Paul and Charlie were scrupulous about checking and double-checking each other's calculations.
Over by the patio doors Debbie was in a separate huddle with Grayson and Bilbo. Robin squeezed his way over to them.
'Everything alright?' he asked her.
'Oh, yes, I was just asking Gray if he could be on stand-by in case someone knocks one of the bending poles in the water. The water is over my boots through the middle, and it's freezing. I don't want wet feet!'
'I can hang around nearby,' offered Bilbo. He said to Grayson 'You wanted me to go along the section of track over on that side of the field next week, and check all the rails were secure. I could make a start

today, and then if the poles get knocked over I'll row the boat and put them back up.'
Content that between them they had resolved a potential issue, Robin accepted a bacon roll from Caroline, and stood in the corner letting the noise wash over him. After all of the tension and drama the previous day he was feeling drained, and with everyone else so busy he was surprised to find himself at a loose end.
Patricia clapped her hands 'Come on everyone, let's get to our positions! The first competitors will be warming up, and we don't want to start late or we'll never catch up.'
General agreements and exclamations of 'gosh is that the time' rippled through the room, along with the scraping of chair legs on the tiled floor, and the noise of plates and mugs being washed up in the sink.
'Leave that, I'll do it!' called Caroline. 'Make sure you take your lunch bags; they are all named.'
'Thank you' came repeated calls as they handed bags to the right person, and found their own.
Robin watched as the kitchen emptied of everyone except for Caroline, Grayson and Bilbo.
'Time for another coffee,' commented Grayson, and the three men sat down around Madeleine's table, where Caroline joined them once she'd refreshed the coffee jug and teapot.
She gestured to a plate she had piled with sausages, bacon and toast. 'Please eat this lot.'
Bilbo didn't need to be asked twice, and even Grayson and Robin found themselves making a sandwich out of the leftovers.
'Bad business yesterday,' said Grayson. 'Tricia said the police are involved.'

‘I think they always do get involved with an unexpected death,’ said Robin, knowing full well that this was the case but not wanting to present himself as an expert.
‘Fell off her horse, didn’t she?’ asked Bilbo. ‘I’ll miss seeing her around the auctions. She was a nice lady, and a very knowledgeable dealer.’
Robin didn’t want to go into details about how she was found, and nodded non-committedly, using his mouthful of toast and bacon as an excuse not to expand.
‘I’m surprised the camp continued,’ Grayson reached over for another piece of toast.
‘No reason to stop it,’ said Bilbo. ‘Just because someone fell off their horse. Must happen all the time. We’ve certainly seen a few accidents here,’ he gestured towards the fields.
‘True,’ nodded Grayson.
Robin could feel the brief lifting of his spirits plummet again, and checking his watch said ‘I’d better get going.’
In truth he wasn’t needed anywhere, but he couldn’t bear to sit and listen to comment and speculation. He wanted to be back in amongst the positivity generated by the competitors.
‘Don’t forget this,’ said Caroline, as she went over to the side where a few lunch bags remained. ‘I’ve made one for each of you, too,’ she said as she handed over Bilbo and Grayson’s brown paper bags with their names on. Grayson looked genuinely touched by the gesture.
‘Thank you. We weren’t expecting anything. We’re paid to be here by Mrs Higston.’
‘I know,’ said Caroline, ‘but Robin knows how much you two do behind the scenes to ensure their events can

run smoothly, and he felt the least he could do was include you in the lunch provision.'
'That's right, thanks chaps,' said Robin, as he left the room.
The electric gates were opening, and PC Ian McClure drove into the carpark. Robin was used to dealing with the police in a professional capacity, and had no reason to think that Ian was coming for any other reason than to update him on something about yesterday's death. But then he saw that two other cars had followed Ian's marked police car, but these were unmarked and the occupants didn't look as though they were coming for a horse riding lesson. A frisson of fear ran through him. Surely they weren't coming to arrest him on a manslaughter charge for some administrative error he'd made?
'Robin, hello,' said Ian. 'Is Grayson Bragg around?'
'Yes, he's just in there,' Robin indicated the open front door to Madeleine's cottage.
Without another word, Ian gestured for his colleagues to precede him through the door, leaving Robin standing in the carpark with his lunch bag dangling from his hand. He went to follow them, then stopped as indecision flooded over him. His professional persona took charge, and he started to walk back to Madeleine's cottage determined to retrieve some control over events, but stopped as Grayson Bragg was led out of the cottage in handcuffs.
'What?' Robin didn't know what else to say.
Grayson looked furious, but didn't say a word as he allowed himself to be put into the back seat of one of the unmarked cars.
'We'll be in touch,' was all Ian said, as he walked past Robin to his patrol car, and then the convoy drove out of the electric gates. Robin turned to see Bilbo and

Caroline standing in the doorway of the cottage, both looking as shocked as he felt.
Caroline was the first to speak. 'They've arrested him on suspicion of murdering Linda!'
Bilbo found his voice 'This is not true; this can't be happening. There is no way that Gray would murder anyone. We have to do something.'
Not for the first time that weekend, Robin felt helpless.

Chapter 31

Sunday 3rd November 2019, 9.30am

Several people had seen the arrival and departure of the police cars, but it appeared that fortunately no one else had witnessed Grayson's arrest. Robin asked Caroline and Bilbo not to speak to anyone about it, although he would go and tell Patricia what was happening. He found her in position in the field, one of the five volunteers who were judging the fifty-metre control of paces course. Jennifer, the first competitor, had already begun her test with her horse Jasper. Robin watched as she and Jasper performed a beautifully controlled canter along the figure of eight course, with a couple of clean flying changes first left to right, and then right to left. He was sure they would be getting the top marks for this test, where the object of the exercise was to complete the distance within the narrowly marked track in as slow a canter as possible, and then follow the same course in reverse in as fast a walk as possible, without breaking either gait. Grayson and Bilbo had recently installed the all-weather surface for the figure of eight, and Debbie was relieved it had been completed in time for the competition, ensuring that the test was not affected by patches of frozen ground which would have made cantering too dangerous. Robin continued to watch as Jennifer and

Jasper completed the first part of the test and left the track, before re-entering in a long energetic walk. For those few minutes he was able to appreciate that this was what the weekend should be about, and he knew the competitors had been right to push him to keep the weekend going.

As Jennifer and Jasper strolled away towards the start of the three-kilometre obstacle course, Robin walked over to Patricia where she was standing on one side between the two circles of the eight, and touched her arm.

'Patricia, can I have a word with you over there please?' Robin asked quietly, in a practised tone he normally used with nervous clients.

'Of course,' said Patricia, assuming he was going to take her up on her offer to be Zoe's assistant. She signalled to the nearest judge that she had to go, and received a smile and a thumbs up in reply. All so normal, no drama, thought Robin as the other four judges shuffled their positions so that Patricia's vantage point was covered.

They had almost reached the indoor school before Robin brought them both to a halt. He checked that no one was within earshot, and said 'I am so sorry Patricia, but Gray has just been arrested for Linda's murder.'

Patricia's eyes widened and the colour drained from her face. 'What? No! How can the police be so stupid? Where have they taken him? I have to get there.'

She turned and began running in the direction of the track where her horse lorry was parked, obviously intent on driving it to whichever police station now held her husband. Foreseeing a lot of fuss and trouble as she tried to extricate her vehicle from its place embedded with the others which also lined the track,

Robin called after her as he ran to catch up 'Hang on Patricia, wait a minute!' and to his relief she came to an abrupt halt.
Panting, he reached where she had stopped, surprised that such a little woman could out-run his long legs. 'Why don't you take your husband's truck. It will be easier for you to get into any car parks which have a head room limiter,' he suggested. 'If they have taken him to Woodford police station you won't have a problem, but I would have thought that something as serious as murder will be dealt with in Swanwick.'
'Didn't you ask where they were taking him?' she said, furiously.
Aware that they were starting to attract attention, Robin again took her arm, and led her away from the competitors who were preparing for their competition. They were still in the proximity of the indoor school, and he managed to guide her into there, conscious that Zoe was nearby but knowing that he needed to update her on what was happening anyway.
He immediately apologised to Patricia. 'I'm sorry I didn't ask anything, no, I was taken by surprise by the speed with which they came in and arrested him. He'll need a lawyer; does he have one? If not, then I can give you the name of someone I recommend.'
'Yes, he does have a lawyer. We have the same one we use for all of our family business,' nodded Patricia. 'I'll phone her now.'
While Patricia rang Grayson's lawyer, Robin telephoned Swanwick police station to find out what they knew about Grayson Bragg's arrest. Although the police station would not be open to the public on a Sunday, he used his professional contacts telephone list to find the information they needed. Patricia was still talking to the lawyer, but Robin interrupted her with

'yes, they're taking him to Swanwick.' Patricia nodded and passed on the information to the lawyer. Her face was now infused with colour, and Robin ascertained that the lawyer was telling Patricia there was no point in her going to the police station because they wouldn't tell her anything, she wouldn't be able to see her husband, and she couldn't help him from there.
'Argh!' She shouted. 'This is so frustrating. Of course Gray hasn't murdered Linda bloody Beecham. How can the police be so stupid?'
'Why do you think they suspect him?' asked Robin.
Patricia had been pacing in the sandy surface of the manege and stopped suddenly, her mouth open but issuing no sound. Robin saw something flash across her face, a sly look which he'd seen many times before on the faces of clients. Immediately it was gone, and the forceful self-righteous Patricia was back 'Right, I'm not having this. I don't care what that lawyer said, I'm going up to that police station and I'm going to tell them all how stupid they are being.'
She stormed out of the indoor school, and Robin turned to Zoe who had been standing in front of the score board throughout the whole episode, not daring to move or speak.
'What was all that about?' she said, with an astonished look on her face.
'Gray has been arrested for the murder of Linda Beecham,' Robin told her. 'I'm not sure I believe he did it, but the police must have their reasons for arresting him.'
'Murder? They think that Linda has been murdered?' Zoe was more upset by this news than Grayson's arrest, and Robin thought it was interesting that Patricia hadn't picked up on this point. But then, it wasn't Zoe's husband who had just been arrested, and

if Grayson was proved either guilty or not guilty, Robin was sure that Patricia's prime feeling would be embarrassment.

'I know the coroner had asked for a post-mortem to be carried out last night, so presumably the results of that have confirmed that she was murdered.'

Zoe was shocked. 'Oh no, that is terrible news. Krista and Debbie had no idea. They must have destroyed evidence, because they thought she'd been ill. All those piles of vomit everywhere.'

Seeing that Zoe was looking as though she too was going to be sick, Robin guided her towards a chair. He found the bright yellow bottle she always carried with her, and said 'Is this water?'

She nodded, and took it from him. 'Thank you,' she muttered as she took a big gulp. 'This is awful. I must let Krista know. They were tramping all over the place. But honestly Robin, I don't think there was anything there to convict Gray, Krista said that Linda was just lying on the grass verge. There weren't any sticks or metal pipes or anything around her, and no sign of blood or broken bones.' Zoe buried her face in her hands and sobbed.

Robin recognised that she was experiencing delayed shock from the tragic events of the day before, and crouched down next to her as he put one arm around her shoulders, while he sent Caroline a text requesting tea to be brought to the indoor school as a matter of urgency.

By the time Caroline appeared with a tea tray containing a teapot, water jug, milk, sugar lumps and four mugs, the worst of the shock had passed, and Zoe was sitting quietly sharing a typed conversation on WhatsApp with Krista.

'Thank you, Caroline,' Robin said as he took the tray from her. Seeing the number of mugs he raised his eyebrows. She shrugged and said 'I wasn't sure how many of you were in here. I assumed it was Patricia who needed tea and sympathy.'

'Oh no, Patricia drove off to find her husband about ten minutes ago,' said Robin as he poured tea into three of the mugs, offering one to Caroline. Feeling awash with coffee, and not really wanting it, she could see that Zoe was in a bit of a state and so took it as an act of kinship. Caroline carried a chair over and placed it next to Zoe, before sitting down and taking a sip of tea.

'It's all a bit of an upset, isn't it,' she said.

Zoe nodded. 'I can't believe Linda was murdered. I didn't really know her, but still, it's a horrible thing to happen.'

Krista came into the indoor school, looking calmer than her friend, but obviously shocked. She had been watching the competitors on the obstacle course, ready to assist with first aid if required. All of the volunteers had her phone number, and she had one of the group's walkie talkies, so there was no danger that she would not be able to rush to someone's assistance if required. Zoe's messages had seemed more urgent than anything that was happening out in the fields.

'Krista, would you like a cup of tea?' Robin was pouring one for her even as he asked the question.

'You know me, I have never been known to turn down a cuppa,' she grinned.

'Zoe's had a bit of a shock,' Robin explained. 'Someone has just been arrested for Linda's murder.'

'Yes, Gray,' said Krista, gesturing to her phone in its holder on her uniform. 'Zoe just told me. I can't believe it. He's such a nice man.' She shivered, as the

memory of sitting next to Linda's body while she waited for the ambulance came back to her. If she had known she was sitting down enjoying the sunshine in the middle of a murder scene she would never have been able to stay there.
Caroline nodded her agreement, and although with all of his years in the legal system Robin knew you could never judge a person by appearances, he felt the same as they did. He had not for one moment thought that Grayson could be guilty, having known him for many years as a quiet hard-working man who had the reputation throughout Brackenshire and surrounding counties for excellent customer service, value for money, and quality workmanship. There had never been any hint of illegal practices or violence, although his predilection for young girls when he was a teenager and in his early twenties had left a stain on his reputation, and rumours of numerous affairs since then, albeit with women of his own age, certainly made his character open to question. But meeting up with someone who was not his wife a couple of times a week for some afternoon delight was a giant leap from cold-blooded murder.
'Did the police say how he did it?' asked Krista.
Robin shook his head. 'They didn't say very much to me at all.'
'Ian walked into Madeleine's kitchen, read Gray his rights, someone else put handcuffs on him, and they all walked back out,' explained Caroline.
'What, and Gray let them do it? Didn't he ask any questions, or shout his innocence, or anything?' asked Krista.
'Nope, he didn't say a word.'
'He must know something then, even if he didn't do it,' concluded Krista.

'Bilbo and I sat there watching it all going on in front of us,' said Caroline. 'I don't think I've ever seen anyone arrested in real life before, but it was exactly as it is on the television.'
'I've never been in a murder scene before,' said Krista quietly, 'and it is the complete opposite of how it is on the television. Debbie and I had no idea. I can't think of anything that Gray could have given her to make Linda throw up like that. I mean, vomiting can be an effect of concussion, but she was still wearing her riding hat when we found her, and when we removed it there was no sign of a head injury. He must have poisoned her.'
'It is beginning to look like it if he's been arrested. Is there a chance there is another reason why she was sick, and choked on her own vomit? Is it definitely murder?' asked Caroline.
Krista shook her head. 'I don't know. I checked her airways were clear in an attempt to start resuscitation so I don't believe she choked on anything, but she was too far gone to be saved. Her neck wasn't broken, there was no sign she had been shot, no sign of an attempt at strangulation. Poisoning appears to be the obvious answer. I wonder how he did it?'
'You're assuming Gray did murder her,' Robin said.
'Well, yes, he's been arrested,' said Krista confidently.
'How do we find out about the results of the post-mortem?' asked Zoe.
'As members of the public we won't know that until the inquest, and that could be several weeks from now,' said Robin.
'I'm sure we'll hear the rumours long before that,' said Caroline. 'I bet you by the end of today we'll know more than we do now.'

Chapter 32

Sunday 3rd November 2019, 11.00am

Jennifer finished brushing Jasper's coat of the small amount of sweat which had worked up under his girth, and gave him a kiss on his lovely warm grey neck.
'You are such a super pony,' she murmured, breathing in the wonderful aroma. Together they shared a few minutes of mutual calm after a hectic couple of days' competition. All around them people were riding or judging, poo-picking corrals and packing up sleeping bags. Eventually she made the effort to push herself away from Jasper's comforting body, and tidy away his saddle and bridle. The Woodford Riding Club had a spacious and secure room where tack and rugs for the livery and riding school horses were kept, and she would take the time later that day to thoroughly clean everything they had been using that weekend. Although she only lived a few minutes away with Paul behind Black's Auction House, Jennifer had chosen to camp in the veterinary horse lorry to show solidarity with her fellow competitors. After all, if Madeleine who lived on site could do it, so could she. Paul had declined her invitation to join her and Lucy, and although it wasn't something she wanted to do on a regular basis in winter, she had thoroughly enjoyed snuggling down with her greyhound under layers of

duvets and blankets. Lucy wore a navy blue jumper and a matching coat over the top, and still managed to demand to be let underneath a couple of Jennifer's blankets.
Once she was happy she had done everything she could in preparation for their departure later that day, Jennifer went in search of Zoe or Debbie to see what she could do to help for the remainder of the day.
News of Grayson Bragg's arrest had inevitably leaked, but the processes of competing and packing up camp overrode any personal tragedies. Neither Zoe nor Debbie had anything for her to do, and so she took the opportunity to make herself a cup of tomato soup, and join a few other competitors who were watching the competition from the vantage point of the hill in the furthest field. Jennifer loved these moments, where even though everyone was competing against each other, and wanted to win the prize of the stunning three tiered red and gold rosette for first place, they also wanted everyone else to do their very best.
'Oh well done!' commented Jimmy, as Amelia and Blackie demonstrated a perfect one-handed canter in a figure of eight.
'Doh!' said Jennifer, as she watched Kim's horse Maggie take fright when Kim tried to pour fizzy liquid from a bottle into a plastic glass. 'Well sat!'
'She did well to stay on there,' agreed Jimmy. 'Uh oh, she's not having any of that!' he said, as Kim tried again, and Maggie stepped smartly sideways.
'Ouch,' exclaimed Phil, as Kim executed a sideways roll off her horse in slow-motion until the last few inches where she crash-landed on the ground. Maggie bent her head down to her as if to say 'Whatcha doing down there?'

‘I’d better go and check she’s OK,’ said Krista over her shoulder, already running towards Kim carrying the big green medical bag.
‘She’s OK,’ Jimmy laughed, ‘look at her.’
The spectators could see that Kim was shaking with laughter, as Maggie began to frisk her pockets for treats, while Kim continued to lie on the cold and wet ground trying to defend her space from her cheeky horse. She didn’t stay there for long, and was able to stand up and lead Maggie away before Krista reached her, and before the next competitor, Amelia and Blackie, appeared for their turn at the obstacles.
‘Perfection,’ muttered Jennifer, as Amelia poured what looked from that distance like a perfect glass of champagne.
‘This was one of the few obstacles I am sure we scored full marks,’ said Phil, as they watched Amelia steer Blackie from the bar, while she safely carried the champagne flute and placed it on the table. The pair easily negotiated Caroline’s food van where Amelia unwrapped a sandwich and re-wrapped it again, and then over to the auctioneer’s gavel, where Amelia gave it a hearty bang and shouted ‘SOLD!’
The spectators watched in silence as Amelia and Blackie cantered in a long wide sweep around the edge of the field towards the water. As expected, Blackie responded to Amelia’s quiet request to steady, and the pair began to canter a controlled weave through the water, when suddenly Blackie spooked at something in the water, and it was Amelia’s turn to fall off sideways, although her landing was a lot wetter and colder than Kim’s had been. Blackie took fright at his rider’s departure, and shot out of the water, reins and stirrups flapping in an alarming and dangerous manner.

The spectators were too far away to do anything to help, and many competitors and volunteers were unaware of the drama going on in their midst, but the judge on the scene was calling Krista's phone, and she was already running towards the obstacles. Kim was back on board, and she and Maggie were now attempting to unwrap the sandwich at Caroline's food van, together, which was not the point of the exercise, but Maggie was convinced the sandwich was for her and wasn't going to let Kim lean in far enough to reach it first. The competitor on the control of paces course had just finished their canter, and were turning around ready to start their walk, as Blackie shot past, heading for his corral. The nearest judge held up his hand to ask her to wait, and within a few seconds one of the competitors who had been poo-picking her horse's corral had hold of Blackie's reins and was leading him out of harm's way. Satisfied, the judge signalled for the competitor to start her fast walk, and as if nothing had happened the competition continued as before.

Seeing that Amelia was now walking away from the water with Krista, looking none-the-worse for her dunking, the spectators began to chatter about the latest events regarding Grayson Bragg. The general consensus was that the police had got it wrong, and it was far more likely to have been Patricia Bragg who had killed Linda because she had found out that her husband was having an affair with her. No one actually knew if Linda and Grayson had been having an affair, but it quickly became assumed fact because of his reputation, and no one knew if Linda was in a relationship with anyone else, male or female.

'It could have been one of us,' Phil said to Jimmy. 'We both ate one of those chocolate brownies she was handing out at the checkpoint.'

'I had two,' confessed Jennifer. 'They were delicious.'
'How do the police think he poisoned her?' asked Jimmy to no one in particular.
Everyone shrugged and looked at each other for the answer.
'Ugh,' shivered Jennifer, 'it's just too awful to think that someone here would do that to one of us. Oh look, Kim and Maggie are trotting that weave through the water beautifully!'
'Hurray for Kim,' said Phil. 'She did well to get back on and keep going. I don't bounce as well as I used to. I hope no one else falls off. It's not usual for one person to come off, let alone two.'
'Kim's going to have some impressive bruising after that,' observed Jimmy. 'Poor Robin, this is quite the baptism of fire for his first time organising an event. One death, probably murder, and two falls, one of whom is his wife. I wonder if he'll ever agree to organise another one.'

Robin didn't have time to think about organising a future event. He was sitting at Madeleine's kitchen table having received a telephone call from Grayson Bragg to say he had been released from police custody and was on his way back to Woodford, but that Patricia was being detained on suspicion of murdering Linda Beecham. As he finished talking to Grayson, a dripping Amelia was being ushered into Madeleine's cottage by Krista. They were standing in the porch, with the front door open, and Robin jumped up to see what was going on. He could not believe his eyes when he saw that it was the paramedic with one of the most, if not *the* most, experienced competitors on site, who was drenched from head to toe.

In reply to Robin's silent question, Amelia said 'I'm fine! I took a quick swim in the water without Blackie, and Madeleine has kindly said I can use her shower to warm-up. Now that's a luxury we don't usually have access to at these events,' she winked as she began to strip off her soaking breeches and socks.
'Oh, er, I'm glad you're alright,' said Robin. 'I'll get out of your way,' and he left her and Krista in the porch, as he strode out to the fields.
Seeing Zoe standing next to Blackie's corral, he walked up to join her. 'Is he OK?'
'Yes, he's fine. Poor Amelia is soaked, and Krista has ordered her to go and shower in Madeleine's cottage. The water temperature is very cold, and Krista is worried hypothermia will set in.'
'Yes, I've just seen them both.'
'Kim's alright, though,' said Zoe.
'What?' Robin was alarmed, but tried not to show it.
'Didn't you know? She slid off Maggie at the pub obstacle,' Zoe laughed. 'She's fine, she got back on and they finished the course. Look, she's over there untacking Maggie in their corral.'
'Thanks,' said Robin, as he headed over to his wife. 'Hello darling, I hear you've had a bit of a tumble.'
'Oh god, it's so embarrassing,' laughed Kim. 'Maggie just stepped sideways, and I was so busy concentrating on pouring the wine I didn't go with her! I'm bagsying first bath when we get home. I'm going to ache tomorrow. How's things with you? You're looking a little more worried than when I last saw you.'
'I have no idea what is going on. First the police came and arrested Gray for Linda's murder, then he's just rung me to tell me he's been released and is on his way back here, and now Patricia has been arrested.'

'No! Patricia Bragg? She's a bitch and first-class complainer, but surely she's not a murderer. No, I don't believe it.'
'But you believed it of Gray?'
'Well, yes,' said Kim. 'He's very manipulative and controlling, you know. Don't tell me you've fallen for his quiet, always-ready-to help persona?'
Robin shook his head. 'I don't think I know anything about anything anymore.'
'Yes, you do,' she gave him a big hug. 'You know how to make a girl a cup of tea. Go on, I'm sure Heather will appreciate one too. There she is, she and Molly have finished and are heading our way now. I'll help her with Molly, while you make the tea, and cut us both a slice of fruitcake please.'
Robin scanned the fields, but everything looked as though it was running smoothly. 'I will happily make you both a cup of tea, and treat you both to a slice of cake.'
He returned to Madeleine's cottage, and found Paul, Charlie and Amelia sitting at the kitchen table.
Paul jumped up as he walked in, and said 'The scoring is all up to date. We're having a quick tea break before we go back for the second half. The kettle's boiled; what would you like to drink.'
'No, no, you sit down,' he said. 'I'm on drinks duty for my wife, who also had an unplanned dismount. How are you feeling now, Amelia?'
'Oh, I'm absolutely fine, thank you. Madeleine's guest room has the most powerfully hot shower I have ever experienced, and I'm feeling much warmer than when you last saw me!' she laughed. 'How is Kim?'
'She's fine, a bit sore.'
'That's good to hear,' said Amelia. 'While we have a moment, I'd like to thank you for your hard work, and

for allowing us to continue with this weekend. I have never been at an event where someone has died before, and I am so sorry that it has happened during your first time as an organiser.'

'Thank you,' Robin appreciated Amelia's words. For someone with so much experience to express their support was reassuring. 'In my line of work I am often involved with disputes, often violent ones, but I must admit that this is my first murder.'

'Murder?' Amelia put her mug down more heavily than she intended. 'You're not telling me that Linda Beecham was murdered are you?'

'Sorry Amelia, I assumed you knew. First Gray has been arrested for her murder, but he was released a short while ago, and now Patricia has been arrested.'

'Ah,' Amelia nodded. 'I think we can dismiss Patricia's arrest as a temporary situation, and I am sure she will be released without charge. I wonder why he did it? And how?'

Robin stopped what he was doing, and turned to look at her properly. 'You think he did it? Are you not surprised that Gray has been accused of murder?'

She shrugged, and picked up her mug again. 'No, I'm not surprised. I think that a man like that is capable of anything.'

'Well I certainly am surprised!' exclaimed Charlie. 'Why on earth would someone as quiet and helpful as Gray murder anyone?'

'Grayson Bragg is one of those men who controls every aspect of his life, and those around him,' Amelia explained. 'Look at how he has made himself indispensable around here,' she gestured through the window. 'How would Madeleine be able to afford the development and upkeep of these facilities without his apparent generosity? He still has his former wife dependent on him, his children will struggle to break the ties and still fulfil their dreams, and his current wife is one of the most unhappy people I have met. Somehow Linda must have threatened an important aspect of his life.'

Charlie said 'Well, I would never have seen him in that light. Surely he is just an innocuous bloke?'

Amelia shrugged. 'You may well be right.'

Charlie studied her thoughtfully. He had met Amelia at numerous equestrian events over the years, and had always found her to be pleasant company, with a good sense of perspective. He did not wish to dismiss what she had to say, but he was struggling to see things in the way she did. Eventually he said 'I only met Linda recently, and am shocked that she has been murdered. Until this weekend I would have believed that Patricia was capable of murder, but now I have spent a lot of time with her, I don't think she could. I hear what you are saying about Gray, but he still doesn't seem like the murdering type to me.'

'I have known Linda for years,' said Paul sadly. 'She was one of the good guys in the antiques business. Hard working, fair and honest. I never knew her to be involved in any scandals, and she was very supportive of Cliff during his troubles with the antiques centre a few years ago. Since all this money laundering bollocks has been brought up she has been equally supportive to me. Someone I would describe as a really nice person. It makes my blood boil to think that some selfish bastard has chosen to end her life.'

Robin looked at him shrewdly 'What do you think about the fact that Gray has been arrested for her murder, Paul?'

Paul was uncharacteristically silent, and mimicked Amelia's shrug of the shoulders. He was desperate to share the information that he and his staff had uncovered about the funding for the Braggs' lifestyle, but knew it would jeopardise the case against those involved in the illegal activities. Everyone was waiting for him to answer, and so eventually he said 'I suppose the police must have their reasons, or they wouldn't have arrested him. They have certainly moved quickly.'

'He's been released and is coming back here,' said Robin. 'Now they have Patricia in custody for Linda's murder.'

'Now that does surprise me,' said Amelia, furrowing her brow. 'I don't see Patricia as the murdering type, unless he manipulated her in some way. Why on earth would she murder Linda?'

Paul kept his eyes focused on the bottom of his empty mug. He did not want to hear that Grayson Bragg had been released. He needed to speak to Ieuan Davies as soon as possible, and find out what was going on.

Chapter 33

Sunday 3rd November 2019, 17.00pm

Robin, Madeleine and Zoe waved the last of the volunteers out of the gates. Debbie Tolstoy waved back enthusiastically, ashamed to admit that this had been the most invigorating weekend she had enjoyed for a long time. At seventy-two years old she had been expecting to retire from planning and organising events such as this one, and had decided it would be her last. But being part of such an enthusiastic and pro-active team, who had managed to persevere despite the murder of one of their number and the arrest of another, during a very cold November weekend, had encouraged her to put such thoughts out of her head. She still had a lot to offer, and was eager to continue to support the group.

'Well done, Robin. Despite all of the traumas that was a successful weekend for Brackenshire HOOFING,' Madeleine gave him a hug. 'All of the competitors had a great competition, and Debbie should be congratulated for her fantastic orienteering course, and the obstacle course was both testing and fun!'

'Madeleine's right. You did an amazing job of setting us all up for success, and when things went badly wrong, everyone was able to keep going,' Zoe also gave him a hug. 'I know I teased you about your lists,

but thanks to your diligence we were able to give our members a weekend which will be remembered for the right reasons, as well as the tragic one.'
'Oh stop it,' Robin laughed, 'you'll have me in tears! We all did a tremendous job, and I am very grateful to you two and Debbie in particular. But don't ever ask me to run one of these again.'
'On the contrary,' grinned Madeleine. 'You are now our expert winter camp organiser. Come on, jump in, I'll run you both home.'
Kim and Heather had left half an hour earlier with the horses, although Kim had intended to stay until the very end her body was stiffening at an alarming rate, and Robin had persuaded her to leave. She and Heather still had to take Maggie and Mollie back to their yard, and settle both mares and the rest of the herd in their fields for the night, before Kim could go home and treat her bruises. The night was hurrying in, and everything was being done by the light of head torches and moonlight. Robin walked over to the track and surveyed the fields, where only a few hours ago around fifty humans and thirty-two horses had been actively using sixteen obstacles and the control of paces track. Now two of the fields were empty, and one was home to a number of horses contentedly munching on the grass. He joined Zoe and Madeleine as they leaned on the wooden fencing which separated the field from the track.
'Thank god that's over with,' he murmured.
Madeleine grimaced. 'Well, it isn't is it? Yes, the weekend camp and competitions are all done and dusted, and I think everyone went home happy with our achievements, but having one member of our club in custody for the murder of another means we can't put this to bed just yet.'

'No, you are right,' agreed Robin with a sigh. 'I don't know what to think about it all.'
'I must say I am surprised to hear the police have now arrested Patricia. I mean, she is a baggage, always complaining about other people and showing off her own achievements, or at least things that she sees as achievements, but I wouldn't have thought she was the violent-type.'
'Now this is something I keep coming back to,' said Robin. 'Why was everyone so happy to accept that Gray was the murderer? He's been one of us for years, always willing to help out with anything we did at the Woodford Riding Club, he's done some excellent work for people I know around the county, I've never heard or seen him get into any kind of altercation with anyone, and yet hardly anyone else this weekend has been surprised at his arrest?'
Madeleine shivered. 'You are right; of the two of them he has always been the more willing to help, and I have never heard him say anything derogatory about people, unlike his wife, but there is something unsettling about him. On the surface he and Patricia do seem like an odd couple, but they have stayed together for over forty years, so she can't be all bad. With his money he could leave her at any time, so why does he stay? And we have seen a better side to her in recent weeks, haven't we?'
'All I can say is it's been a long time coming, this better side,' muttered Robin, who had been at the receiving end of Patricia's complaints on numerous occasions. 'But now she is the one in a police cell, and he is on his way back to Woodford.'
'I haven't met her before,' said Zoe 'but I really liked her. I have known Gray for years through the running club, and he's always been a bit too familiar for my

liking. That makes me sound like a right prude, but do you know what I mean Madeleine?'
'Yes I do. I wish someone had warned me about him when I first came here. He has never done anything inappropriate, but his presence is quite menacing. He isn't someone I feel comfortable to be around. If it does turn out that Patricia murdered Linda then I think we will find out that Gray is involved somehow, and this probably has something to do with Paul's situation. If you think about it, Linda is, I mean was, an antiques dealer, and Patricia regularly puts stuff through Paul's auction.'
'How do you know?' asked Robin. 'Auction houses are not allowed to reveal the names of their clients.'
'She's always boasting about how much this sold for, and that cost. Maybe she's the one who has been laundering money, and Linda found out about it!' said Madeleine.
'Possibly,' said Zoe.
'Either that, or it is Gray who has been laundering the money, and Linda found out about it, and so Patricia murdered her before Patricia's rich lifestyle and her perceived status in the community were dashed to the ground,' said Madeleine. 'If you think about it, Gray is the one who is the grafter in that relationship. With his regular so-called fishing trips to France, he could easily be using that as a front to pick up smuggled goods, and yes, we all know how hard he works building properties and equestrian yards, but can he really be earning enough to pay for all those dressage horses next door, their posh lorry, let alone their electricity and water bills for that place. A boat isn't cheap to run, and Patricia certainly isn't used to working within a budget judging by her expensive beauty treatments, clothes and jewellery. I have always

thought it was strange that he refused to buy a family home with land so that Patricia could keep her horse at home, which I know is what she would prefer to do. Instead, he makes her keep her horse at my yard which, don't misunderstand me is absolutely the way I would choose to keep my horses if money was no object, but it is within feet of his former wife and their children's palatial expensive equestrian palace. For someone with Patricia's tastes that has got to hurt.'

'Mmmh, I hadn't thought of that,' agreed Robin.

'Must sting a bit,' said Zoe. 'But surely by your logic it places the spotlight back onto Gray as the murderer. If he is the one behind the money-laundering through Paul's auction, and Linda found out about it, surely he would be the one to get rid of her.'

'Whoever did it, I'd like to know how they did it,' mused Robin. 'According to Krista, Linda was exhibiting all the outwards signs of anaphylaxis, a severe allergic reaction to something, although there wouldn't usually be so much if any vomit.'

'It was Patricia who was handing out the chocolate brownies,' pointed out Zoe.

'Oh they were delicious!' said Madeleine. 'My money's on Gray. I think Patricia is a lonely woman who has committed to spending her life with an unappreciative, manipulative, cheating and controlling man.'

'I just don't see it,' said Robin. 'Patricia is argumentative, disagreeable, bossy, and Gray has stuck with her through misplaced loyalty. I think we'll find out that he was having an affair with Linda and was finally plucking up the courage to leave Patricia. Patricia found out and disposed of her love rival.'

‘We never really know what goes on in other people’s lives do we. I don’t suppose any of us need to be taking extra precautions, do we?’ asked Zoe.
‘What do you mean?’ asked Robin.
‘Well, one of our group has been murdered; we don’t know why; we don’t know by whom. Are we in any danger?’
‘I hadn’t thought of that, either,’ said Robin.
‘Nor me,’ said Madeleine. ‘I think that if we were in any danger then Ian or one of the other policemen would have said something. I can’t imagine they would have let us carry on with our weekend’s activities if there was a hint of danger. I still think this is mixed up with Paul’s business. No one believes he is part of the criminal activities he has been accused of, but the police appear to be certain that something illegal has been going on. It would be a bit of a coincidence if a murder took place at the same time, even for a town with Woodford’s reputation.’
They heard the noise of electronic gates opening, and together walked down to the yard to see who was arriving. Grayson Bragg’s familiar battered red truck pulled up outside Madeleine’s cottage, and she shivered. She did not want to have to deal with him this evening.
Before he had opened the driver’s door, the gates swung open again, and a black van followed by one marked police car were driven through into the yard. Immediately Grayson started up the truck and swung around the vehicles, aiming for the gates, the truck’s headlights on main beam and the row of lights on the roof turned on, effectively blinding Zoe, Madeleine and Robin. They could hear the crash as one vehicle hit another, and the smashing of glass, followed by more noises of car, truck and van coming into violent

contact. The three of them stood still as their sight cleared, and the shouts of men and women as Grayson Bragg attempted to run away from his pursuers. Boots on hardcore replaced the noise of the vehicles, and in seconds they could see Grayson Bragg flattened face down with three policemen holding him to the ground. Unseen and unheard, Ian McClure had walked up to them, and he made them jump when he said 'Are you all OK?'
'Bloody hell' yelled Zoe, as she punched her friend on the arm. 'You frightened the life out of me! Don't creep up on people like that.'
'Sorry, sorry,' said Ian, holding his hands up as an apology. 'I didn't realise you hadn't seen me.'
'That was absolutely terrifying,' said Madeleine, before she started to giggle. Zoe soon joined in.
'We had no idea any of this was going to happen,' Robin attempted to admonish Ian, but gave up when he was overtaken by laughter, and Ian looked on as the three of them convulsed in hysterics, their breath coming out in fits, and their attempts to speak in voices higher than normal.
Zoe was the first one to recover. 'Sorry mate,' she apologised to Ian, rubbing the spot where she had punched him on the arm. 'We have had a helluva weekend, and Madeleine was about to drive us home when all that drama started.'
'But you are all alright?' Ian wanted to be sure no one had been injured in the chaos which had surround the vehicles.
'Yes, yes, we're fine,' Robin assured him. 'I take it you have just re-arrested Grayson Bragg for the murder of Linda Beecham?'

Ian nodded. ‘Yes, we have, and for the running a money laundering scheme. I am very sorry about your friend, Linda.’
‘Thank you,’ Madeleine said. ‘I don’t think any of us really knew her, but it was a terrible thing to happen, and she seemed like a lovely person.’
‘Are we free to go?’ Robin was overwhelmed with tiredness, and wanted to go home to his family.
‘Of course.’ Ian checked the situation with his colleagues and their prisoner. ‘Come with me, and I’ll see you out of the yard.’
‘I’ll be coming back in about half an hour,’ said Madeleine. ‘Will any of you still be here?’
‘Yes, I’ll be here. Someone has to clear up this mess. You are going to have a disturbed evening with recovery lorries and people sweeping up that broken glass.’
‘I’d rather that than have any of the glass getting stuck in the horses’ hooves.’
The three of them climbed into Madeleine’s truck, and Ian waved them through the electric gates..

Chapter 34

Wednesday 6th November 2019, 9.00am

'Good morning everyone,' Paul beamed at his staff, all present and correct in the reception area of Black's Auction House. 'Cheers!'
He opened a bottle of champagne, and made a big show of pouring it into the flutes Rebecca had laid out on a tray. Everyone took a glass, even Richard who didn't like champagne, and they all chorused 'Cheers!'
'Right, that's the first and last time we'll be drinking at this time of the morning at work' laughed Paul. 'Ah, here they come.'
Doug pulled open the glass doors, and indicated for the police to come in. One by one the boxes containing paperwork and computers were brought back into the auction house from the vans parked outside. Rebecca and Paul directed the officers so that almost everything ended up in approximately the correct area of the offices, while Daniel, Doug and Richard helped to unload the vans. The process took less than half an hour before the vans were empty, and Paul was cheerily waving police off his property. Daniel, Doug and Richard were very happy to be back in the huge warehouse which was housed in the old chapel building, and Paul watched them working together for a while, familiarising themselves with the goods that

were already sorted and prepped for the next six auctions. When he returned to the reception area, he found Rebecca deep in conversation with the Welsh blond-haired policeman in charge of the investigation, Ieuan Davies.
'Hi Paul,' he said. 'I hope everything has been returned. Let me know if anything is missing.'
Paul and Ieuan had been in regular contact in recent weeks, and were on first-name terms. After his initial fury at the policeman's actions in closing down his auction house and freezing his bank accounts, Paul had realised that the sooner the illegal activity operating through his auction was flushed out, the sooner he could get back to work. Ieuan had appreciated Paul's willingness to help, and the auction house staff had been able to provide the police with invaluable information. Natasha Holmes had been as good as her word, and managed to stall a number of Paul's regular clients who wanted to divert their stock to her auction, although as she had informed him with a chuckle on the telephone on Monday, now that he and his business were in the clear they were back to being mortal enemies.
'I will check it all today and let you know either way, thanks,' said Paul. 'I saw Patricia Bragg yesterday. That poor woman looks broken. After some of the conversations we've had in the past where she has been outrageously rude to me, I never thought I would feel sorry for her, but I do.'
'She's had a shock, that's for sure,' nodded Ieuan.
'I do feel foolish,' admitted Paul, as he sat down in a chair near Rebecca's desk. 'I did not notice what Gray was doing, and nor did my dad. To think that for twenty-five years he was quietly pushing goods through here, and walking away with a total of two

million pounds, tax-free. Once Rebecca started looking through our records, we could see that the stamp album was the last of many transactions where we assume Gray had bought it from another auction for cash, and then put it through ours where someone else bought it for cash but he was paid out through his bank account.'
'But not the bank account that Patricia knew about,' added Rebecca. 'Do you know how many other auctions he was doing it to?'
'We think we do. Yours was one of forty-two around the country we have tracked down. We reckon he has made over thirty million pounds in that time. He had established several different identities, enabling him to easily buy and sell the same item but appearing to be two different people.'
Rebecca said 'I can't believe that someone like Grayson Bragg has the brains to do it. As far as I knew he didn't even manage his own bank account; Patricia was the one who took care of all the invoices. He couldn't even manage to use a cash machine! How on earth did he become a suspect?'
'We could trace how drugs were being imported into this country on his boat, or at least the boat which appeared to belong to four different people but who were actually all aliases for Grayson Bragg, but then the money seemed to disappear. Initially we were looking for a large group of people, believing that Grayson Bragg was a small cog in the wheel being turned by a criminal mastermind, but our investigations for the past eighteen months have narrowed it down to Grayson Bragg being a sole operator. He is part of a group who import drugs for which he is paid in cash, so he doesn't source or distribute the drugs, and he then launders the money through auction houses and building projects. But you are right Rebecca, as far as

Patricia was concerned that was exactly how their joint finances were managed. But she did not know about the millions of pounds he was manipulating through numerous other accounts. He was careful to set-up business accounts with building merchants through which he legitimately bought some building supplies, with corresponding invoices for the clients to show how they were being bought and paid for. But a major part of the high-end business supplies were paid for in cash, and the invoices for those clients went into bank accounts of which Patricia had no knowledge. That entire equestrian property he has built and maintains for his wife and daughters is paid for with drugs money.'
Paul narrowed his eyes 'Oh come on, are you really trying to tell me that Patricia didn't know anything about it? How is that possible?'
Ieuan nodded 'I really am telling you that. When we first started investigating him it became obvious very quickly that she was ignorant of much of his daily activities. He was using the fact that she chose to ignore his affairs with women to conceal his illegal business dealings. These rumours which have circulated for years about his affairs are untrue, and probably all emanate from Grayson himself.'
Paul shifted uncomfortably. There had been a time in his life when he had created an illusion that he was more popular with women than in truth he was.
'How did you manage to find that out?' asked Rebecca.
Ieuan hesitated before answering. 'We had someone who was able to give us insider information, and with that information we could join the dots.'
'Was that Linda?' asked Rebecca.

'I can neither confirm nor deny who it was. Please don't ask me, as I don't want to give away that person's identity. The people who Grayson couriered the drugs into this country for are mightily pissed off that their lucrative route has been cut off.'
Paul spoke carefully 'So, did you know that I was innocent all along?'
Ieuan said 'We suspected that you were innocent, but we had to be sure. We still think that Grayson must have had at least one accomplice, maybe more, because of the sheer amount of time managing this side of his income must have taken. But we can find no trace or evidence of another person. It would have been convenient for us if it had been you, or another auctioneer, or another antiques dealer. Your compensation should come through fairly quickly, but I hope our investigation doesn't adversely affect your business in the medium to long term. Our media bods have been working hard to ensure your reputation is shining and sparkling.'
'Yes, I've noticed the social media traffic is looking very positive!' said Rebecca.
Paul gave her a look. He wasn't quite so ready to forgive the police for the devastating upheaval they had put him through, even if his business was being given a boost beyond the place it was when the nightmare began. The compensation was going to be very useful for his and Jennifer's wedding and honeymoon too, as well as paying for staff loyalty bonuses and covering all bills for at least the next twelve months. It was substantial, and went a long way to making him feel more kindly towards the man who had started it all.
'I am confident that the reputation of Black's Auction House can be recovered, especially with all of the

publicity about how we have been extremely helpful to the police in their investigation,' Paul said. 'But personally I could have done without the stress.'
'Poor Linda,' said Rebecca, her eyes filling with tears. 'She was such a nice person. I shall miss seeing her around here. She was one of the few dealers who always took the time to speak to me whenever I visited Cliff at the antiques centre, and here she was always a pleasure to deal with. Did Gray kill her because she was your informant?'
Again Ieuan hesitated. 'We think that Linda was killed because Grayson Bragg believed she was our informant.'
'How did he manage to kill her?' asked Paul.
'Until the inquest has taken place into her death, I cannot tell you anything officially,' prefaced Ieuan, 'but it appears that he persuaded her to turn off the official orienteering course to talk to him about something, and he gave her one of Patricia's chocolate brownies which had been smeared with a toxin found in seafood. The effects of these toxins can range in severity, and it would appear that this one had an immediate and catastrophic effect.'
Rebecca shook her head. 'I just cannot believe that someone like Gray Bragg, who can build a wall which will stand for hundreds of years, and is a first-class carpenter, is also an international drugs dealer, who launders millions of pounds, and get his hands on and successfully engineer the correct dose of a deadly toxin.'
'That is because the Gray Bragg that you know has been cultivating this Woodford persona all of his life, and with Patricia as his wife he was able to manipulate everyone into believing it because she was innocently playing her part as the loud, brash extrovert, with an

opinion about everyone and everything. It was easy for him to hide in her shadow, make everyone feel sorry for him, and pull her strings.'

'He has played us all for fools,' said Paul.

'I do feel foolish for writing him off as a bit of stupid perv,' said Rebecca. 'I wonder what will happen to Patricia now? Presumably everything will be claimed by the government as the proceeds of money laundering?'

'At the moment we are concentrating on prosecuting him for the murder of Linda Beecham, because the financial side of things is going to take a long time to untangle, but yes, both the first and second Mrs Braggs need to be prepared to lose a large amount of tangible assets they believed belonged to them.'

'I can understand what they are going through, because that was what I have been facing for the past few weeks. If Patricia really is innocent then I will do what I can to help her. Well, I had better get my office straight now that I have it back,' Paul said as he stood up and went to his desk, shutting the glass door behind him. A casual glance back revealed Rebecca and Ieuan deep in conversation again. Something was brewing there, he was sure of it.

Once in his office, Paul spent a happy couple of hours sorting, filing, and re-discovering both the history and the current state of his business. The majority of the auction's work had been computerised for many years, but there were still some things which were kept on paper, like catalogues, copies of provenences for special items, and invoices for some of the cracking house clearances the firm had undertaken. Once he was satisfied that his business could hit the ground running later that week, he turned his attention to his and Jennifer's forth-coming wedding. During his enforced

time away from work, Paul had been making the most of it to concentrate on their wedding preparations. He could understand why Jennifer had been so reluctant to take time out of work to do it herself, especially with the changes that she and her father had been making to the way the equine veterinary business was run. This would be his third wedding, and the first one he had taken any active part of in the preparation, and he was thoroughly enjoying it.
Of course, one small headache was the wedding arch, because there was no way he was going to be using the one Grayson Bragg had created.

Chapter 35

Friday 15th November 2019, 11.00am

The sun shone weakly in the winter sky as Jennifer and Alison walked from the equine veterinary hospital along the unmade track to the back of The Woodford Tearooms. Their long brown hair was entwined with crimson roses, and Jennifer had one gold-coloured rose in hers. They were dressed in matching dark green suede ankle boots with three-inch heels, long crimson fitted skirts, and each wore a fitted shirt. Jennifer's was gold with crimson detail, and Alison's was crimson with gold detail. Their father, Peter Isaac, was walking between them, dressed in a dark grey suit with a crimson shirt and a dark green tie. Waiting for them on The Green, standing under an archway decorated with bridles, rope halters, stirrups, gavels, weighing scales, eye-glasses, surgical instruments, and, of course, vet wrap in red, yellow and green, were Paul and Cliff, also wearing dark grey suits and crimson shirts, with Cliff wearing a dark green tie like Peter's, and Paul wearing a gold tie.

Paul could feel an enormous lump in his throat, as Jennifer walked towards him, picking her way carefully across the slightly muddy grass, and with a broad grin on her face. She was stunning, and she had agreed to marry him. Right up until this moment he

had not truly believed she would turn up, but now she was here he couldn't believe he had doubted her.
Surrounding them were as many friends and relatives as could make it on a winter's weekday morning. Glancing around, Jennifer could see that most of the town had turned out to support them, and she was thrilled that so many of the men had worn their best suits, and the women had made a special effort with hair and make-up. Only a select few had been invited to the wedding luncheon, but Paul had promised a free bar at The Ship Inn from six o'clock that evening until the money ran out. It looked as though it wouldn't be a late evening, if the number of people who had made the effort to come out for a few minutes of formal ceremony on a miserable cold November morning was anything to go by.
The sky was threatening a downpour, and the registrar performed the ceremony with as much speed as she could, while ensuring it was not rushed. Huge droplets began to tease towards the end, and then with a roar the heavens opened and everyone dashed into the tearooms or the back of the antiques centre, depending on whether they were invited guests or happy onlookers.
Inside the tearooms Lisa, Caroline, Gemma and Daniel had decorated the room with the theme of the archway, adding saddles, watchmakers' tools, and lots and lots of photographs of Paul and Jennifer. In seconds the room was filled with dripping, laughing guests, and Lisa was glad she had lit the wood burner in plenty of time so the room was warm and cosy, and wet hair and clothes could begin to dry out.
'Who organises an outdoor wedding in November!' laughed Jennifer, as she gave Paul a big kiss.
Paul had told Jennifer about his plans the previous week, but she already knew because everyone he had

trusted to keep the secret had told her, believing, correctly, that it was something she should have a say in. She had kept their secret, and had willingly given her wishes when they asked on style of wedding outfit, wedding food, and guest list. The one thing she had no input into was the honeymoon. Paul had booked a fortnight off through Peter, and Alison had colluded to make sure that nothing was put into Jennifer's diary which could not be postponed or performed by their father. When Paul nervously but with an attempt at casual, told her over lasagne in The Ship Inn that if she wanted to they could get married next Friday, Jennifer had willingly said yes.
'You knew, didn't you?' he asked suspiciously.
'Yes, I did,' she replied. 'Thank you for doing all of this. You were right; I would never have got around to it. So, where are we going on honeymoon?'
Trying not to sulk or feel betrayed by people he had counted on, Paul said 'Now that you are going to have to wait and see.'
The informal lunch in the tearooms was exactly what Jennifer wanted, and she was able to laugh and joke and chat with her friends and family without any formal and stuffy constraints. The only nod to tradition was when her dad stood up and made a speech, but he was then joined by her mum in a rare moment of unity after many years of separation, and Alison joined them too. Paul's mum and dad also stood up and told a few stories about him, and it wasn't long before everyone was telling childhood and teenage stories about each other.
It was four o'clock before the wedding lunch drew to a natural close, and as the rain had stopped Jennifer and Alison went home and swapped their heeled boots for wellies, and the wedding party went for a stroll along

The Trailway, with dogs and children running and splashing in the puddles, and coming back by torch light.

As planned, six o'clock on the dot the wedding luncheon party moved to The Ship Inn, where the decorations from the wedding arch and the tearooms had been relocated to the garden room, and the celebrations continued. Amanda the pub's chef had produced a fantastic buffet which just kept coming throughout the evening, with bowls of vegetable chilli, spicy chicken fajitas, onion bhajis, ham sandwiches, her legendary hotpot, jacket potatoes, a variety of salads, and finally an array of cakes to ensure that even the sweetest-toothed amongst the guests was satisfied.

The pub was full to bursting, as clients of Paul's and the human clients of Jennifer popped in to pass on their congratulations, and wish the couple all the luck in the world. The entire Woodford Streakers Wearing Clothes club members were there as were all of the other livery owners at the Woodford Riding Club, and several members of Brackenshire HOOFING. Patricia Bragg put in a subdued appearance, and both Jennifer and Paul gave her a big hug, and said they were very pleased to see her.

'I'm sure her boobs have shrunk,' Paul whispered to Jennifer.

'We've only been married a few hours and you're already looking at other women's boobs! But I think you're right, she's almost flat-chested now. Oh look who's here!' and Jennifer put the mystery of Patricia's disappearing boobs to one side as she rushed to embrace Charlie Lichmann, who had driven for almost two hours to join them, bringing his new girlfriend for their first public date together.

By nine o'clock many people were flagging, and there was a thinning out of the party, but there were enough people still upright to carry on.
'I've hardly drunk any alcohol,' commented Jennifer to her new husband in surprise.
'Nor me, I can't understand it. I think I'm spending so much time talking to people I've not had time to drink,' Paul laughed. 'I could do with a cup of tea now.'
'Me too, I'll go and ask Sarah for a pot of tea for two.'
Paul put his head around the curtain of the snug, and found it was full of antiques dealers and his staff, all still clearly enjoying the free bar.
'Paul!' yelled Bilbo above the noise. 'Congratulations mate!'
'Congratulations!' they all chorused.
'Thank you,' said Paul, and for a moment he and Bilbo locked eyes. Paul was pretty sure that Bilbo was the insider Ieuan had spoken about, and he was equally sure that Bilbo was not as drunk as he was making out. He had never paid much attention to the part-time dealer before, always believing him to be a wannabe without the aptitude to make a living as an antiques dealer, but if he was right and Bilbo was in league with the police, then there was more to Bilbo than Paul had realised. He resolved to keep an eye on Bilbo's dealings in future. 'Enjoy yourselves, I'm really pleased to see you all.'
Finally the last guests and locals emptied from the pub just after midnight, leaving an exhausted Tom, Sarah and Amanda to finish clearing up after them.
Paul and Jennifer walked hand-in-hand across the road to their home. 'Now can you tell me where we are going on honeymoon?' begged Jennifer.

'The taxi is coming to collect us at ten o'clock tomorrow morning, and she's going to drive us all the way there, and will collect us when it's time to come home again. I have booked us into a self-catering cottage in Scotland, by the sea in Cromarty. We are next to a pub which serves superb food, and twenty minutes walk from another which is also an excellent food venue. The cottage has an open fire and a wood burner, and is dog-friendly so Lucy can come too. We can spend two weeks walking, reading, sleeping, and of course shagging.'
'You mean making love, Jennifer admonished him with a giggle. 'It sounds perfect darling, thank you.' She was slightly disappointed that they weren't going to somewhere hot and sunny, after all November in Scotland wasn't going to be the warmest or driest place to be, but to go somewhere romantic with guaranteed sunshine and warm sea water would probably have meant innoculations and visas, and altogether more hassle than either of them wanted after the last few weeks of stress. 'You really have thought of everything.'
'Next year, for our anniversary, if you would like to, I thought that we could book a super luxury holiday somewhere abroad. We would have to leave Lucy behind, negotiate the minefield of post-Brexit travel, and endure a horrific long flight both ways, but if we start planning now we could do it?'
'Definitely, let's go!' said Jennifer. 'November 2020 will see us jetting off to a sandy beach for two, maybe three weeks.'
They clinked their wine glasses together and toasted their future.

Thank you for reading Deadly Philately, and I hope you enjoyed it. Please leave a review with your favourite retailer, because it will help to promote this book to a wider audience, and therefore assist me to produce the next one.

For more information about me, please join us on the Kathy Morgan Facebook page, and @KathyM2016 on Twitter.

Kathy

Printed in Great Britain
by Amazon